DESOLATION

DESOLATION

BERNARD STOCKS

authorHOUSE®

AuthorHouse™
1663 Liberty Drive
Bloomington, IN 47403
www.authorhouse.com
Phone: 1-800-839-8640

This book is a work of fiction. People, places, events and situations are the product of the author's imagination. Any resemblance to actual persons, living or dead, or historical events, is purely coincidental.

Published by AuthorHouse   07/25/2012

ISBN: 978-1-4772-1930-0 (sc)
ISBN: 978-1-4772-1931-7 (e)

Any people depicted in stock imagery provided by Thinkstock are models, and such images are being used for illustrative purposes only.
Certain stock imagery © Thinkstock.

This book is printed on acid-free paper.

Because of the dynamic nature of the Internet, any web addresses or links contained in this book may have changed since publication and may no longer be valid. The views expressed in this work are solely those of the author and do not necessarily reflect the views of the publisher, and the publisher hereby disclaims any responsibility for them.

Books By Bernard Stocks

The Guardians
The Teenage Pensioner
The Lannan Project
The Far Side Of Nowhere
The Lannan Diary
Half Alien
A Leap Too Far
Cara Iv
The Lannan Memoirs

CHAPTER ONE

C aves have always held a fascination for me. It all started when I was about seven or eight. We were spending the September weekend in Arbroath at the time. The weather was unusually warm for that time of the year and on the Saturday my father took my mother and I on a boat trip to the sea caves just north of the town. I was overwhelmed. From then on, whenever talk of holidays came up my only request was to go somewhere that we could visit caves. A couple of years later my wish was granted.

On a tour of the north and west Highlands we first went to Smoo Cave at Durness. Though a lot smaller than those at Arbroath I was in my element at being able to walk around. At that time visitors weren't allowed into the inner chamber, the access being deemed too dangerous. I wanted to try it nevertheless and recall having a rare fit of temper because my father physically restrained me. From the north coast we went to spend a week in Wester Ross and included a trip to the world famous Fingal's Cave on the island of Staffa.

Sadly that was the last family holiday I was to experience. Less than a year later my father deserted us and set up home with his secretary. Maintenance cheques arrived promptly for six or seven months, then stopped altogether. Shortly thereafter the Child Support Agency reported that the two of them had run off to New Zealand and couldn't be traced. My mother sold our comfortable semi-detached home and with the proceeds after the mortgage was paid off bought a three room and kitchen flat in a nearby high rise block. She took a job in a local factory and somehow managed to keep us in essentials. Holidays were beyond our means, but we got by without too much hardship. Sadly my mother never got over the breakup of the marriage and at the age of fifty suffered a massive stroke and passed away three days later. I had just turned seventeen.

1

By good fortune and the help of one of my teachers I got a job in the I.T. section of a nearby branch of a well known multinational company. Though not a great scholar I had done well in computer studies. There were fifteen other applicants for the post but I did well at the interview and even better at the practical tests that we were set. I got a shock when I was told what my salary would be. It was far higher than I expected! I was able to stay on in the flat, live comfortably, enjoy a full social life and still save towards a pension plan. Promotion came within two years and I was able to invest in a second hand car as well.

Best of all I could use my holidays to further my love affair with caves. Over the next few years I visited many of the longer caves in Scotland including one memorable trip to Assynt in south west Sutherland to Uamh An Claonite, our longest cave at around three kilometres. I also spent ten days in Somerset and Devon where I visited Wookey Hole, the caves in the Cheddar gorge and England's longest cave, Baker's Pit. In fact it is the longest cave in the British Isles at three and a half kilometres.

My excitement knew no bounds when I heard on the news one night that a party of potholers had stumbled by accident on a large cave in the hills north-west of Dunkeld. The following day I made some enquiries, only to learn that a great deal of work would have to be done before the cave could be opened to the public. The man that I spoke to eventually, who simply gave his name as Eric, seemed to sense my enthusiasm and went into great detail. A road would have to be laid so that vehicles could get close to the cave, the entrance had to be widened to facilitate access, lighting had to be put in and handrails installed to meet health and safety rules. He also told me the main cave was close to three kilometres long and that visitors would be able to walk the full distance to the far end. I gave him my name and address and he promised to send me word once a date had been fixed for the official opening.

Though I scanned newspapers, watched the TV news and scoured the internet I found very little further reference for the next fifteen months. Occasionally I came across a couple of lines in a paper saying that work was progressing but that was all. To be honest I'd almost forgotten about it until one day in mid July I came home from work and found a letter on the mat. At first I thought it was simply yet another piece of junk mail, then I looked at the enclosed leaflet and my excitement grew. McLaren's Cave would be open to the public from Monday the third of August. Details were given as to how to get there, the cave would be open from ten a.m. to six p.m. seven days a week and admission would be £5 per adult and £2 for senior citizens and children under sixteen.

I'd hoped to be able to get that week off, but with the holiday season in full swing I was told bluntly that I couldn't be spared. I begged for just two days but my pleas fell on deaf ears. In the end I had to settle for the week beginning the seventeenth of August. I promptly phoned the telephone number supplied and managed to secure a place in a party at four o'clock on Tuesday the eighteenth. Having ascertained that I knew where to go and didn't wish to reserve a seat on the minibus leaving Perth at two thirty, the disembodied female voice on the phone instructed me to report to the guide, one Duncan Petrie, not later than three thirty on the day in question. She took my credit card details, sounding totally bored, curtly told me to notify immediately if I had to cancel and rang off without saying goodbye.

After trying unsuccessfully to book a hotel in Dunkeld itself for a couple of nights I finally struck lucky with the Salutation Hotel in Perth. The next three weeks seemed to drag by on leaden feet. I found it hard to concentrate on the daily grind and it was sheer good fortune that I managed to get through without making any major blunders. There was a last minute scare when a rush job landed on my plate just after lunch on Friday the fourteenth. Thankfully my boss was only too happy to grant my request to come in on the Saturday and Sunday without overtime pay. I finally got it finished and reached home just after four o'clock on the Sunday afternoon. After a quick bite to eat I did my packing. My previous encounters with the longer caves warned me that it would probably be quite chilly inside, so I included a track suit and a thick sweater and at the last minute added a pair of woollen gloves.

After a light lunch on Monday I drove up to Perth in the early afternoon. I checked in at the hotel, dumped my bag and went for a walk round. I noticed that there was a show on at the theatre that evening, so I booked a seat and went for a meal. Next morning I resisted an inclination to go up to the cave entrance before noon and simply watch people going in and out and listen to their comments. Instead, feeling restless, I had another wander round the town and a salad lunch in a small cafe. Back at the hotel I changed into my track suit, stuck the gloves in a pocket, collected the car from the car park and set off northwards at half past two thinking I had plenty of time. I would have had if there hadn't been a bad accident five miles up the A9 and what should have been a twenty minute journey took me nearly an hour. Thankfully the way from Dunkeld town centre to the cave was well signposted and I arrived at the car parking area just one minute late.

Although boasting a signpost bearing the legend 'Visitors Car Park' I was confronted by a reasonably level area of rough gravel and weeds.

Little pieces of stone rattled under the wheel arches of my seven year old Mondeo as I crawled towards a vacant area. There were perhaps a dozen other cars scattered around plus a yellow minibus with 'McLaren's Cave' printed on the side in large purple letters. A fingerpost in the same colours directed visitors along a narrow gully to the cave entrance. Locking the car I set off hurriedly along the gully. It was perhaps two hundred and fifty yards long with a couple of sharp bends, the second of which was less than five yards from the end of the path. I emerged from gloom into bright sunshine and a fair sized clearing. Directly in front of the far side the ground, of solid rock, rose steeply and facing me was an arched entrance. A group of people were standing close to that and I walked quickly to join them.

I just had time to notice that most of the group were fairly young before my attention was drawn to a much older man who was standing a little apart. Dressed in a heavy sweater and corduroy trousers he was slim and of medium height, with thinning grey hair and blue eyes. He held a clipboard in one hand and by his side was a large sack. As I drew level with the others he looked up and spoke.

"Mr. Barclay?" I replied in the affirmative, and he made a mark on his clipboard.

"Good," he said. "Now we're all here." Laying the clipboard beside the sack he thrust his hands into the pockets of his trousers. "Would you like to form a semi circle round me while we go through the preliminaries." We did as he asked. As the last arrival I was on one end. Once we were in position he spoke again.

"I always like to start off by getting everyone to introduce themselves. That way we can use Christian names from here on in and it makes for a better atmosphere. I'll start the ball rolling. I'm Duncan Petrie, aged seventy-one, and a widower with family in Australia and Canada. I'm originally from Pitlochry though I now stay in Dunkeld and I retired four years ago after nearly fifty years working at the Blair Atholl Distillery, the last twenty-five as head stillman. This is my first job since then." He paused, then looked at me. "Your turn, Mr. Barclay."

Even though I'd had to do something similar at work dozens of times, I'd always felt uncomfortable about it. Taking a deep breath I tried to keep my voice at a level pitch. "My name is Dean Barclay. I'm twenty-seven, single and with no meaningful attachments at present. My parents are dead and I have no close relatives. I stay in Motherwell and work as a recruitment and training officer for a large multinational company in East Kilbride."

My immediate neighbour was a lady, somewhat older than the rest of the group, dressed in a dark green track suit similar to my own. I put her at about thirty-five to forty. She was small and fairly slim with jet black hair that I suspected was dyed and was smoking a cigarette in a short black holder. When she spoke her voice was low pitched and without any discernable accent.

"Esme Collins. Let's just say I'm over twenty-one. I'm divorced with no children and hail from Dunfermline. I'm the co-owner with a lifelong friend of a small fashion boutique."

Next in line was a stocky individual about five feet ten who was also smoking. His hair was light brown and close-cropped surmounting a square face and determined mouth and chin. He spoke with a distinct Glasgow accent. "The name's Robbie Crawford, the Robbie being short for Robert. I'm thirty-one and a professional soldier in the Royal Regiment of Scotland, currently on leave after a spell of service overseas. I came originally from Govan, in Glasgow, but joined up at sixteen and have seldom been home since. My rank is Corporal and I'm not married."

Robbie had hardly uttered the last word when his neighbour chimed in. I saw a tall, lanky youth, one of two in the line up without warm clothing. His choice was a tee shirt with a large thistle printed on the front, a smart looking pair of jeans and sandals. Surprisingly he had a very deep voice. "Daniel McKay from Perth, known to everyone as Danny, aged nineteen. I'm in my last year as an apprentice joiner. I've a mother, father, two sisters and a brother, all older than me."

Another young lad was next, but one very different from Danny. The first word that came into my head as I looked at him was 'chubby'. He'd a round, rather childish looking face, a somewhat vacant look and with another half stone or so would certainly be described as fat. He also looked incredibly nervous and stammered slightly as he spoke. "My n-name is Brian Forbes and I'm just eighteen. I'm an only c-child and stay with my parents in Bridge of Earn. I'm unemployed and g-going to college part time to t-take 'O' levels that I didn't get at school." By the time he'd finished his face was bright red.

There was a slight gap between Brian and the rest of the semicircle. Then came two girls standing very close together. One didn't need to be a detective to realise they were proclaiming to the world that they were an item, to use the modern idiom. The first of the two was tall, possibly just an inch short of my own five feet eleven. She was passably good looking with long dark hair hanging over her shoulders, brown eyes and a pleasant open face that I suspected would look even more attractive if she was smiling. Her partner was almost an exact opposite, five inches shorter with tightly curled blonde hair, what some men would call deliciously plump, and a face that a model would have envied. Like Brian she looked really nervous. The dark girl spoke up in what I've always called a university drawl, but with overtones of the east coast. "My name is Lindsay Stevenson and this is my friend Claire Roberts. We're both twenty and students at Abertay University in Dundee. We share a flat. Both of us have families but we don't get on with them and have little contact. We're originally from Fife, Kinghorn and Dalgety Bay respectively." She looked round defiantly, as if ready to challenge anyone who suggested that Claire should speak for herself.

Next to the two girls was another couple. They also stood close to each other, the girl's hand resting lightly on the boy's arm. They were both of average height. The girl had mousey brown hair with a fringe over a plain face that was wearing a sulky expression She spoke reluctantly but without hesitation in a very English accent. "Sian Jackson from Huddersfield, in Pitlochry on holiday. I'm twenty, a waitress and have my own flat. I've a mother, father and two brothers. I met Michael here a couple of days ago."

Michael cleared his throat. He was tall and thin with a long face, a prominent Roman nose, full lips and a bad case of acne. He looked sulky too and I wondered if he and Sian had had an argument. His accent was unmistakably local. "Michael Brown, twenty-one and unemployed. I stay in Dunkeld with my mother and older sister, but I'm moving into my own place next week." He stopped abruptly and looked down at his feet. At the same moment noises from within the cave entrance heralded the arrival of the previous party. A group similar to our own, also with the emphasis on youth, emerged to be followed by a guide much younger than Duncan. The two of them had a quick word in low tones before our predecessors moved away towards the car park. We all looked towards our guide.

"Good," Duncan Petrie enthused. "From now on we'll use first names. Now before we go in there are a few things I need to say. In case anyone asks the cave was named after George McLaren, the leader of the group of potholers who discovered it. Everything possible has been done to make sure the cave is safe but nothing can ever be one hundred per cent foolproof. So each one of you please concentrate on what you're doing at all times and don't take unnecessary risks or stray away from the group. From the entrance that you see before you we negotiate a narrow tunnel for about fifty yards. We go along that in single file. After the second bend we'll come to the only difficult part. If you'll forgive the comparison this is like the U-bend underneath a lavatory but on a much bigger scale. Twelve steps have been put in place on either side so that you can get down and up the other side. There's about six feet of headroom, so Danny and Michael may have to bend slightly. We go into the U-bend one at a time. There's a bell at each side. Each person as they reach the other side rings the bell to let the next one know the way is clear. On no account start to come down until you hear the bell."

"From the U-bend we'll come up into a circular chamber just big enough to take all of us. Then comes another narrow tunnel that we'll go through in single file, even though it's just wide enough to go two abreast. This second tunnel runs for thirty yards, then there's a sharp bend. Five yards further on we'll come out on to the gallery that overlooks the cave proper. From that gallery a ramp leads down to the floor. Everything is well lighted so you'll be able to see where you're going at all times. There are also three powerful torches in case of emergency. I'll take one and Robbie and Lindsay can take the other two. Any questions so far?" No-one spoke. "Final two points, then. We all wear hard hats from this point on. I've got a selection of sizes in the sack here so you should all get one that's a reasonable fit. We go in single file. I lead the way and then Dean follows me and the rest of you line up behind Dean. Now come and get your headgear."

So saying he upended the sack and spread a couple of dozen bright yellow helmets on the ground. I half expected a kind of rugby scrum but everyone moved quietly forward. The third hat I tried on was a perfect fit and a minute or two later everyone seemed happy. Putting the remaining hats back in the sack Duncan motioned us towards the entrance and the rest of us lined up in single file behind him as instructed. He looked back, gave a nod of approval and waved an arm. "Let's go," was all he said.

CHAPTER TWO

I'd stayed reasonably calm during the foregoing, but now that we were actually on our way the excitement started to build up inside me. I kept a full two yards behind Duncan as he walked at a steady pace through the tunnel. This sloped marginally downwards and there were a couple of shallow bends, otherwise it was easy going and there was at least fifteen inches of headroom. Just before the end the tunnel widened slightly and here Duncan stopped and turned. As he had promised, the lighting was good and I could see an open hole just beyond him. He raised his voice. "I'm at the edge of the U-bend now and am about to go down. I repeat, don't start down when your turn comes until you hear the bell. It's quite loud, so you'll have no trouble hearing it. I think you'll find it easier and safer to go down the first set of steps backwards. See you all on the other side."

At that he turned and started to descend. I moved forwards and peered over the edge of the hole. The shaft, circular in shape, went straight down and wasn't more than five feet wide. The twelve steps were quite narrow and almost vertical. They were made of aluminium and reminded me of the loft ladder we'd had in our first house. I mused that it was just as well none of the ladies in the party was wearing high heels! I saw Duncan reach the bottom, turn and disappear from view. It must have been about twenty-five seconds before we heard the shrill note of the bell. I turned and grinned at Esme behind me. "Don't try taking the steps two at a time," I joked. She grinned back at me. "No chance," she replied emphatically.

I descended slowly and carefully. The treads were even narrower than I'd thought, probably not much more than three inches wide. At the bottom I waved vaguely upwards, turned and went into the opening in front of me. Beneath my feet the ground sloped gently down for some four yards, then gently upwards again to another vertical shaft identical to the one I'd come down. At the lowest point I noticed on my right a circular hole in the rock wall some fourteen inches in diameter. The light here was at its weakest and I could see nothing when I peered into the hole except that there seemed to be an upward sloping vent. Shrugging my shoulders I moved on and climbed up to where Duncan was looking down at me. As I got to the third last step he held out a hand and helped me to the surface. The chamber that I found myself in was exactly as he had described it. Wordlessly he pointed at an electric bell push at head height near my left hand. I put my thumb on it and held it there for a good three seconds. Then I rejoined Duncan at the mouth of the shaft. Less than a minute later Esme's head could be seen ascending. Duncan and I helped her out between us.

One by one the others followed and the circular chamber began to fill up. Thankfully there were no mishaps, though Claire gave us a fright when she missed her footing halfway up and almost fell. We were all itching to move on and get into the cave proper as Sian started her upward climb and only Michael remained on the other side. I was standing by the bell as Sian reached the top and my hand had just started to move towards it when we heard a rumble from beneath. A second or two later the rumble turned into a roar, seemingly coming from beneath our feet, the lights went out and we were engulfed in a cloud of dust. Then the noise died away and we were left coughing and confused. I heard Duncan trying to speak and choking before he could get a word out. Suddenly I remembered the bottle of water in my pocket. I pulled it out, took a mouthful and rinsed it around my mouth before spitting it out at where I knew the wall must be.

At the second attempt I found my voice. "Can someone get a torch over here," I croaked. "Move carefully, a step at a time. I'm right at the edge of the hole."

I heard a click and then a beam of light cut through the darkness. At first I couldn't see who was behind it but as it moved closer I spotted the shadowy shape of Robbie approaching. Silently he reached my side and pointed the torch into the shaft. We both gasped just as another torch was switched on. Someone, I think it was Duncan, immediately ordered it to be switched off again to conserve the battery. I took all this in subconsciously as all my attention was focussed on what lay beneath. The shaft was filled to within a foot of the top with rocks of all shapes and sizes. I looked at Robbie and he looked at me. "The hole in the side," we both said simultaneously. Duncan joined us at the edge looking white and strained. "There must have been a landslide," he whispered. He looked on the edge of panic.

9

The air was still thick with dust and nearly everyone was coughing. I raised my voice as much as I could. "The best thing we can do is get out of here at least until the dust settles. If we stay here much longer we'll all choke to death. Duncan, will you take your torch and lead the way to the gallery that you mentioned. Robbie, would you bring up the rear and shine your torch over everyone's head." Duncan's torch went on and like a zombie he pushed his way through the crowd and on into the next tunnel. We followed him in single file with Robbie at the back, myself just in front of him and Sian in front of me. Barely had we gone ten yards when Sian let out a wail, stopped and turned towards me. "Michael," she cried. "What's happened to Michael?"

I put what I hoped would be a comforting hand on her shoulder. "Michael will be fine," I consoled her. "The bell wasn't rung, so he won't have started down the steps and the landslide won't have reached him. Right now he's probably outside phoning for help." I hoped that was true. At least it seemed to ease her worries as she turned back and resumed walking. As soon as we'd left the tunnel and entered the gallery Robbie swung his torch around. We were in an area similar to a giant box in a theatre. At a guess it could have accommodated around eighty people standing up. Waist high railings formed almost all of the three sides, with a narrow exit to our left. As Robbie flicked his torch off Duncan moved to a bank of switches on the wall to our right. One by one he depressed them. Nothing happened until he got to the fifth, when a dim radiance appeared below and beyond our platform. There was just enough light filtering upwards for us to see ourselves.

I took a moment to look at everyone in turn. Everyone was covered in a fine layer of grey dust. Claire and Sian were crying. Duncan, Danny and Brian seemed in total shock. Lindsay looked calm, but kept a protective arm around Claire's waist. Esme was nervously twisting a handkerchief round and round in shaking hands. Only Robbie appeared unmoved.

"First things first," I said in as normal a voice as I could muster. "Would you all try your mobile phones. It's almost certain we won't get a signal down here but there's an outside chance someone will be lucky." Suiting the action to the words I got mine out. As I expected I got nothing. One by one the others gave a shake of the head. Claire started sobbing uncontrollably and Sian let out another long wail. I realised that I needed to raise their spirits.

"Come on now, girls," I looked directly at the two of them. "Things aren't as bad as they appear. By now Michael will have called for help and rescue teams will soon be on their way. They may take a little time to get through to us, but in the meantime we have enough air to breathe so we're not in the slightest danger of suffocating. Before we do anything else, how much food and drink do we have with us?"

Once everyone had emptied their pockets and bags I took stock. There were six bottles of water, none less than three quarters full, and four of various fizzy drinks. Food wasn't quite so plentiful, amounting to three bars of chocolate, four packets of crisps, half a packet of biscuits and a bag of mixed sweets. I'd hoped for more. Though I was confident of rescue I realised that it could take anything up to forty-eight hours. That, however, was a piece of knowledge that I intended to keep to myself.

At this point Duncan seemed to pull himself together somewhat. "Water's not a problem," he said. "There's a burn that runs the length of the cave. The water in it has been analysed and it's perfectly fit for drinking."

I tried to sound cheerful. "There you are then. We may be hungry by the time we get out but at least we're not going to die of thirst. The best thing to do right now is to try and relax. Try and get rid of some of the dust from your clothes and find yourselves a seat. If you start feeling cold walk up and down or do some physical jerks. Above all, keep calm." One or two looked as if they wanted to object but no-one said anything. Robbie, Duncan, Lindsay and I remained standing, the rest started to make themselves as comfortable as they could on the hard floor. For a full minute silence reigned.

It was Lindsay who broke it. "Do you think it will be all right to smoke in here?" she asked.

Duncan thought for a moment. "Should be. The cave's over a mile and a quarter long, half a mile wide and nearly two hundred feet high. That makes enough air to last us for several days." So saying he took out a pipe and started to fill it.

Unseen by anyone else I made a sign to Robbie to follow me and moved along the gallery out of earshot. He was lighting a cigarette as he came.

"When you've finished that," I said quietly, "I'd like to take another look at the U-bend. Bring your torch along." He nodded assent and I began to try and clean the dust out of my hair, face and clothes as I moved back to rejoin the others. Most of them were following my example. When Robbie indicated he was ready I looked round.

"We're going to take another look at the damage," I told them quietly. "We won't be long." Nobody said anything and only Danny and Lindsay looked remotely interested. Robbie and I walked in silence back up the tunnel. When we came to the pit we stood for a few moments looking down. It was my companion who broke the silence. "What's on your mind?" he asked softly.

I marshalled my thoughts. "Morale's low enough so I didn't want to say too much in front of the others but I don't think we should rely too much on Michael raising the alarm. The other side of the U-bend could have overflowed into the passage way and knocked him out or even buried him. There's also the possibility that he disobeyed orders, didn't wait for the bell and was coming down the steps. Either way he may be dead or unconscious for hours. That means that the alarm won't be raised until the minibus going back is overdue and that could be as late as nine tonight."

I saw Robbie frown in the dim light of the torch. "Worse than that, I'm afraid. Duncan takes the minibus home overnight. He told us that just before you arrived. Not only that, he's off tomorrow so no-one will know what's happened until tomorrow's first party gets here at ten o'clock. Are you thinking what I'm thinking?"

I tried to manufacture a smile and failed dismally. "I'm thinking that could mean we're here for anything up to forty-eight hours. There may not be a problem with thirst but we're all going to be gey hungry by then."

"Suggestions?" he queried.

"I think we should start clearing the blockage ourselves. It'll serve more than one purpose. It will keep everyone active and therefore help keep us warm." Despite my heavy clothing I was beginning to feel the chill of the place. "It will keep people's minds from dwelling too much on our plight and most important of all it will make life easier and quicker for the rescue teams when they do arrive."

Robbie considered my proposal for a full minute. "There's just one wee problem with that. Once we shift a quantity of the debris more will come down that shaft."

"True," I agreed. "But sooner or later it's all got to be shifted before we can get out. Optimistically there has to be a finite amount of rock to come down. Also the shaft was only about a foot or so wide, so surely sooner or later a bigger block will jam it up."

Just as I'd finished speaking I heard footsteps coming down the tunnel behind us. Robbie swung his torch around and a moment later Lindsay appeared. She'd cleaned most of the dust off herself and her black hair almost shone even in that dim light. She gave us a searching look, but before she could speak I asked how the others were bearing up.

"Esme and Danny have got themselves together," she reported. "Claire and Sian have stopped crying. Duncan still seems overwhelmed and Brian's just sitting there with a vacant look on his face. I don't think he's said a word since it happened. Meantime what are you two cooking up?"

In a few brief words we outlined our thoughts and the action we proposed. She nodded approvingly. "Good thinking. How do you want to organise it?"

I hadn't got that far in my thinking but thankfully Robbie had. "One person in the hole lifting the rocks and passing them to someone at the side. Then a chain all the way down the tunnel. The rocks passed from one to the other and the last person tosses them over the gallery rail."

Lindsay grinned. "Duncan won't like having the floor of his precious cave mucked up."

"Duncan will have to grin and bear it," I said firmly. "Getting us all out of here is a shade more important. O.K. We might as well make a start. I'll take first shift in the hole and Robbie can be at the side. Lindsay, will you go back and get the others sorted out. Most of the rocks can be lifted easily by the girls and any bigger ones we can leave in here temporarily for one of us to carry later. One hour on and then a fifteen minute break. After each break we'll change positions."

"Leave Danny to do the throwing at the end," Robbie instructed. "That takes a bit more strength than just passing from one to another. If anyone objects tell them to come up here and talk to us. This needs to be a team effort and we want everyone joining in with a bit of enthusiasm. And for heaven's sake don't mention our fears about Michael."

Lindsay turned towards him with a scornful look on her face. "I'm not a complete idiot, believe it or not." She moved off down the tunnel with head held high.

I grinned at Robbie. "You asked for that," I told him. He grinned back and said nothing. "I'll take the first shift at the coal face," I carried on. "You post yourself at the side. Lindsay seems to know what she's doing so we'll leave her to organise the chain."

"Fine by me," Robbie assented. "Just watch what you're doing down there and don't take any chances. Once we get started the rocks may shift position and the last thing we need is someone with a broken arm or leg."

"Caution is my middle name," I assured him. "I'll be like a cat on hot bricks."

It was about fifteen minutes before Lindsay had everyone organised. She'd stationed herself at the mouth of the tunnel. Robbie asked her if she'd had any trouble persuading the others; she just shook her head. Robbie managed to jam a torch at the side of the pit so that a certain amount of light filtered down. Carefully I got down on my stomach and swung my legs over the side before gingerly rising to my feet. There was a little bit of movement among the smaller rocks but not as much as I'd expected. Pulling on my gloves I looked round and selected a medium sized chunk about eight inches in diameter and handed it up to Robbie.

"Here we go folks," he called out at the top of his voice. "Post early for Christmas. First delivery on its way." For the first time since the rock fall I heard laughter.

CHAPTER THREE

I very soon got into a rhythm. Bend, lift, stretch, hand over, bend, lift, stretch, hand over. I said the words in my head as I performed the actions. For twenty minutes I felt fine, then one or two muscles began to make their presence felt. This despite the fact that I was in pretty good condition. Right away I made a mental note that the position in the pit would be too heavy for the ladies of our party. On the half hour mark I got a second wind, but by the end of an hour I was exhausted and ached all over. Apart from the physical effort dust was a problem. Whenever I lifted a stone a small amount of fine powder wafted upwards. There wasn't enough to affect anyone outside the hole. I managed some relief by tying a handkerchief over my mouth and nose, but often had to pause and cough. I was thankful when Robbie announced it was time to break.

At least our efforts hadn't been in vain. The level of rock had gone down by about three feet. Though I'd been half expecting another fall from the shaft and held myself ready for such an eventuality there'd not been so much as a tremor under my feet. Robbie and Lindsay between them helped me out and we all trooped back to the gallery. The first thing I did was to take a couple of mouthfuls of water to rinse out my mouth. Then I turned round and leaned on the railing. By this time all the rest were seated. Duncan had his pipe going and Esme, Robbie and Lindsay were smoking. I thought a word of encouragement wouldn't be amiss.

"Well done everyone," I praised. "We're making real progress. The level of rock has gone down by at least three feet. At this rate we'll be at the foot of this side of the U-bend by nine o'clock. If the rescue team gets here quickly and makes the same progress we could be out by ten o'clock. However, it's quite likely that there's more rock to come down, so don't get your hopes up too high." I paused but nobody made any comment, so I carried on. "For the next hour we'll change positions and I want to make one amendment. A full hour in the hole is a bit too much for anyone, so the person at the side will change places with the one in the hole every half hour. Now I don't want to be accused of being sexist, but frankly it's too much for a girl or woman." I looked straight at Lindsay, pretty certain that she would object. I was right. She opened her mouth but I forestalled her. "All right, Lindsay. You can have a go if you want to but on one condition. If you do find it too much of a strain you say so immediately. You've nothing to prove to any of us and if you get yourself crocked you'll just be a burden on us. Deal?" She nodded, though with some obvious reluctance.

"Robbie will take the next shift in the hole with Danny at the side," I continued. "At the half hour mark they'll change places. Brian can go up to the mouth of the tunnel and I'll stay at this end and do the final throw. The rest of you take up your previous positions." I looked at my watch. "We'll make the breaks twenty minutes instead of fifteen. There's ten minutes left of this one so I suggest we all relax; maybe even doze off. It could be a long day."

The next few hours were the stuff of which nightmares are made. Despite the chill the sweat was pouring off us. We could only use one torch for fear of the batteries running out so those in the tunnel were working in near darkness. Our bodies were sore and aching with the unaccustomed effort. Both Brian and Lindsay had taken a turn in the hole but only managed fifteen and twenty minutes respectively before giving in. I extended the breaks to half an hour. I think the only thing that kept us going was the progress we were making. By half past seven we were down eight feet and had uncovered nine of the twelve steps on the ladder. I was back in the hole for the third time when the disaster we'd all feared arrived. The first intimation was a rumble under my feet. Luckily I was close to the ladder at the time. I grabbed at the handrail and climbed quickly.

By the time I was out the rumble had become a roar and the hole started to fill up again. Others came running in from the tunnel and we watched in silence. Once more dust filled the air. Coughing and spluttering we waited for it to settle. To my stunned senses it seemed as if the noise continued for five minutes though in fact it wasn't much more than twenty seconds. When the dust finally settled we looked down. It was Danny who sounded the note of optimism.

"It's not as high as it was when we started," he exclaimed. "The fourth rung down is clear and the level is close to the fifth." This was true.

"One of two things must have happened," Robbie reflected. "To look on the bright side, this is the level on both sides of the U-bend adjusting itself. If you want to be pessimistic though it's more debris coming down the shaft. Take your pick." He turned to me. "Any thoughts, Dean?"

"Yes," I replied. "I think we should take a couple of hours off and try and rest. Right now we're all exhausted. What's the water position?" It transpired we had practically none left. "O.K. Danny and I will take the bottles down to the floor of the cave and refill them from the burn. The rest of you settle yourselves down, take a drink and try to get some sleep. Anyone got an alarm on their watch?" Robbie held up his hand. "Set it for nine thirty and give us all a call."

Uncomfortable though the floor was it took me less than ten minutes to fall into a heavy slumber. It seemed that just a few seconds had passed before Robbie was shaking me awake. "Nine thirty," he said softly. One by one we woke the others to a chorus of groans. We all had mouthful of water and a square of chocolate from our precious rations. I felt stiff as a board and aching in every limb so I could appreciate what everyone else was suffering. I half expected some protests when I suggested we get back to work but there weren't any, just more groans.

By just after midnight we were nine feet down when for the second time a rumble underground heralded a new fall of rock. This time the dust stayed relatively low and when it cleared we were encouraged to see that the level of the rock had only risen by just under three feet. Robbie had been 'down below' at the time and he turned round and gave the thumbs up sign.

"This looks as though the stuff in the bend is levelling out," he beamed. "If more had come down the shaft it would almost certainly have risen higher than this."

Only Esme seemed unconvinced. "If this is what we've been able to do what the hell are those on the other side doing. They should be nearly through to us by now." Robbie and Lindsay both looked at me and I gave a slight shake of my head. This was no time to mention our fears for Michael. I didn't want to dampen the optimism and I particularly didn't want to cause Sian any more distress.

"We don't know what they have to contend with," I told Esme. "They could have much more to move than we have. Let's keep at it. Think what a triumph it would be if we managed to get out through our own efforts."

By two a.m. we revised our timetable to half an hour on and half an hour off. Even so we made progress, slow though it was. The first of the torches gave out at five past three, but by that time we were below the roof of the connecting tunnel. There were three more rock falls, each smaller than the last and by now we were certain that it was simply the debris evening itself out in the two vertical shafts. When it was possible to move into the bottom level without too much difficulty I took a torch and shone it into the shaft that had caused all the trouble. As I'd hoped far up the opening I could see a larger rock wedging the channel shut. My relief was tempered by the fact that there were no sounds of people working on the other side. I feared for Michael. By now it was approaching quarter to six. I went back to the chamber where everyone had slumped to the ground in exhaustion.

"Good news and bad news," I announced. "Unless we're very unlucky there'll be no more rock coming down the shaft. It seems to be blocked. Another half hour should see the last of the fall cleared and we can get out. The bad news is that I can't hear any sounds from the other side to suggest a rescue party is working towards us. Of course they may just be having a break. Let's hope so. In any case we're almost home and dry. I know everyone's tired, but one last effort should do it."

Somehow aching limbs responded and by twenty past six just a scattering of small rocks and rubble was left. Taking one of the torches I went down and across and up to the other side. On the bottom bit I tried to clear as much debris out of the way as I could with my feet. I went up the steps on the other side and shone the torch along the exit tunnel. More debris on the floor there indicated that there'd been an overflow on that side but the tunnel was passable with care. The faintest light was coming from up ahead. Once more I listened intently but I couldn't hear a sound. Returning whence I'd come I gave a thumbs up sign. Before speaking I tested the bell but there was no sound from the other side.

"The way out is clear, ladies and gentlemen." A ragged cheer greeted my announcement. "Take it slowly and watch where you're putting your feet. There's still a lot of rubble and small pieces of rock underfoot. Having come so far the last thing we want now is a sprained or broken ankle. I'll go ahead with one torch, then hand it to whoever follows me and so on down the line. Danny, will you bring up the rear with the other torch. As soon as you get to the other side give a yell and all follow me out. If you're all ready let's go."

As soon as I reached the other side of the U-bend and handed the torch to Robbie who was hard on my heels I moved up the tunnel a few yards. There was still no sound from up ahead. I wondered what had happened to Michael. I had begun to think that he had been knocked out or worse, but there was no sign of a body anywhere. My reverie was interrupted by the sound of Danny's voice shouting that everyone was out. There was just enough light for me to see where I was putting my feet as I started moving further along the tunnel. As I rounded the final bend I turned to

Robbie, who was just behind me. "Wait there for a moment while I take a look outside."

I walked the final five yards or so and came to the entrance. Up above the sky was bright and blue with not a single cloud to be seen. A number of floodlights were in place and switched on. The sun was still low down behind the hills but the reflected light threw everything before me into sharp relief. The scene that met my eyes will be engraved in my mind for the rest of my life. A dozen or so bodies, two women among them, were lying on the ground in close proximity. Michael was one of them. I prayed silently that they were simply sleeping but I knew with some certainty that it was a sleep from which they'd never awaken. Nevertheless I checked for a pulse in every one. There was nothing, nor was there anything to indicate the cause of death. There was no sign of strain or suffering on any of the faces as I closed the eyes of the four that were open. I felt weak at the knees but I knew I had to pull myself together and find the words to tell the rest of them the disastrous news. As I made my way back to the cave entrance I noticed piles of rock on either side; obviously the rescuers had been working for some time before they were overcome. The first thing I did when I rejoined the group was to whisper to Robbie. "Go and take a look." He pushed past me.

I raised my voice. "Listen everyone. I've got some dreadful news. There's no easy way to break it to you, I'm afraid, so brace yourselves. There is a rescue party outside, twelve or more, but they're all dead." I heard one or two gasps as Sian called out with a trembling voice. "Is Michael there?"

There was no point in delaying the impact. "I'm sorry, Sian, but I'm afraid he is." I couldn't see her, but I heard the wail of distress and could picture the tears that accompanied it. I heard Esme trying to soothe her. I had one more instruction to give. "When you get out into the open don't linger at the entrance. Make your way straight to the car park." I turned and led the way.

Thankfully everybody did as I'd suggested. The minibus, a fire engine and a dozen cars plus my own Mondeo were scattered around but thankfully no more bodies. As soon as we reached the car park I spoke again. "Try your mobiles now and see if you can raise family and friends. I'll get on to the police." Taking my own phone out I keyed 999. I could hear the pulse of the ring tone but though I held on for a full two minutes there was no reply. Then I tried the Salutation Hotel, reasoning that by half past six there should be staff up and about and preparing for breakfast. Again there was nothing. I looked around. Despair showed on every face.

"I tried Fort George," Robbie was standing next to me and spoke in an undertone. "No reply, yet there's always someone on duty twenty-four hours a day." Hardly were the words out of his mouth when there came a cry from Danny.

"Hey, come and look at this." We crowded round him. He had the news headlines on his phone. I scanned down them as he read them aloud.

3.05 a.m. All contact lost with Ireland.

2.57 a.m. All contact lost with the Americas.

2.50 a.m. Gas cloud 'minutes away'.

2.38 a.m. Scientists baffled.

But it was the fifth item down that provided the clue to the mystery. Timed at two twenty it simply said: 'Huge gas cloud approaching the Earth at high speed from outer space'.

I didn't time it but I'd swear the silence that followed lasted a full thirty seconds. Then Robbie's voice sounded in disbelief. "Holy Moses. Global disaster." He then swore briefly and fluently. Another silence followed his outburst. I couldn't look up or around and stayed for a long time staring at my feet. They seemed miles away. When I finally managed to raise my sight I got a minor shock. Everyone was looking at me. Somehow I'd assumed that as the oldest among us Duncan, Robbie or Esme would have taken charge of the situation. But they looked as stunned as the younger ones. Little as I fancied the role I realised that it was up to me to provide the lead. All of a sudden the panic that had seized my brain evaporated and as if by divine guidance my mind became clear and I knew what had to be done.

"There's no point in hanging around here," I declared. "I know that everybody's instinct is to rush off home and if anyone wants to do that then of course you should, but until we know the full extent of the disaster I think we should stay together. If we separate now we may never link up again. Our best move would be to head for Perth, see if we can find out exactly what happened, get some food into us and get cleaned up. Then we'll have council of war. How many of you can drive?" It emerged that Claire, Brian and Sian were non drivers.

"If things are as bad as I suspect we're going to need cars, so we'll leave the minibus behind and take the cars that are here. Not all of them may have the keys in them, so does anyone know how to start a car without keys?" Robbie held up a hand. "Right," I continued. "Give us a demonstration. It's a skill we'll all probably need to learn."

"Wait a minute." It was Lindsay, speaking for the first time since our exit from the cave entrance. "We can't just leave all those people lying there. We ought to bury them before we go."

I spoke as gently as I could. "It's just not practicable. Much as I'd like to do it the ground for some distance around is solid rock. I'm more sorry than I can say but seeing dead bodies around is something we're going to have to get used to. If the situation is as bad as it looks at present there will be over five million in Scotland alone. Burying even a fraction of them just isn't possible. Now, when we get the cars going I'll lead the way. Follow me in convoy. I'll be keeping my speed down in case of obstacles in the road. Keep your eyes peeled for any sign of life anywhere and if you see anything honk your horn and we'll all stop. Danny, am I right in thinking the Esso garage on the outskirts of Perth is open all night?" He nodded. "We'll pull in there and fill up all the cars. The fact that the floodlights were on suggests that the electricity is still working so we'll be able to turn the pumps on. Claire, you go with Lindsay, Sian and Brian you come with me. I'll be heading for the Salutation Hotel when we get to Perth. There'll be plenty of food there and showers etc." Less than ten minutes later I led the way out of the car park and on to the single track approach road.

CHAPTER FOUR

I maintained a sedate twenty-five miles an hour until I came on to the double carriageway that led to the A9. Even then I didn't go above forty. Nothing moved anywhere. The sun was beginning to climb and it bade fair to being a hot day ahead. We saw no other signs of traffic until we turned on to the A9 itself. Neither Brian nor Sian had uttered a word since getting into the car. Over the next twenty miles we saw evidence that people had been on the road when the gas cloud struck. A number of lorries and several private cars littered the verges and the surrounding fields. The southbound carriageway remained clear, but on the northbound there'd been a four car shunt about seven miles from Perth. I slowed right down but there was no point in stopping. The occupants of all four vehicles were unquestionably beyond human aid. Even more worrying was the sight of sheep, cows and horses lying in fields by the side of the road. I didn't need to stop and examine these either; they were patently dead. At twenty to eight I pulled the Mondeo into the twenty-four hour garage and lined up at one of the pumps. Danny and Esme followed me into the shop, the latter intending to grab some sandwiches, filled rolls or bars of chocolate to hand around. At my suggestion she added some bottles of water and other beverages. Danny quickly grasped the method of turning the pumps on and called everyone in for a demonstration. We filled up, Robbie thankfully remembering that the car he'd chosen was diesel driven.

There were three or four crashed cars in the city itself as we drove on to the hotel. Telling the others to stay back I took Robbie and Danny in with me, wanting to make sure there were no corpses in the working areas when the girls and Esme came in. I blessed my foresight moments later. Between the three of us we manhandled the bodies of a porter, two chefs and a waitress out of the back door of the kitchen. Once the rest of the party arrived I led the way to the lounge and switched on the television. First I tried the main channels; all were blank. Then I pressed the teletext key. The headlines were much as they'd been on Danny's phone. I scanned down to the first mention of the gas cloud. Silently we read the entry.

'Astronomers have reported that a massive cloud of what appears to be gas has been sighted heading directly towards the Earth at a phenomenal speed. Estimates suggest that it is something approaching twenty thousand miles in diameter and will reach us in just over an hour. Further information will be posted here as soon as it is received.'

The next entry was equally brief. 'BBC News has contacted a number of scientists both here and in the U.S.A. All say the same thing. Spectroanalysis proves that the gas is not one that we know here on Earth. The only item of new information that has been given is that there does not appear to be any solid matter within the cloud. Here in London the cabinet has been summoned to an emergency meeting. In the meantime people are instructed to stay indoors and close all doors and windows until further notice.'

The remaining entries briefly stated that all radio and TV stations in North and South America had gone off the air and the last piece of news was that Ireland had followed suit.

"So now we know," someone said softly. Yet again I felt that all eyes were on me.

"The toilets on the ground floor are empty. I suggest that first we all get cleaned up as best we can. Than can I ask the ladies to prepare some sort of breakfast while we look around the hotel for tools and anything else that may prove useful. By the time we've eaten I'll have worked out our immediate prospects." Much to my surprise there was no dissension and everyone moved obediently towards the toilets. I nipped upstairs to my room and dug my electric shaver out of the suitcase along with its charger. The stubble around my chin was beginning to annoy me and I suspected the other men would be similarly afflicted.

By the time we'd washed and shaved encouraging sounds were emanating from the kitchens. As we laid a table in the dining room I gave out instructions. "Would the three of you have a hunt around and see what you can find in the way of tools. There's bound to be some somewhere. Ideally we need jemmies, crowbars and sledge hammers but even ordinary hammers and screwdrivers will be useful. We're mostly going to have to break into shops for the things we'll need. I'm going to see if I can find some maps."

I hit gold immediately. Over half a dozen street maps of Perth were on display near the main entrance. In the manager's office I found a wall map of central Scotland and several ordnance survey maps of the surrounding districts. When I returned to the dining room the others had assembled a haul that included two crowbars, three jemmies, a sledge hammer and several ordinary hammers and screwdrivers. By this time breakfast was ready and the ladies had done us proud. There was no porridge, but they'd made up sandwiches and rolls with a choice of bacon, fried egg, sausage or black pudding. Toast and butter, not to mention pots of tea and coffee also appeared as if by magic. Conversation was limited in the extreme while we ate and that gave me a chance to marshal my thoughts. When we reached the tea and coffee stage I cleared my throat.

"Once again can I say that if anyone wants to go home then of course you must do so. I've nobody close so it's easy for me to decide. But think carefully. There is nothing you can do now for your loved ones other than say goodbye and it will cause you needless distress." I paused for a full thirty seconds but nobody moved, so I carried on. "Before we make any plans for the future I think we should check around the area to see if there are any other survivors. There's one other thing that should be done as soon as possible. Danny, you know the area. Check at home if you want to, then will you and Robbie get hold of a large van and go around the police stations and Territorial Army premises and collect up all the guns and ammunition that you can find."

Before I could continue I was interrupted by Lindsay. "God help us. The human race has just about been wiped out and now you want to start a war!" Her tone was scathing.

"I want to stop one, not start one," I snapped back. "The more guns we can confiscate the less chance there is of them falling into less scrupulous hands. In any case, we'll need guns for protection. It's odds on a few dogs will have survived; possibly even some wild animals from safari parks and zoos. Before long they're going to be hungry. Do you really fancy facing a starving Rottweiler with your bare hands?" Lindsay subsided, holding up a hand as if to acknowledge the point I'd made.

I held up the sheaf of street maps. "I've divided the area into sections. Lindsay and Claire, will you go to the fire station and the infirmary first. You'll find them on the map. They're the two most likely places to find survivors. Fire crews have protective clothing and breathing apparatus and hospitals have oxygen cylinders. After that do a tour of the western half. Esme and Brian, will you head across the river, take a quick trip round Barnhill and then up to Scone. Duncan and Sian, yours is the southern section, down as far as Bridge of Earn. Send anyone you find back here. Take an hour or so, certainly not longer than an hour and a half. In the meantime I'll lay on a hot lunch for all of us. After that we'll sort out what to do next." As they prepared to leave the room I signed Robbie to hang back.

"I feel a bit embarrassed telling everyone what to do," I said to him when the others had gone. "You've had more experience of dealing with a crisis than I have. You should be giving the orders."

He shook his head decisively. "One thing I've learned in life is that I'm better at taking orders than giving them. Anyway, you're making a pretty good job of it so far. Just keep on the way you're doing and you'll get my full support. Don't worry. If I feel you're getting too big for your boots I'll soon cut you down to size." He turned abruptly and left.

Once he'd gone I headed for the kitchens and checked the stores. In the cold store I found several five kilogram packs of rump steak among other meats. Taking two of them I put them into one of the ovens to defrost. Next I found a large cauldron, put a couple of litres of water and a handful of salt into it and put it on to boil. An adjacent cupboard yielded half a sack of Maris Piper potatoes, a large polythene bag of carrots and half a dozen swedes. I'd just laid them out by the sink when I heard a voice calling in the distance. Going back through to the front doors I found a young girl standing just inside. As I looked at her the old Scots word 'shilpit' came into my mind. There isn't a direct English translation; possibly the nearest one could get to it is dowdy or down at heel. Her light brown hair hung down in rats' tails and looked as if it hadn't seen a brush or comb for some days. She was wearing a grubby orange tee shirt and torn jeans. Only the sandals on her feet looked new. I reckoned she was anywhere between thirteen and seventeen.

"Are you Dean?" she asked in a strong local accent.

"I am," I replied. "Who are you, how old are you and where did you come from?"

"I'm Kirsty. I'm fifteen. A woman and a boy in a car told me to come here and ask for Dean."

"Come along in then. Tell me, Kirsty, can you peel potatoes?"

"Course I can," she said scornfully. "I've done it often enough at the hostel."

"Good. There's ten of us now and I'm making lunch for them. That means a whole heap of tatties and carrots need to be peeled."

She looked down at her feet and spoke hesitatntly. "Is it O.K. if I go outside for a smoke first?"

I tried not to laugh. "Of course. But why do you want to go outside? What's wrong with in here?"

She looked at me as if I was off my head. "We're no' allowed to smoke indoors."

This time I was unable to prevent a slight chuckle escaping my lips. "So who's going to complain? In case you haven't realised it yet, nearly everybody in the world is dead. There aren't any policemen left to arrest you, nor any courts left to try you. Come on into the lounge and tell me how you escaped the gas."

Bit by bit I got the story from her. She'd been in care for most of her life and for the last year had been living in a council run hostel. Sometime during the night she'd awoken feeling cold and had snuggled down right under the blanket. I deduced that she must have cut off her air supply altogether and been breathing the trapped air within the bed. She awoke again a little later gasping for breath.

"When I woke up next I looked at my watch and saw it was after nine o'clock," she continued. "At first I thought I must have slept through the alarm bell, then I saw that all the others were still in their beds. It was only when I went to waken them I realised they were all dead. I went downstairs and switched on the radio but nothing came out. Then I tried the teletext and that's when I found out about the gas cloud. The night warden was in her room but she was dead too. I had some toast and made a cup of tea. Since then I've been walking the streets looking for other people. The two in the car were the first I saw."

I put her to work preparing the vegetables. The water in the cauldron was boiling by this time and the steak was defrosted. Cutting it into cubes I dumped it into the boiling water. As Kirsty handed over the vegetables I cut them up and added them to the stew. Rummaging around I came across a tin of gravy granules and they too went into the mix. Finally I unearthed a couple of gateaux from the massive fridge and put them out to defrost. Just as I finished doing that I heard voices in the lounge. Leaving Kirsty to supervise the cooking I went through. Five strangers stood there looking around. The two oldest were a woman in her thirties and a Chinese man about the same age or slightly older. Standing to one side were a slim dark Asian looking lad in his early twenties and two girls slightly younger, one black, one white. The woman was the first to speak.

"You must be Dean," she stated in a warm, cultured voice. "We're all from the Royal Infirmary. I'm Myra McAuley, this is Doctor Sen Chi Ling, over there is Paul Leggatt who's a staff nurse and the two girls are nurses, Selma Dupres and Lily Lawson respectively." As she introduced each one I moved around and shook hands.

"I'm very pleased to see you, Doctor," I began. I tried to say more but she held up her hand.

"Please, no titles," she instructed. "I'm Myra."

"And I'm Ling." The Chinese doctor spoke for the first time. "In the circumstances it seems rather foolish to be formal with each other." His English was faultless and without accent.

I smiled. "O.K. Myra and Ling it is. I don't know how much the girls told you, but there are another six in our party out searching for signs of life. One more person has turned up so far and we're getting some lunch together. After that we'll get down to making some plans. I think I know how you survived but tell me anyway."

My assessment had been almost correct. They'd been on duty in the intensive care unit. On hearing about the approaching gas cloud they'd broken out a number of oxygen cylinders and set up two large oxygen tents into which the five of them had packed.

"Ling rang round the wards to colleagues suggesting they took similar precautions but they just laughed at him," Myra explained. "We stayed in the tents for as long as the oxygen held out. That was nearly an hour and a half later. We'd taken masks in with us, which we put on when we emerged. Then we drew lots to see which of us would remove their mask and test the air. Paul lost! When we found that it was breathable we went round the entire hospital but there was no-one else alive. Since then we've been loading three ambulances with equipment and supplies ready to head out to the countryside."

"My estimate is that the towns and cities will become disease ridden and unsafe within ten days." Ling contributed. "We suspected that we might be the only ones left alive, so we planned to find a country house somewhere, lay in supplies and start to grow our own food. However, now that we have found there are more people we will be happy to join in with you."

I explained that the others would be back soon for lunch and that afterwards we would start to plan. "I have some ideas to put forward," I added, "but suggestions are always welcome." I called Kirsty through to be introduced.

Esme and Brian were the first to return. The latter headed straight for the toilet without a word. Esme lit a cigarette, placed it in her holder and looked at me with disdain.

"Thanks a bunch for teaming me with Brian. I tried a dozen times to start a conversation. All I got in return was a yes a no and a grunt. He seems to be living in a world of his own. If you want to stay in my good books give him to somebody else next time. I take it the orphan girl got here."

I laughed. "Sorry," I apologised. "I thought you might be good for Brian. Obviously I was wrong. And yes, Kirsty did get here. She's been helping me get the lunch ready."

"I hope she washed her hands first," was the only reply I got.

I took her through and introduced her to the hospital contingent and we chatted for a few minutes. I learned that Paul's Asian look was due to his mother having been a Filipino. Then I headed back to the kitchen. The stew was coming along nicely and the gateaux were fully thawed. I sent Kirsty in to lay the tables in the dining room while I put plates in the oven to warm. Over the next fifteen minutes the remaining couples arrived in. A shake of the head from both Lindsay and Duncan told me they'd found no other survivors. Robbie and Danny were the last to get back.

"There isn't a gun left in public places anywhere," Robbie reported. "We even cleared out a couple of gun shops. I've added some fishing gear as well. Never know when it might come in handy."

As with breakfast there was little talk while we ate. My hastily flung together stew drew approval and I was relieved to find there were no vegetarians among us. I used the time to prepare my opening speech for the forthcoming conference. When the meal was over we took our tea and coffee into the lounge. Once everyone was seated I took up a standing position in front of the fireplace, looked round and smiled.

CHAPTER FIVE

"While I've been doing my impression of Jamie Oliver this morning," I began, "I've been trying to think ahead. One thing came to my mind right away. I've always been an avid follower of science fiction. I've read a lot of the books that tell of a situation similar to ours and seen just about all of the TV series. The thing that stuck in my mind in every case was that the survivors spent the first weeks and months travelling round the country looking for somewhere to settle, scavenging enough food for two or three days at a time. I presume that was for dramatic effect, but in my view it's a recipe for disaster. I would suggest that we decide here and now where we're going to live. Then we'll spend the next week or so building up a stock of food, clothing and other essentials. After that it won't be safe to venture into populated areas. Before I enlarge on that, is there anybody that disagrees with me so far?"

I looked first at Lindsay. If anyone was going to argue she was the most likely candidate. But she shook her head, as did all the others. With more confidence than before I spoke again.

"At present there are fifteen of us, but there's nothing to say that we won't come across more survivors in the days and weeks to come. Though it's optimistic I think we should be looking at somewhere that can accommodate at least fifty people. It has to be well away from housing and have ample storage space. That means we're looking for a hotel or school in its own grounds. Though there are larger houses and the odd castle here and there I doubt if they would be suitable. As to location we have two choices. One is to find somewhere on the coast or on the banks of a large loch. The advantage there is that we'd have access to a regular supply of fresh fish. The disadvantage is that coastal areas and those near lochs do not usually have adjacent areas of good growing soil. The second choice is an inland area with good soil and a good sized area for cultivating. It would need to have a river nearby to ensure water supplies and if that river had fish in it that would be a double bonus. I think the best thing to do would take a vote on it. A show of hands will be sufficient."

It was a fairly emphatic decision in favour of an inland site, ten to four while I abstained. Had I voted I would have been one of the minority. To my mind the lure of a constant supply of fish was overwhelming. I kept my thoughts to myself, though.

"Now we get down to the nitty-gritty." I tried to think of a gentle way to make my next point and failed. I'd have to give it to them straight. "Wherever we go there'll be dead bodies. They'll have to be disposed of before we can take up residence. It won't be pleasant but it will have to be done and done quickly. We daren't risk disease. With that in mind can any of you come up with somewhere suitable?"

I wasn't expecting any replies, but to my surprise Myra McAuley stood up immediately. "I know just the place. There's a new hotel been built near the A9 just north of Gleneagles. It's not due to open until the middle of September so there's only security staff and maybe a couple of workmen staying there at present. I was called down there last week to treat one of the brickies who'd fallen off the roof and broken his arm. The assistant manager was there at the time and gave me a tour of the place. It's ideal for our purpose. The hotel is built round an old mansion house. There's something like a hundred bedrooms, it's got its own power supply via solar panels and there's several acres of newly flattened ground around it. Better still there's a river on one boundary within two hundred yards of the buildings."

I asked if there were any objections. Nobody spoke or moved. "That settles it then. Now there's no point in us all going there straightaway and empty handed. If the hotel's not due to open for another couple of weeks it's doubtful if there'll be much food in the place. So what we'll do is this." I turned to the two doctors. "Would you go ahead, check the place over and remove any corpses? I know it's a ghastly job, but you're best fitted to do it."

"Of course we will." It was Ling who replied. "The three ambulances outside are fully loaded with medical supplies and equipment so we can head off immediately." He rose, as did the other medics, but I held up my hand to restrain them.

"A couple of things before you go. Hopefully the phones will continue to work for a day or two. I'll give everybody my mobile number and Robbie's too. When you get to the hotel will you phone one of us and report on whether the road is clear, please? I'll take everybody else's number and if there's a blockage I'll ring round and instruct as to detour. Secondly, how many of the five of you drive?"

"We all do," Myra responded, "though Lily hasn't passed her test yet."

"Good," I said. "You'll find a van outside loaded with guns and ammunition. Would one of you take that along with the ambulances, please?"

When they'd departed I looked at Danny. "How many supermarkets are there in Perth?" I asked.

He grinned. "We've got them all. Asda, Tesco, Morrisons, Aldi, Lidl. There's also a Tesco storage depot on the boundary."

I wished I'd made out a list of priorities, but I didn't want to delay any longer than was necessary. "Danny, will you and Brian take the Tesco depot. Lindsay and Claire, yours will be the Asda store. The Tesco supermarket for Robbie and Sian and Aldi for Duncan and Esme. Kirsty and I will look after Morrisons. You know what we need. All manner of tinned stuff and dried food like flour, sugar, salt, pulses, that sort of stuff. Lindsay and Claire only, will you get a few dozen loaves of wrapped bread. There'll be freezer storage at the hotel to keep it fresh for a week or two. Also get butter, margarine, cheese and cold meats for sandwiches. There should be trucks on site; if not get one somewhere nearby. If the teams with two drivers can load more than one lorry, fine. But whatever stage you're at around half past five, knock off and leave. There'll be a lot to do this evening and after what we've been through in the last twenty-four hours an early night is indicated. Write your mobile numbers on this sheet of paper for me before you go. If I don't call you you'll know the road to the hotel is clear. Danny will show everyone where their target is on the map."

Kirsty and I were the last to leave. The time was two thirty-five. I drove the few hundred yards to the Morrisons store and parked around the back. Luck seemed to be with us. A lorry was already backed on to the loading bay. Telling Kirsty to stay in the car I went to explore. The lorry had obviously been discharging and was still more than half full. Six bodies, all male, were around the tail end. As quickly as I could I dragged them behind a stack of boxes and covered them with a tarpaulin. I blessed fortune once again when I examined the goods remaining inside the lorry. Most of it was tinned stuff. There were pallets of sugar plus a few dozen boxes labelled as jam and marmalade. Though they weren't high on my priority list I realised that a little bit of luxury would help morale. I certainly didn't intend to waste time unloading them. Then I called to Kirsty to come in.

"You go into the main part and start loading trolleys. Concentrate on tinned meat and fish, flour, dried yeast, dried milk, sugar and salt. Put the first half dozen trolleys into the lorry as they are. After that empty them out and reuse the trolley. O.K.?"

She nodded and turned to go. Then she wheeled round. "Will it be all right if I take some cigarettes as well?"

"Yes, but don't put them in the back of the lorry. Fill three or four carrier bags to take in the driver's cab."

The three forklift trucks near the bay weren't working, but another couple were plugged into the recharger. Taking one of those I made a start. It took me a few minutes to get the hang of lifting pallets on the trucks and putting them down again in the back of the lorry but once I did I worked fairly fast. Soon after we got started my phoned bleeped. It was Myra, reporting that the road was clear. Kirsty was finding it hard to push full trolleys the length of the storeroom, but she worked away bravely and never once complained. By twenty to four the lorry was full. I made a last visit into the front shop itself and collected a bundle of notebooks and a handful of ballpoint pens. Telling Kirsty to go and collect her cigarettes I climbed into the cab. The keys were in the ignition and when I turned the engine on I was pleased to see that the fuel tank was three-quarters full. Kirsty appeared and heaved five full shopping bags in to the space behind driver and passenger before climbing in herself. I let in the clutch, gingerly engaged first gear and we moved slowly around the building and out into the road. For the first three or four miles I kept the speed down to around twenty while getting used to the vehicle. After that I felt confident enough to move into top gear and settle down at around forty miles an hour. More traffic had gone off the road into the surrounding countryside than on the trip down from the cave to Perth. Once again dead animals littered the fields.

Although Myra had given precise directions I wasn't entirely sure where the hotel was situated and slowed down appreciably just short of the turn off for Auchterarder. A short while later Kirsty gave a cry.

"There it is. Muirton Grange Hotel. Go left here."

I turned into a side road. Less than a quarter of a mile further on there was a sharp bend and just past that another signpost led us to a metal fence with double iron gates. These in turn led us to a driveway and another quarter of a mile brought us to the car park next to the front entrance. There was no sign of the ambulances, though five or six private cars and two vans were scattered around. The original mansion house had been made of grey stone and was four storeys high. Modern wings had been added on either side but with no attempt to blend with the original. They were constructed of brick and also rose to four storeys. Later I discovered other stone buildings to the rear of the original mansion house that had at one time been stables. Parking the lorry, we dismounted and went through the front door into a reception area, with Kirsty still clutching her precious cargo. A sign at one side showed the way to a lounge bar. Feeling thirsty I made for that.

The bar was large and well stocked. To my delight there were three or four pumps of real ale. I drew myself a pint while Kirsty settled for draught cola. She sat down at one of the tables and lit a cigarette while I wandered over to the window, glass in hand. The view was towards the rear and in the far distance I could see a thin column of smoke rising into the still air. I'd just turned away when the door opened and Myra walked in looking white as a sheet. She acknowledged our presence with a nod before wordlessly heading for the bar and taking a double shot of brandy from the gantry. This she drank in one gulp. Then she took a refill and came to the table to join us. Seeing Kirsty's open packet of cigarettes she took one without asking and used the lighter. Still she hadn't spoken.

"I never thought I'd live to see a doctor smoking," I remarked with a smile.

"I gave up five years ago," she said sadly. "I think it was a mistake. Even though I'm case hardened the last hour or so has been an absolute nightmare. There were more bodies than I anticipated. Twenty-two in all, including three young children."

"What have you done with them?" I asked.

"We loaded them on to stretchers and took them to just beyond the back gate. Then we dug a pit six feet deep and put all the bodies into it. Ling siphoned off some petrol from one of the vehicles and when I left they were setting light to them all. That's when I felt faint and came away. Once the fire burns down they'll fill in the pit again. Strange that I should be so squeamish. The young ones and Ling seemed to take it in their stride."

I thought it best to change the subject. "Where are the ambulances and the guns?"

"Round the back," she replied. "Apart from getting the stretchers off we left the unloading until you came."

Leaving the two of them I went back into the reception area and studied the plan on the wall. The whole of the ground floor was given over to kitchens, restaurants, offices, a committee room, lounges and a ballroom, plus an area at the back marked conservatory. I explored the kitchens first and was delighted to find a cold store that was as big as an average living room. We could raid the supermarkets and fill it with enough frozen meat to last for a good three months. Two massive freezers stood in one of the two kitchens. I switched everything on. There were thirty bedrooms in the mansion house itself and each wing held thirty-six. I was pleased to see that the keys hanging behind the desk were the old-fashioned mortise type and not the modern electronic card variety. I explored the ground floor first, ending up in the conservatory. This was huge and ideal for turning into a greenhouse. Next I went down to the basement, which covered the whole length and width of the original house. The roof was a good ten or eleven feet high and it was plain we could store a huge quantity of food and other items in that alone. Going back to the bar I noticed that Kirsty had made some effort to tidy herself up. Her hair was neater and she was wearing a light sweater over the grubby tee shirt. I guessed she'd picked it up in Morrisons. I was still thirsty, so I made myself a shandy and went back to the table.

"I suggest you take a key and pick a bedroom for yourselves. We'll stick to the ones in the mansion house for the moment. The power seems to be on so it will be all right to use the lifts. I'm hoping Lindsay and Claire will be back first so we can make up a pile of sandwiches for everybody when they're all here."

They did as I suggested and I followed suit. Rooms one to ten were on the first floor. I took eight, my lucky number, Myra grabbed five and Kirsty seven. Each bedroom had toilet and shower attached, a double bed and all the other usual fittings. They were spacious. The beds weren't made but sheets, pillows and duvets had been placed, neatly folded, at the foot of each. Towels were stacked on the dressing table. Alone again I made up the bed, stripped and took a much needed cold shower. My room overlooked the front drive and moments after I was dressed I heard the sound of an engine. I dashed to the window in time to see Lindsay descending from the cab of an Asda lorry. Fortune was still smiling, I thought. I met the two of them as they came into reception. Lindsay gave me a big smile, the first I'd had from her, and saluted.

"Asda party present and correct," she laughed. "The bread and stuff is at the back of the lorry."

"Well done," I said as I returned her salute. "Pick yourselves a room or rooms from one to thirty and relax for a bit. I'll start unloading what we need for tonight." I left them to it and went to the lorry they'd brought. True to her word the back was piled from floor to roof with loaves of wrapped sliced bread. About to grab an armful I stopped, turned and went to the lorry I'd brought. With difficulty I got to one of the trolleys that Kirsty had filled, emptied it and used it to unload the bread and other items. Myra had reappeared by this time, also looking fresher. I dug out a second trolley and between us we carted load after load into the kitchen. Leaving enough and to spare for that evening we put the rest into one of the freezers. The two girls had selected wisely when it came to the fillings. Slabs of cheese, packets of ham and chicken and tins of salmon followed the bread into the hotel, not to mention butter, margarine and even several assorted jars of pickles.

The rest of the hospital contingent appeared as we were taking in the last lot, followed a minute later by Esme and Duncan in a plain van. I sent them all to get rooms. Kirsty had also reappeared. She and Myra volunteered to make a start on the sandwiches, tea and coffee. As soon as they'd taken off for the kitchen Robbie and Sian drove up and hard on their heels came Danny and Brian. Both teams reported full loads.

CHAPTER SIX

Once the sandwiches were ready I took a handful, grabbed a cup of coffee and went outside. Barely had I taken my first bite when Robbie materialised at my side. We chewed without speaking for a couple of minutes.

Eventually I broke the silence. "How was Sian this afternoon?"

"Quite bright. She seems to have got herself together," Robbie replied. "Apparently she'd only known Michael since Saturday. They met at a disco and yesterday was their first outing together. I get the impression that she quite liked him but was treating it as a holiday romance."

"Good." Already my mind had switched to another subject that was bothering me. "Robbie, how much do you know about electricity?"

"Absolutely nothing," he said cheerfully. "Why?"

"I'm wondering just how reliable those solar panels are. Sooner or later the main grid is going to break down. Should we tell people not to use the lifts? If there's no current the alarm bell won't work, so someone could be stuck for hours."

He gave it some thought. "There's an escape hatch in the roof of the lifts," he said at last. "It shouldn't be too difficult to free anyone that gets stuck. As to raising the alarm there'll not be a lot of noise around the place. We'd hear any shouting and banging quite quickly. Hallo, who's this?"

A car was coming down the driveway. As it got nearer I realised it was a Corsa, one that had seen better days, and that there were two occupants. It drew up in front of us and an elderly man and woman emerged. The man leaned heavily on a walking stick. We moved forward, shook hands and introduced ourselves.

"James and Margaret Tulloch," the man said in return. "We're from Aucterrarder. We saw the smoke in the distance and it looked too regular to be a normal fire so we thought we'd investigate."

I hadn't realised that the smoke from the funeral pyre would have attracted attention. The new arrivals went on to tell us how they had survived.

"We don't sleep too well," the husband explained, "so we heard the warnings at the back of one o'clock. We got all the blankets and things we could find, shut ourselves in the bedroom and made the place as airtight as we could. It was after midday before we dared come out and go outside. That's when we found that everyone was dead."

Between us Robbie and I gave a potted version of our own experiences and what we planned to do in the next few days.

"I'm afraid we're not going to be a lot of use to you," James apologised. "We're both seventy-five and I'm suffering from arthritis. Lifting things is a bit beyond us."

"On the contrary," I protested. "You're going to be very valuable. We'll need to leave someone here to look after the place while we're out foraging. I assume you can cook, Margaret." She nodded energetically. "There you are then, you're our catering officer. For the next few days it'll be a matter of sandwiches, tea and coffee for the teams as they come in with their loads and a cooked evening meal. We've got an odd number at present, so there'll be one person left with you every day to help with anything heavy."

We took the new arrivals into the dining room and introduced them to everybody. Once that was done I held up a hand for silence.

"In view of all that's happened in the last twenty-four hours or so I think an early night would do us all good. We'll leave the unloading of the vans till morning, but there are two things to be done this evening. First of all Robbie is going to issue guns and show us how to use them. From now on we carry them everywhere we go. I hope we'll never have to use them but as the old saying goes it's better to be safe than sorry. Once we've done that I'll rough out the programme for tomorrow and then we'll all get to bed." I half expected a complaint from Lindsay but there were no protests.

The rifle that Robbie had picked out for us was the Kalashnikov AK 47. As he explained, it was light and easy to handle and was probably the most efficient weapon in the world. He spent ten minutes instilling into us the use of the safety catch and the need for safe handling at all times. Then he showed us how to hold, aim and fire the rifle. Finally, one at a time we fired single rounds and a burst of fire into the distance, without aiming at anything in particular. He promised that would come the following evening.

On the way back into the hotel I cornered our two doctors. "Do either of you know anything about dentistry?" I asked. Myra shook her head immediately.

"I know a little of the theory," Ling admitted. "Extracting a tooth would be no problem and I think I could manage to fill one. Making dentures would be beyond me though."

Once everyone was settled and had drinks I moved across and stood with my back to the bar. "I'll try and make this as short as possible," I began. "First off, there are alarm clocks in every room. I suggest we set them for eight tomorrow morning. If anyone wants to get up earlier they could maybe make a start on getting breakfast. There's not much available for a fry up I'm afraid, but there's oatmeal, so perhaps the first person down could put some porridge on. Other than that it's more sandwiches or toast. First job after breakfast will be to unload the trucks. The cellar has columns supporting the roof and these divide it nicely into compartments. James, I'd like you to direct operations down there and have a separate space for each type of tinned and dried goods. We'll fill the cellar before we start storing anything on the ground floor. Also I want the medical staff to choose where they want to set up shop before leaving tomorrow."

"Take your guns with you at all times from now on. Would each team also take a notebook and pen from the pile I've left on the bar here. While you're driving around make a note of anything you see in the countryside that might be useful to us. Fields of potatoes and other vegetables, fruit trees and bushes, farm machinery, that sort of thing. Obviously if you see any live animals, note those down. If we don't find some cows or goats milk is soon going to be a thing of the past. Likewise eggs if we can't find any poultry. But even more important, keep your eyes open for dogs and cats. The most likely species to have survived the gas are those which burrow in airtight compartments like rats and mice. A few cats and dogs are vital to deal with that menace. And it goes without saying if you meet other people direct them back here."

"Now as to deployment tomorrow. Robbie and Danny, I'd like you to concentrate on fuel. Take one of the cars over to Grangemouth and start bringing back every tanker you can fill with petrol and diesel. You may even find some tankers en route. Park them away from the hotel in and behind the stables. Keep doing that for as long as you can. Myra and Selma, would you carry on collecting medical supplies and equipment. Raid the chemists' shops and grab everything you think will be useful. Can you also get a dentist's chair and tools. Ling and Lily, will you make a start on clothing and footwear. Remember that winter is not far away, so put the accent on warm, long lasting items in a variety of sizes. The rest of us will carry on bringing in food, but this time we'll hit Stirling instead of Perth."

Quickly I detailed the pairings, making one or two changes. "Brian, you're with me tomorrow and our target is Tesco. Kirsty, you're the odd one out. Would you stay here and help Margaret with the catering. We'll have a different person staying every day." There was method in my last two deployments. Kirsty still wasn't fully developed physically and she'd done a lot of heavy lifting the previous day. A day on lighter duties would give her a chance to recover. As for Brian, I wanted to get to know him better. He was the only one who didn't seem to fit in and that worried me. He spoke seldom and then only in monosyllables. Even while we'd been eating he was sitting apart from everybody else. I hadn't even seen him smile up to that point; in fact his expression never varied from its normal look of blankness. Esme and Danny had got nothing out of him. Maybe I could get him to relax.

It was coming up to half past ten before we completed the unloading and got on the road next morning. Sunshine and blue skies had greeted us once more. True to form Brian had said nothing to anyone all morning. I let a few miles of the A9 slip by before I spoke. I'd decided on shock tactics.

"Brian, I'm not going to beat about the bush," I began. "I'm worried about you. You've hardly said a word in the last two days and you don't seem willing or able to mix with the others. I know we're all grieving over what's happened, but is something troubling you in particular? If so, tell me what it is and we'll see what we can do about it."

He was staring straight ahead through the windscreen and was silent for so long that I started to think he intended to ignore my approach. Then I felt rather than saw him turn his face towards me.

"I just feel so helpless," he mumbled. "I'm not much good at anything practical and I've never mixed much with other people." Bit by bit I got his life story, though it was like pulling teeth. His parents were in their late forties when he was born and he was their only child. He'd been sickly in his younger days, so his doting parents had spoiled and pampered him. For a while he was deemed too unfit to attend school so he'd had private tutors until he was twelve. Once he did go to school he was very much a loner and had never made any friends. His only interests were reading and classical music.

By the time I'd wheedled all this out of him we'd arrived at Tesco and started to load. I used the time to consider the problem. What he really needed was a strong minded girl friend to knock him into shape, but I couldn't see any of the girls in our group who could fit the bill apart from

Lindsay and her interests obviously lay in other directions. My musings were interrupted by a cry from Brian. I was in the shop at the time and he was in the back store. I ran through, gun at the ready. My first thought was that someone had appeared on the scene. When I reached him, however he pointed at a stack of boxes containing tinned salmon.

"I heard a noise from behind there," he whispered. "It sounded like a faint cry." I walked round the stack, which appeared to be unbroken. We'd be taking it any way so I told Brian to start pulling the boxes off gently. We were almost down to floor level when a space in the middle was exposed and in that space was an emaciated mother cat and four kittens. The kittens were still moving and I saw signs of breathing in the mother. Telling Brian to go and get some cat food and milk and a couple of bowls I spoke softly to the brood as I stroked the adult cat. She lifted her head and tried to stand, but the effort was too much for her. We laid the food and milk by her side and left her to dine in peace.

We carried on with our loading, including a large supply of cat food. When we finished we went back to check on our litter. The mother looked much stronger and the kittens were feeding off her. Taking a trolley we laid towels on the base and gently lifted the family on to them. I cut off some wire from another trolley and fastened it over the top.

All the time we'd been working I was pondering the best way to deal with Brian's problems. Once we were on the road I'd made up my mind. Wryly I thought to myself that I was acting almost as a father to him.

"You know, Brian, there's nothing much wrong with you," I opened. "What you need is self confidence and that will come with responsibility. Have you ever done any gardening?"

He looked a little more animated as he replied. "I used to cut the grass and do some of the digging."

"Right." I tried to put a note of encouragement into my voice. "That's probably as much as any of us have done. Now my plan is to turn the conservatory into a huge greenhouse and I want you to take charge of it. That'll be your personal project for the future. We'll get you some gardening books out of one of the libraries and you can study them. We'll talk more about it in a couple of weeks' time." When he didn't reply I stole a sideways look at him. It was difficult to read his expression but I thought he looked pleased.

For the next few days we all worked like Trojans. Apart from food and clothing we laid in large stocks of water purifiers and chemical toilets. Like the electricity service mains water supply was almost entirely automated, but it would need only one burst main to cut us off. I wasn't even sure that a fault in the electricity circuits wouldn't also affect the water delivery. I also deployed teams to plunder the garden centres. In the conservatory and outside the back entrance piles of pots, barrels and tubs grew, as did the sacks of compost and fertilizer. Hundreds if not thousands of packets of seeds went into cupboards in the conservatory and elsewhere on the ground floor. By the Monday evening very little stock was left in the supermarkets in Stirling, Perth and Dundee, not to mention more modest stores in the smaller towns. The hotel cold store was packed from floor to ceiling with frozen meat, fish and poultry. Robbie and Duncan had done particularly well. At the back of the stables there were twenty-two tankers of petrol and twelve of diesel. In the car park in addition to eight or nine cars we now had six all terrain vehicles and had also collected and stored a couple of dozen bicycles and six motor bikes.

Over that period our complement of humans and animals increased. Lewis Miller, a twenty-two year old salesman from Aberdeen, drove in on the Wednesday evening, followed on Thursday morning by Dundonian accountant Gary Laird, his wife Sophie and their two children. Robin was eight and Emma six. Their stories were identical. They'd been driving home during the night from Birmingham and Chester respectively. As soon as they heard the warnings on the car radio they'd pulled on to the hard shoulder, closed all the windows and turned off all the ventilators. Lewis had waited twelve hours before daring to open a window. Gary and Sophie had to take their chance after five hours when it became difficult to breathe. Eighteen year old history student Tony Kane appeared on Friday morning. He had no idea how he'd survived. He'd been at a stag party on the Monday night, got blind drunk and couldn't remember a thing when he woke up twenty-four hours later in a shed at the back of the pub. Finally on the Saturday another young newly married couple returning from honeymoon were spotted on the road by Lindsay and Claire. They were Ross and Rowena McTear from Aberfeldy. Lindsay gave them the necessary directions and they walked the seven miles to reach us. We'd also acquired three more cats and four dogs, all adults. We never did work out how they'd survived. Esme, who'd kept cats most of her life, estimated our new feline arrivals were between three and six. The dogs, three of which were mongrels and one a Cairn terrier, all looked young, healthy and energetic. Mentally I crossed mousetraps and rat poison off our shopping list.

On the Monday evening, one week on from the tragedy, I professed myself satisfied with the amount of provisions we'd accumulated. When it came time for me to allocate duties for the next day I had another and different list in my hand.

I began my little speech by complimenting everyone on their recent efforts. "Tomorrow is the last day we can guarantee it's safe to go into populated areas, so we're going to be doing something completely different," I went on. "I'm sure you don't need reminding that winter is only a couple of months away. If it's anything like the usual Scottish winter we'll not be able to do very much outside. Now I suspect that after the last week the thought of lazing around doing nothing sounds wonderful. I'm also sure that after a few days of that we'll all be bored to tears. So tomorrow we're going to concentrate on leisure interests. There's a well equipped fitness room here in the hotel so we don't need to bother with that. I've made out a shopping list, but if anyone can think of any additions to it please speak out. For more active pursuits we'll need half a dozen snooker and pool tables and three or four table tennis tables plus all that goes with them. Add plenty of board games and playing cards. There's a TV set in every room. We'll lay in playstations and DVD and blu-ray players for every set and plenty of replacements for when they wear out. Other teams will hit the shops and libraries and bring in all the books and films that they can lay their hands on. If possible add CD players and CDs of a wide variety of music to the list. Wherever you are if you see anything else that may prove useful add it to the load. Even with all that there should be spare capacity in at least some of the trucks, so use that for confectionery. If there aren't any questions I'll detail the teams."

One of the things I'd been trying to do over the previous week was to try and assess the strengths and weaknesses of the group. To that end I'd picked a different partner for myself each day. On that Tuesday I was accompanied by Selma Dupres, the young black nurse. Up till then I'd barely spoken two words to her so it was a good opportunity to get to know her better. As the day wore on I became more and more impressed. She was just eighteen, a second generation Scot from a West Indian family. Bright and lively, she was brimful of confidence and enthusiasm and talked intelligently on a variety of subjects. I found myself enjoying the day and enjoying her company. She wasn't short on physical strength either. Several times she lifted with ease things that I thought would have been beyond her. I knew without a doubt that she would be a major asset to the new society that we would be building.

CHAPTER SEVEN

My Tuesday night address to the troops was short and sweet. As I looked around at my audience all I saw was a sea of tired faces. Practically everyone was showing signs of the exhaustion that I too was feeling. "Tomorrow is a day of complete rest for everyone," I instructed. "Chill out as much as you can, do whatever you feel like doing and recharge your batteries. Thursday we start looting the countryside."

I slept late next morning, having set the alarm for nine o'clock. Even when I did go down to the kitchen only James, Margaret, Sophie and her two children were up and about. The two women were preparing breakfast. I gave them a hand and when mine was ready James and I went into the dining room. Robbie joined us soon afterwards and one by one the rest of the group arrived. When Robbie had finished his third cup of coffee I looked across at him.

"Fancy going for a gentle stroll?" I asked.

He flexed his arms and grinned at me. "As long as it's gentle and not a route march and there's no lifting involved."

"It will be gentle," I assured him. "Mainly I want to walk round the grounds and work out some sort of plan for cultivating them."

The weather that morning was showing signs of change. Ever since the disaster we'd been favoured with long sunny days. Now the clouds were gathering and I reckoned on rain before the end of the day. For a few minutes we strolled in companionable silence. It was Robbie who broke it.

"What's on your mind, Dean? I guess you didn't want my company just to talk about crops."

"You read me too easily," I smiled. "The truth is that I'm still not entirely happy with my position. I'm beginning to feel like a dictator the way everyone meekly does what I tell them. I really feel that we should have some kind of democratically elected council or that someone else should take over." Even as I said the words I realised that there was no-one who could take over sole control. Robbie himself had already made his position clear. Duncan should have been an obvious leader but he'd become very withdrawn and morose. The medical crew tended to keep themselves to themselves. I'd commented on that fact to Myra one day. Her reply was that as doctors and nurses to the community they would be in receipt of personal information. They therefore had to be discreet and keep their distance, otherwise they'd lose the confidence of their patients. In fact the only two of our group that showed leadership qualities were Danny and Lindsay and both were too young to take over at present.

Robbie took some time before replying. "I can only repeat what I said before. The reason we're all doing what you tell us is that you're making all the right decisions. You're the only one who's shown the vision to assess our needs for the future. In addition you're a born organiser. Go ahead if you want to and suggest at the meeting tonight the idea of having a committee. But I've talked to nearly everybody and I'll almost guarantee that the verdict will be for you to carry on as you're doing. So let's get down to something more practical. How are we going to allocate the grounds."

We stayed outside for most of the morning. By lunchtime we'd decided that the front should be devoted to growing fruit and the rear ploughed into four equal sized fields for cereals and vegetables. To the south of the hotel grounds was an area of trees and grassland and here we would turn loose any cows and sheep we might hopefully acquire.

I spent the afternoon in my room going through all the notebooks that had been handed in. Taking a dozen photocopies of the local map I marked in various areas for the teams to forage on the morrow. There'd been no actual sighting of any animals but two or three people thought they had seen movement in the far distance so I included those areas for special exploration. Once I'd finished I went downstairs again. I'd intended to have another chat with Robbie but before I'd taken two steps from the foot of the stairs I was waylaid. First it was Lewis Miller, the young Aberdonian.

"My dad was a radio enthusiast," he said without preamble. "I never got into it in a big way, but I picked up quite a lot from him. While we've been out scavenging I've collected up all the necessary equipment to put together a fairly powerful transmitter. Could I take over one of the top floor rooms and set it up? If there are other groups elsewhere radio would be the most likely way to contact them."

"By all means," I said with enthusiasm. "You're right, of course. I should have thought of that."

Barely had he trotted off when I was accosted again. This time it was Dr. Myra and a radiant looking Rowena. Myra spoke first. "Ling and I have been doing checks on all those that wanted one. Rowena here is three months pregnant."

"That's great news," I said. "Congratulations. It's light duties for you from now on."

"I'm perfectly fit to work for another four or five months," Rowena protested.

"I'm sure you are," I replied. "But children are our future and we can't take any chances. I'm not suggesting you put your feet up but we don't want you running around digging up potatoes or shifting heavy machinery. Would you help out Margaret in the kitchen? She could do with an assistant."

Rowena seemed quite happy with that and rushed off to tell her husband the good news. I finally made my way into the bar, which by now had become the focal point when we were all together. I was surprised to find it deserted. Bemused I went on a tour of the building. Despite the fact that I'd declared a day of rest I found that nearly everyone had taken up a task of some kind. One group was busy setting up the snooker and table tennis tables. Another was erecting shelving for the books, games and films that we'd collected. Brian was arranging and filling containers in the conservatory with some assistance from Claire. For the first time the glum look on his face had disappeared and while not actually smiling he looked absorbed and was even carrying on a sporadic conversation with his blonde assistant. Myra had gone back to the area reserved for the medical group. I found them all there filling out forms or entering data into computers. Ling grabbed me as soon as I walked in the door and insisted I had a check-up. "It will set a good example for those who are hanging back," he stated by way of persuasion. Fifteen minutes later I got up from the couch having been given a clean bill of health. Without giving away too many details the two doctors professed themselves happy with the overall physical condition of our community.

"Hard work, fresh air and a minimum of fancy foods over the last week have toughened everyone up," was Ling's verdict.

Despite Robbie's warning I was determined to give the group the chance to elect a committee to take over from me. To that end I put the proposal to the meeting that evening. There was silence for some twenty seconds before Myra got to her feet.

"Committees are a waste of time," she said forcefully. "I know. I've been on plenty. If we'd had a committee from the start I doubt if we'd have accomplished half of what we have. There'd have been too much talking and too many arguments. Dean's done a damn good job on his own and I suggest we let him carry on doing it. Who agrees with me?" To my embarrassment nearly every hand in the room shot into the air. I'm sure I was blushing as I mumbled a few words of thanks.

Spreading my notes out in front of me I started on the allocation of duties for the following day, beginning with a reference to the weather. "I'm no expert, but I wouldn't be surprised if this rain keeps up for a day or two. Now there's no great urgency about the next phase of operations so if it does rain we stay indoors. There's plenty to be done here though none of it is urgent. Whenever we do get out these are the things we need. First and foremost we explore the possible sightings of animals. Then we want some farm machinery. In case you wonder why I've listed four ploughs, just remember that if anything breaks down we can't go somewhere and get replacement parts so we need the additional safeguard. Other machinery on the list includes things for cutting and threshing cereals crops, bulldozers and anything else you see that might prove useful. Several fields of potatoes have been spotted. We can lift them all and store them. If you can find some sacks then use them; if not just load them loose. As far as fruit and green vegetables are concerned we'll just bring in a few days' supply at a time. There's no point in getting too much and seeing it go bad. Every team takes a couple of spades with them. Take any fruit trees and bushes that can be dug up without too much difficulty and replant them in front of the hotel. Duncan will plan a layout."

I read out the pairings and as I did so handed out the maps and instruction sheets that I'd prepared. "Before we break up Doctor Ling would like to say a few words."

Ling made his way to my side, turned and spoke. "We're coming to the time when disease will be a factor. Therefore you will please follow my instructions to the letter. The medical staff will come round and issue each of you with a protective face mask and gloves. You will put the gloves on before leaving here and wear them continuously until you return except when eating and drinking. Only eat and drink in your vehicle with all the windows closed. Wash your hands before and after meals wherever possible. If you're anywhere near dead animals and people put on the face masks immediately. Do not go into any buildings other than sheds and greenhouses. Do not touch any dead humans or animals that you see. We have been checking during the day that everyone has been vaccinated against typhoid and smallpox. Anyone that hasn't spoken to us please come forward as soon as possible. Finally if anyone feels the least unwell at any time come and see Myra or myself immediately. Even if you think it's something trivial, still come and see us. We simply cannot afford an epidemic of anything. That is all."

My prediction as to the weather proved correct. The next day, Thursday, was one of continuous rain, heavy at times. I wasn't too unhappy. We had the whole of September and October to scour the countryside so two or three days would make no difference. Most of us were still showing signs of weariness anyway so a second day of rest would improve rather than hinder our work rate. We passed the time doing some cleaning around the mansion house. I spent a large part of the day observing those around me and getting to know individuals better. I noted with some amusement that liaisons were beginning to form. Paul Leggatt, the staff nurse, spent most of the day with Sian. Esme and Duncan were rarely apart and the same applied to Danny and Selma, the black nurse. That was one linking that I hoped would prove permanent. The two complemented each other. Late arrival Tony Kane was paying a lot attention to Lily, the other nurse. Lewis looked like being the odd man out, but I saw little of him. Early in the morning he disappeared into his top floor room to work on his transmitter and we only saw him briefly at meal times.

Unfortunately the reverse side of the coin became apparent to me in the shape of clashes of personality. I overheard heated words in mid morning between Esme and Myra. An hour later a row broke out between Danny and Paul over something trivial. I debated intervening but decided against it. The parties concerned would have to deal with things in their own way. All I could do was ensure that I didn't pair the protagonists together on a work detail.

With Brian now happily occupied my one real concern was Kirsty. She was very much the odd one out; too young to relate to the older teenagers and too old to be interested in Gary and Sophie's children. During that Thursday she tended to follow me around in the guise of wanting to help. I wasn't sure whether she had romantic notions about me or whether she just saw me as some sort of father figure. Without sounding too inquisitive I learned most of her story that day. It was a not uncommon scenario. Her unmarried mother was addicted to heroin and she never found out who her father was. She was taken into care when she was five and from then on it was a succession of short lived foster parents and longer spells in care homes. She knew of no relations and the constant movement gave her little chance to make friends. Within our group the only ones she felt comfortable with apart from myself were Esme, Robbie and Lindsay. She seemed to feel that she had a bond with the only others who smoked.

The issue of smoking raised its head that afternoon. I was resting in my room before the evening meal when a knock on the door heralded a small deputation consisting of our two married couples. Ross was the appointed spokesperson.

"We've come to ask if smoking can be banned in the main rooms," he pleaded. "I know that there's no-one to enforce the ban now, but until we draw up new ones presumably the old laws still apply. Although we want to be on good terms with everyone some of us do find it annoying."

Sophie Laird was more vehement. "I don't want my children to be exposed to tobacco smoke or even to see anyone smoking," she declared. "If something's not done about it I'm going to have to keep them apart from everyone else."

Though I was reluctant to start laying down rules and regulations I realised that I couldn't simply ignore the request. After giving the matter some careful thought I called the four smokers together along with Duncan who still used his pipe. I suggested that they take a room of their own.

"Is that an order?" Lindsay demanded with passion.

Diplomacy was obviously called for. "No. Let's say it's a request designed to promote harmony in the camp."

To my relief Robbie came to my rescue. "It's a pity that with so few of us left the others can't be more tolerant, but we have to respect their wishes. I'll go along with you." Esme and Duncan nodded and Kirsty looked disinterested. Lindsay was still simmering but gave in, albeit with ill grace. The only room not in use on the ground floor was the manager's office. There and then we removed the desk and the filing cabinets and brought in comfortable chairs and two occasional tables. Rebellious to the last Lindsay found a large square of cardboard and printed on it with magic marker the words 'Private—Keep Out'. From that moment on I was the only non-smoker ever allowed in the room. Even Claire was excluded.

These minor flurries of discontent caused me some concern. Up to that point we'd all pulled together and worked as a team. I hoped that we hadn't lost the community spirit. There was a long winter ahead when perforce we would be confined to the hotel with little to do. The one consolation was that the place was big enough to keep any warring factions apart.

CHAPTER EIGHT

Thursday dawned overcast but dry. Refreshed from two days' rest everyone set out with a will to start plundering the countryside. Although there was still plenty of heavy lifting to be done the sense of urgency was no longer evident. On the debit side the protection that we'd been told to wear was a constant irritant. I took Kirsty with me each day thereafter. Our task was to track down and dig up all the potatoes we could find. About a fifth of what we collected was put aside for the following year's sowing; the rest went to the kitchen for cooking or storing. I'd have liked an expert available to tell us which variety each was. As it was, all I could do was segregate according to looks.

We spent the whole of September and most of October scouring the countryside for many miles around. Our efforts didn't go unrewarded. Most importantly we'd found surviving livestock: two sickly looking calves, two baby goats, one male one female, half a dozen lambs and an incubator containing over sixty baby chicks. The whole of the ground in the front of the hotel was planted with young fruit trees and with row upon row of blackcurrant, redcurrant, raspberry and gooseberry bushes. We'd also found plenty of strawberry plants and clumps of rhubarb. Older trees were marked down for future use. Duncan revelled in his role as head gardener. He lost his air of despair and became as focussed as the rest of us. I was amused watching him at work. From somewhere he'd unearthed a measuring tape and whenever a new tree was ready to be planted he meticulously measured off the exact distance from the previous one. Woe betide anyone who planted a tree without his supervision! Now and again he had help from Brian, who seemed to have taken to the role of greenhouse keeper like a duck to water. Kirsty appointed herself keeper of the chicks and once our outdoor duties started to wind down spent all her time in the heated room containing the incubator. Inevitably some didn't survive and she'd be wiping the tears away each time she came to tell me the bad news. It was the first sign of real emotion that I'd seen from her.

Our first few days in the countryside were eerie to say the least. It took me an hour on the first day to realise why. There was complete and utter silence. Neither bird, animal nor insect could be seen or heard. In normal times the rotting carcases of sheep and cows would have been buzzing, each with its cloud of flies. The smell of decaying flesh was everywhere. We'd been somewhat lax about following Ling's instructions, but after a couple of days we all took to wearing face masks wherever we were.

Shortly after we'd started plundering the countryside Lewis came to find me one evening about nine thirty. In a state of suppressed excitement he told me he'd made radio contact with a group of survivors in the south of Ireland. Eagerly I went back upstairs with him and had a long talk with their leader, a farmer called Patrick O'Hanlon. His farm was very isolated, he told me, and when he heard the warnings about the gas cloud he'd called in his two workers and their families. Along with his own fairly large family he sealed them all in the big farmhouse kitchen. Thereafter they'd worked along similar lines to ourselves, scavenging in the nearest towns and villages and building up large reserves of food and other necessities. In their wanderings they'd come across other survivors and their group was now some thirty-five strong. They'd had contact by radio with one or two similar groups in Spain, France, Wales and Italy. Patrick promised to stay in touch. This was a useful contact to have made. No-one in our party had any knowledge of farming. Now we at least had someone to consult with any problems we encountered. Lewis had taken note of the wavelengths of the other groups that Patrick had been in contact with and from then on spent his evenings talking to them. In due course they linked up with more groups, two of which were in England. He hadn't come across another Scottish settlement though.

A cold snap with flurries of snow in the last week of October warned us that winter was fast approaching. I scaled down outside activities to the bare minimum needed to keep us in fresh vegetables. Meantime another problem had arisen. One Sunday morning late in September Robbie called Danny and I outside saying he had something to show us. Walking across the grounds at the rear he pointed to the fields beyond the boundary. It took me a moment to realise what he was indicating. Then I saw them, dozens of rabbits.

"We're going to have to do something about them," Robbie stated. "They'll destroy any crops we try to raise next year if we don't." For once I was at a loss. "Any suggestions?" I asked him.

"We've a few airguns in the weapons store," he reflected. "If half a dozen of us spend the afternoon here we can reduce the number considerably. The only thing against that is when we come to eat them. Lead pellets aren't good for the digestion. Maybe somebody can work out a way to make traps."

I had to make up my mind quickly. "Even if we do find a way to make traps it will be a few days before we get them positioned. By that time the rabbit population could easily double. I think we'll have a shooting party this afternoon to reduce the numbers. We'll warn Margaret and Rowena about the pellets. They can maybe find a way of getting rid of them before cooking."

In the end the hunting party consisted of the three of us plus Lewis and Tony. We stayed out for some four hours, at the end of which time we'd bagged over seventy, covering a radius of about half a mile. Robbie and Duncan between them took on the task of skinning them. The pelts we put aside for possible future use. A few days later Danny worked out a way of making traps. We had to send a party into Perth in protective clothing to get the materials we needed. On their return they reported a number of fires burning and many signs of decomposition among the bodies of both humans and animals. Cocooned in our small area memories of the disaster had been slowly fading over the weeks. This news brought it home to us once again and cast a cloud over our community.

While we were scouring the countryside I'd put a couple of minor projects in hand. I call them minor, but if successful I knew they would go far to improving our future prospects. There was no way of knowing how long the supplies of electricity and water would be maintained. I suspected that when the former broke down the latter would follow. My knowledge of the utilities was non-existent, but I assumed that the pumps that circulated the water were electrically driven. After talking to everyone I decided that Robbie, Danny and Tony were the most mechanically minded among us. I called them together.

"I'd like you to dig out what books on engineering you can find among the ones we've taken from libraries. Try and work out a system for pumping water from the river up to the storage tank on the roof. You'll need at least one filter in the chain, if not two to remove plant and animal matter. The solar panels should give us enough electricity to run the pump. You'll need a pretty powerful pump. The cold water tank is on the roof of the north annexe, four storeys up." They set to work with a will.

The water system for the hotel was quite simple. A huge square cold water tank held around eighteen thousand gallons when full. The smaller hot water tank was next to it, both being enclosed in a solidly built boiler house. It took the team three weeks to design the system they wanted to use and another week to gather all the basic bits and pieces. These included a strong wooden hut in which to house the pumps. They collected four pumps altogether, two electric and two diesel driven, all big enough that only one pump would need to be in use at any one time. But as they pointed out, we needed reserves in case of breakdowns.

The system they'd designed was fairly simple. A funnel shaped tube picked up the water from near the bed of the river. The business end of this funnel was some nine inches in diameter and was covered with a fine wire mesh to act as an initial filter. A two inch copper pipe was attached to the narrow end of the funnel and ran from there to the pump house, situated half way between the river and the hotel. Another two inch copper pipe took it to the side of the hotel, then up and on to the tank on the roof. A second filter guarded the entrance into the tank. The funnel could be lifted easily from the river bed when the filter needed to be cleaned and an ingenious switching system ensured that we could change pumps at the touch of a button. It was late November before everything was in place and we could trial the finished product. It worked perfectly first time. I put Tony in charge of overseeing the whole shooting match as and when we had to bring it into use.

The second project I put in motion wasn't of the same importance. The river that formed our northern boundary was singularly devoid of fish, at least none of us had ever seen any in it. In conversation one day I learned that both Duncan and Gary Laird had been keen anglers. Once the main bulk of the outside work was completed I put them to scouring all the rivers and lochs within a reasonable distance looking for trout and salmon. They took large containers of water with them and if they found any their instructions were to bring anything they caught back alive and put them into our river. They put in a lot of travelling and hard work with little success, but by the time they were finished they'd transferred around forty adult fish, all trout. I'd hoped for more but with luck and no natural enemies I trusted that the forty would multiply rapidly. I said as much to Gary.

"Don't hold your breath," he advised. "There's not even any guarantee that they'll stay around this stretch of the river."

Early in December I took Danny and a light van and set off southwards down the A9. We hadn't been far in that direction since the first week or so and I wanted to check out a few things. My intention was to go as far as Stirling and detour back through Bridge of Allan and Dunblane. We had face masks and gloves but no other protective clothing as I'd no intention of getting out of the vehicle. I drove slowly while Danny scanned the surrounding countryside with binoculars and reported on what he saw. About a mile south of the Dunblane slip road I rounded a shallow bend and then jammed on the brakes in surprise. About a hundred yards ahead a barricade stretched the full width of the road, blocking both north and south carriageways. It was composed of cars, bulldozers and other vehicles of all descriptions, some piled two and three high. In the middle was a wooden gate about six feet wide. Behind this stood a sentry, dressed in army uniform and carrying a rifle on his shoulder. He opened the gate as we came to a standstill and unhitched the rifle, which he then held pointing upwards.

"He doesn't look very welcoming," Danny observed. "Do we turn back?"

"At least he's not actually pointing the gun at us," I remarked. "I think I'll go and talk to him. Cover me without making it too obvious and get ready to fire if he does."

Danny grinned. "Don't worry. If he kills you I'll make sure he doesn't live to tell the tale."

I grinned back. "Thanks, Danny. That's very reassuring."

I dismounted from the driving seat slowly and carefully. As soon as I was on the ground I held my arms out from my side with the palms of my hands outstretched and marched briskly towards the barricade. As soon as I got within hailing distance I halted.

"I'm not armed," I said loudly, "and I come in peace." I started walking again. He kept his rifle pointing upwards but said nothing. I carried on until I was a couple of yards away from him. He was younger than I'd thought, probably no more than eighteen or nineteen. Although his uniform was well worn it had clearly been pressed. Though his hair was long it was clean under the beret and he had certainly shaved that morning.

"We're from up near Perth," I began. "We've just been having a look round the countryside and didn't realise there was another group anywhere around. Is it possible to have a chat with your leader?"

He looked me up and down in a manner that was just short of being insulting. "The Major's not here," he growled in a strong Glasgow accent. "Stay there and don't move while I call the captain." So saying he shouldered the rifle and walked a few yards to an adjacent hut, put his head round the door and spoke for a few seconds. Then he returned to his post.

"The captain's coming," he reported in a slightly more civil tone. "Meantime keep your hands where I can see them." I did as I was told while watching the door of the hut. When it opened some thirty seconds later I received my second surprise of the day. Out stepped a slim blonde woman of medium height. Dressed from head to foot in black leather she too had a rifle slung over her shoulder. She came halfway towards me, giving me a long hard stare as she did so. Then she stopped deliberately, took out a cigarette and lit it. When it was going to her satisfaction she resumed her progress, coming to a halt a yard away but with the gate between us. Seen close up I realised that she was a beautiful woman but there was a hard look in her cold blue eyes and her mouth was set in a straight line.

"Who are you and where are you from?" She almost barked the words at me.

I tried a tentative smile, but determined not to give too much information away. "I'm Dean Barclay, from a group based away up near Perth. And you are?"

There was no answering smile. In fact I thought at first that she didn't even intend to give me her name. When it did come it was given almost reluctantly.

"I'm Captain Louise Buckley, vice-president of the republic of Stirling. The president is Major Wistance. What do you want?"

I was on easier ground here. "Just to establish friendly relations. We'll respect your territory and hope that you would respect ours. There may be things that one or other of us is short of that the other could supply."

"We've got all we need and none to spare for others," she snapped back at me. "Where exactly are you and how many are in your party?"

In view of her hostile attitude I didn't intend to give anything away. "We're in an old mansion house near Perth," I lied. "As to numbers, I've never bothered to count, but I guess there must be around fifty of us. And now I'll bid you good day. There are areas north of here we want to explore. Give my regards to your Major Wistance." I turned on my heel without waiting for her reply.

I walked back to our lorry, did a three point turn and headed north again, all the while giving Danny the gist of the exchange. He hooted with laughter when I came to the bit about 'the republic of Stirling'.

"Talk about delusions of grandeur," he commented. "All the same, they don't sound very friendly. We could have trouble with them in the future. You did the right thing not giving too much away."

Not knowing exactly where the boundaries of the self styled republic lay we abandoned the rest of our trip and headed back to base. There I ran Robbie to earth in the pump house and gave him a report on what had happened. He looked thoughtful.

"I don't like the sound of that, Dean," he reflected. "That name Wistance rings a faint bell with me, though I can't quite place it at the moment. I think I'll take a little recce tonight and see if I can find out more."

"I'll come with you," I said immediately.

"You'll do nothing of the kind," he responded warmly. "I'm trained in jungle warfare and you're not. Neither is anyone else here. If I took someone with me we wouldn't get more than a quarter of a mile without being discovered. This is a one man show."

"Let me at least drive you down," I asked.

He held up his hands in horror. "See what I mean about being trained. A car can be heard from miles away in the dark. I'll take a bicycle. The best thing you can do is go to bed and I'll report in the morning."

"No way." I was emphatic. "The least I can do is stay up and have a hot drink ready for you when you get back."

He grinned. "All right, I'll settle for that. Incidentally it would be better not to tell anyone else what's going on for the moment. Now I want to have a look at the ordnance survey map for the area. You can show me exactly where that barrier is."

It was a chilly and unpleasant night with a thin drizzle falling. Robbie waited until everybody had gone to bed before setting out. He'd changed into an all black outfit and blacked his face and hands. Instead of the AK47 he'd taken a revolver with a silencer attached.

"Don't worry," he assured me. "I don't aim to kill anyone. But it may be necessary to shoot someone in the leg if I should get pursued. You really shouldn't wait up, you know. It'll likely be around four before I get back."

I saw him off from the front door. Returning to the kitchen to get a cup of tea I found Lindsay in pyjamas and dressing gown obviously waiting for me.

"What's going on?" she demanded. There was no point in disseminating so I told her the whole story from start to finish. I knew she would keep it to herself. She offered to keep me company but I saw no point in two of us missing a night's sleep, so after sharing a pot of black coffee she left me to it. My thoughts were not pleasant. The months and years ahead would be difficult enough without the added complication of hostile neighbours. Then, realising that I could make no plans until Robbie returned I found a book and tried to lose myself in the pages of Robert Louis Stevenson. It was a quarter to four before I heard Robbie coming in. Switching on the kettle I went to meet him. He looked tired. Once the coffee was poured he told me his story.

"I managed to get right into the town without being spotted. There I had a huge stroke of good luck. The first person I saw was an old army mate of mine, Tam McPhee. We'd been pretty close at one time and I knew I could rely on him not to give me away. He led me to a quiet spot and answered all my questions freely. Remember I said I thought the name Wistance was familiar? Tam filled in the gaps in my memory. Roy Wistance was a lance corporal in the pay corps five or six years ago. He got caught embezzling funds, was court-martialled, did a year in the military jail at Colchester and was then given a dishonourable discharge. Seemingly he rules his so called republic with a rod of iron. There are about sixty of them all told, most resident in Stirling Castle. More than half are former inmates of Glenochil Young Offenders' prison. How they survived Tam doesn't know, but survive they did. They're a wild bunch but seem to have an affinity to the 'Major'. He treats them like soldiers, has put them in uniform, drills them and has given them weapon training. Your blonde lady captain just turned up one day and attached herself to Wistance. She has never revealed where she came from."

"The whole bunch are living off supplies they scavenge on a daily basis. It's a miracle that no-one's been poisoned, although they did take the precaution of burning every body they came across, human and animal. But they've made no provision for the future and Tam's sure that when supplies run out they'll start attacking other settlements. Apparently there's one deep in the Campsie Fells that's the first target. Now that they know about us we're almost sure to be the second."

"Why doesn't your friend up and leave?" I asked as he paused for breath.

"His wife is there too," Robbie replied. "Wistance has the place so well guarded that it would be difficult and dangerous for the two of them to try and escape. Tam is the only regular soldier in the party, so Wistance relies on him for practical matters and thus keeps a close eye on him." I sat thinking about what Robbie had said. To say I was disturbed would be putting it mildly. The hotel was very open in aspect and would be a difficult place to defend against determined foes.

Eventually I asked the obvious question. "Should we set up an armed guard from now on?"

Robbie shook his head. "Tam and I have worked out a way of meeting secretly on a regular basis. If any attack on us is planned Wistance will get him to formulate the battle plan. Tam will make sure that any action is delayed for forty-eight hours and find a way to let me know. We'll have at least twelve hours' notice of an impending attack. And now I'm off to bed. We'll talk more in the morning. Among other things we'll need to decide how much to tell the others."

CHAPTER NINE

In the end we called a meeting that day and told everyone the full story. While I didn't want to start a panic there was no point in secrecy when we might be called to arms at short notice. There was nothing that could be done to ease the situation but Robbie insisted on setting up some battle training sessions and target practice to improve our shooting skills. From that moment on he made a sortie into the republic's camp every three or four nights. We took it in turns to wait up and have a hot drink and some food awaiting him on his return.

The start of December brought new problems. The mains supply of electricity and water went off on the first Tuesday of the month. There'd been a hard frost for a couple of nights and that must have triggered off the breakdown. We'd always known previously that the electricity was still working, because once darkness fell we could see the faint glow from the street lighting in Auchterrarder a few miles away. When it wasn't visible that Tuesday evening we knew the worst. Simultaneously water stopped flowing into the cold tank. Tony set the pumps going immediately and from then on checked the filters and the level in the tank three times a day. Every other day he cleaned the filter in the river. The trio of learner mechanics had done their job well as the system worked perfectly from then on. Despite the water purifiers we'd collected Ling and Myra gave out orders that from that time on all water for drinking and for cleaning teeth had to be boiled first. Each room had a kettle and we had plenty of empty containers of all shapes and sizes. Everyone was issued with half a dozen and it soon became general practice to spend twenty minutes or so each morning boiling up sufficient water to last the day and night.

For a few days I was worried about how the solar panels would stand up to the test. When there appeared to be very little diminution in the current I relaxed a bit. Despite cloudy days and the long nights of winter the hot water supply remained fairly constant. Occasionally from nine o'clock onwards the lights would dim and the heating drop a few degrees, but that was the only hitch. Robbie and I often discussed how the panels worked. Neither of us had much knowledge of electricity; in fact the only things we were certain about was that it couldn't be stored and that the solar panels didn't generate in darkness. We came up with several wild theories, each more improbable than the last. In the end the most likely explanation we arrived at was that there was some part of the old grid still operative and that somehow the power that our panels produced during the day went round and round a circuit and came back to us when needed. I don't think either of us believed it for a moment! For myself I was just thankful that we had any power at all.

Once the frosts had started we discovered that mice had entered the building. We were pretty sure there hadn't been any when we first moved in and this was confirmed when we identified the first unwelcome visitors as brown field mice. To begin with there were only one or two a night but as the month progressed they came in ever increasing numbers. That's when the cats began to repay the care and attention that we'd lavished on them. Our three, with the occasional help of the mother cat, got to work with gusto. We left all doors on the ground floor and the cellar open at night for them to roam at will. They seemed to work as a team. Each morning three or four heaps of dead mice greeted us when we went into the entrance hall. To prevent any possible infection the medical team burnt the corpses immediately. The dogs soon got their share of the action, though rats were small in number. In the month of December only seven were caught and we saw no more from then on.

All our animals were looking healthy and the young ones were growing fast. We'd cleared out two rooms on the ground floor and brought the farm animals indoors for the winter. Ross and Rowena, with occasional help from Esme and Duncan, volunteered to look after them. The only dissentient voice was Sophie's. She protested long and loud, but I simply turned a deaf ear. The animals were a vital part of our future and took priority in the scheme of things. One thing that pleased me at that time was that most of our people were beginning to show more initiative. Without any instructions from me they took up various tasks on a voluntary basis. Esme and Duncan took charge of the book library. Lindsay and Claire ran the film equivalent. Danny and Selma organised the snooker and table tennis tables, for which a waiting list developed every evening. Lily helped Tony with the overseeing of the water supply, Brian had his greenhouse and Lewis his radio. While for Gary and Sophie the care of the children was a full time job in itself.

The attachments that had been forged in the previous two months became stronger. Without deliberately trying to find out I became aware that Sian had moved in with Paul, Selma with Danny and Lily with Tony. Myra and Ling and Esme and Duncan still kept separate rooms, but were seldom apart. Lewis seemed disinterested in the opposite sex, which left Kirsty and me. More than ever she was somewhere around me for most of the day. Though I wanted to discourage her I hadn't the heart to tell her to get lost. One evening when there were just the two of us in the bar I decided to bring the subject up in a tactful way.

"You know, Kirsty," I began softly, "you should be spending more time with the other younger people instead of with me."

"They've no time for me," she retorted with spirit. "They're all taken up with themselves and they look down on me 'cos I'm not educated like them. I like being with you. You always treat me like an equal and you never talk down to me like the rest do."

"I'm sure they don't," I said with surprise. "Friendship is a two way thing you know. You have to meet other people half way."

"Doesn't work," she sniffed. "Why'd you bring this up? Am I a nuisance?"

"Of course not, Kirsty. Don't ever think that. I just feel that life's hard enough for everybody after what's happened and I'd like to see you getting what little fun and friendship you can from it. There's not much joy hanging around an old fogey like me."

"You're not *that* old," she said with spirit. "You know, you're the first person I've ever met that I know I can trust. I wish you'd been my father." There was no answer to that!

I'd called a halt to the daily tours of the countryside late in November. There was little likelihood of finding much more that could be of use. From then on two people went out about twice a week and gathered in our immediate needs in the way of fresh vegetables. We'd been lucky. Early on we'd found a farm some ten miles away with fields of turnips, cabbages, carrots and parsnips, enough to keep us going throughout the winter. James Tulloch had been meticulous in keeping records of our food stock and usage and once a fortnight gave me a full report. We'd used less than I expected. It was especially pleasing to see that our cold store was still about two thirds full. For that we had Danny to thank. He'd designed a very effective rabbit trap and once he'd tested it made another two dozen or more. These we spread around the nearby fields, catching enough beasts to provide our meat needs for three or four days a week. Among our food stores were plentiful quantities of spices and curry powder, so Margaret was able to introduce variety to the way she prepared the rabbit dishes.

Even with the help of the two married women, Margaret was working long hours in the kitchen. Apart from meals she was now baking seven or eight loaves of bread a day, a hard enough task in itself. With manpower to spare I set up a rota that gave her two extra people to help out during the day. Lewis offered to deal with the breakfast preparation every day. This didn't involve much, merely the cooking of two large cauldrons of porridge. We'd run out of cereals after the first month. To conserve our stock of dried and tinned milk the porridge was taken without, as was all tea and coffee. I'd no idea how old cows and goats had to be before they started giving milk, though I suspected it would be the best part of a year. I wanted to reserve what milk we still had for the two children and the baby on the way.

Three or four days before Christmas Kirsty and I were on duty in the kitchen when Margaret called me aside. "I think we should try and do something a wee bit special for Christmas day," she confided. "It'll not be a proper meal by a long way, but for a start there's still twenty or more turkeys in the cold store. Three of the bigger ones will give everyone a good helping. To go with it I'll roast some potatoes for once. I can make some sort of stuffing and we've plenty brussels. Also I've saved up the corn cobs that were brought in last month. I'll make a big pot of soup. Christmas pudding and dumpling are out of the question, I'm afraid, but I can make up a trifle with some of the tinned fruit. That's as long as you don't mind me using some of the tinned milk."

"Go right ahead and take all you need," I told her. "It may be the last year that we can put any kind of proper Christmas meal together so let's make the most of it. We can all do with a lift."

Although the disaster was still too recent in everyone's thoughts for there to be a real Christmas atmosphere I think we all enjoyed the day in a quiet way. There was just enough turkey left over for sandwiches in the evening. For once the games tables and films were abandoned and unusually everyone spent the evening in the bar. The soft lighting and the hum of conversation was soothing and I found myself sitting back, listening to all that was being said around me and taking no part. I was snapped out of my reverie when someone, I think it was Rowena McTear, asked me a question. I had to get her to repeat it. Basically she wanted to know what I foresaw for us in the year soon to start. All at once the room became silent and everyone looked at me expectantly.

It took me a moment or two to reply. I looked around at all the faces that had become so familiar to me over the past four months and wished with all my heart I could give them some cause for optimism. I knew though that I couldn't disseminate.

"I wish you hadn't asked me that tonight, Rowena," I began. "It's been such a pleasant day that I hate to spoil the mood. I could give you a lot of platitudes and tell you everything will be fine, but you all know by now that that's not my way. We've done wonders to date, but I'm afraid there's more hard work to come. As soon as the weather permits we'll need to get outdoors and get ploughing and planting. After that there'll be hoeing and weeding. Our stores are holding out well but they won't last forever. Sooner or later the only food we'll have is what we can grow ourselves. Our diet is going to be more and more restricted as the months go by. Within eighteen months at the very most the only meat available will be rabbit."

"Our other main worry is that lot down the road at Stirling. Robbie's mole in their camp is fairly certain their food supplies will start to run out within a few months. Once that happens they are likely to attack us at any time. That means more work in the form of guard duty. With luck we'll have an advance warning of the attack but we can't be certain of that. And now drink up, enjoy the rest of today and forget what I've just said. We'll start worrying about the future tomorrow." I think they tried, but the mood was broken. Most people had drifted off to bed by ten o'clock.

One of the things that surprised me in those early days of winter was how abstemious everyone was. With more time on their hands to brood I'd fully expected one or two to hit the bottle seriously, but nobody did. Even on that Christmas Day no-one overdid the liquid intake. Robbie and I were the last to retire and I mentioned it to him.

"I've noticed it too," he admitted. "To be honest I'm even surprised at myself. I was nowhere near being an alcoholic before, but I did take a fair bucket. Somehow I've lost the taste for it. Possibly it's the same with the others. Either that or what happened was so overwhelming that everyone's abandoned their old way of behaving and is trying to adjust to a new set of circumstances." Then he gave a huge grin. "Then again, maybe everybody is scared the booze is going to run out too soon if they pig it. C'mon, it's too late for all this psychology. Go to bed."

Another surprise to me was that nobody ever mentioned religion. In the days following Christmas I made a point of asking more than a dozen of the others the reason. Their replies were almost identical. The scale of the disaster had caused everyone to lose whatever they had in the way of faith. Esme expressed it more dramatically. "How can anyone now believe in a divine power after what's happened? Only the devil incarnate could have perpetrated such an outrage on the world. I prefer to believe in nature. If you look at the general order of things there has always been a system of checks and balances. Birds eat insects, animals eat birds and bigger animals eat smaller animals. In the past wars, famine and disease kept mankind to a reasonable level, but now the population is building up to unacceptable and dangerous levels. So Mother Nature took a hand and condemned us to go back to the beginning again." It was an interesting point of view and to me anyway it carried a certain amount of logic.

Two days later I was in the bar at eight in the evening. There were five of us sitting round a table; I had Lindsay and Claire, Ross and Rowena for company. For once the conversation was on the past and not the future. If I remember correctly we were discussing our favourite TV shows when Lindsay rose and announced she was going for a smoke. Barely had she reached the door when it was flung open, knocking her almost to the floor, and Lewis rushed in. Lindsay called him several rude names but he took no notice of her and came straight to where we were sitting.

"Dean, come quickly," he panted. "I've just made contact with a group from Ayrshire. Their leader wants to speak to you."

I got up and followed him, noticing subconsciously that the others were close behind me. We fairly raced up the stairs to the radio room on the top floor. As he went towards the console Lewis flipped a switch on a control board.

"I've put the speaker on," he said. "That way you won't need to use the headphones and everyone can hear." He motioned me to take the seat in front of the microphone, then picked it up himself and spoke into it.

"Still there, Harvey?" A broad Cockney voice assured him that he was. "I've got our leader here. Is the captain with you?" The voice of Harvey came again from the speaker. "I'm putting him on now."

I heard a noise that sounded like someone pulling up a chair and sitting down. "Captain Phillips, Royal Navy, here. To whom am I speaking please?" The voice was cultured, probably denoting an English public school, but I was able to detect just the trace of a Scottish accent.

"This is Dean Barclay, sir." As he had given his rank I thought it diplomatic to accord him the courtesy of calling him 'sir'.

"You're the leader of your group, I take it?"

"I am, sir, though I should point out that I'm not elected. I got the job by default. Nobody else would take it."

"You must be doing something right or they would have thrown you out long before now," he said with a dry chuckle. "Tell me about yourselves."

I gave him a very brief rundown from the moment we had been trapped in the cave. He listened without interrupting, asked no questions and went straight into an account of his own group. He had been captain of one of the Trident submarines based at Faslane. Along with one of the other subs they'd been cruising in the Atlantic about fifty miles off the west coast of Ireland when the gas cloud struck. The two vessels were in radio contact with each other and agreed to stay submerged for three days before testing the atmosphere. When they finally surfaced Captain Phillips himself went up through the conning tower to check that the atmosphere was safe.

After consulting again with his opposite number, a Captain Jennings, they decided to make for the Ayrshire coast. A return to Faslane was rejected as they felt that it was too isolated. They ran the two vessels aground just north of Turnberry, intending to set up camp in the Turnberry Hotel. When they got there they found a dozen or more survivors in residence already and more than willing to join up. Over the next few days more survivors arrived, drawn by the smoke from a huge bonfire that had been lit in the hotel grounds. From then on they'd followed a similar pattern to us, building up supplies of essentials. In their wanderings they came across several more small groups, all of whom were glad to join a bigger community. In the end they finished up with around two hundred men, women and children. The hotel couldn't accommodate them all, so they cleared all the bodies from Turnberry village, fumigated the whole place and the surplus numbers moved in there. Despite the subs having a predominantly English crew only half a dozen or so had opted to try and return home. The rest seemed quite happy to remain at Turnberry.

Once I realised he'd finished his narrative I had a question to ask him. "I'm sure you've already thought of this, sir, but to be on the safe side I'm going to ask. I presume you were carrying nuclear warheads and that there are more stored at Faslane itself. Can you guarantee that they're safe?"

He gave another dry chuckle. "When we realised the extent of the disaster that was the first thing we thought about. The ones we had on board are safe enough. We dumped them in deep water over a hundred miles from the nearest land. As for the ones at Faslane, they're not armed so they don't pose a threat. The odds are a thousand to one against anyone getting to them, but even so if we can get one of the subs refloated when the weather improves we'll go and pick them up and dump them too. Now if you'll give me a couple of minutes to collect up some notes I'd like to speak to you about the future."

CHAPTER TEN

The other five had been gathered round the chair during the foregoing. I expected some comment as Captain Phillips broke off but there was none. Lindsay lit a cigarette with a defiant look round, but had the decency to step back three or four paces from the group. We waited in silence until a slight cough from the speaker announced the return of the good captain.

"Still there, young man?" he asked. I assured him that I was. "Good. I want to run through some thoughts of mine on the future. We've already made radio contact with seven other groups apart from yours and personal contact with two more, both on the coast. There are twenty-five people encamped just north of Ballantrae and another twenty between Skelmorlie and Wemyss Bay. Now among our group here we have three qualified pilots. They've been up and had a look round Prestwick Airport and reported back that there are several helicopters and ample fuel. I've refused them permission to fly just now; it's just not worth the risk in this weather. But once we get into March they will do an intensive survey of the whole of Scotland and locate as many survivors as possible. Naturally we have wireless experts among our crews. One will go with each pilot and set up transmitters and receivers for every group we come across."

"I think you'll agree that there's no point in trying to form any sort of government. Even if we set one up it would be unworkable once fuel supplies run out. But by being able to keep in radio contact we can monitor everyone's progress and maybe get help to any community in difficulty. Most will have shortages of vital goods; if not now then increasingly as the months and years go by. Which reminds me. Is there anything that you need?"

"We're pretty well set up," I confirmed. "The only thing we're short of is farm animals. We've a few young beasts coming along, but not nearly enough in the short term. However, we can cope with that. How about you?"

He gave yet another dry laugh. "I doubt if you can fill our greatest need. We're desperately short of the fair sex. Although there were women among the crews they were few in number. The ratio of men to women here is three to one. We've even been talking about reversing the Mormon doctrine. Instead of each man being allowed four wives we're considering letting every woman have three husbands!" I wasn't sure if he was joking or not.

We talked for another five minutes, mainly about keeping in touch and letting each other know if we made more radio contacts. Then he handed back to his operator and I gave up my seat to Lewis. Leaving the latter to his own devices the rest of us returned to the bar, all the while discussing what Captain Phillips had told us. I for one felt a lot more optimistic about the future.

As I've mentioned already, when the first severe frost struck early in December we'd cleared a couple of rooms on the ground floor and brought all the young animals inside. Sadly some of the chicks didn't last the course and by the end of the year we were left with only forty-six. These, however, were growing rapidly and looking healthy under Kirsty's tender care. I made a mental note that one of our first tasks when the weather improved would be to build a chicken run. Initially I hadn't been sure of the wisdom of bringing the livestock indoors, but the decision was justified on the last day of the year. A sharp frost preceded a blizzard which lasted for more than forty-eight hours. When the skies cleared we found the ground covered in a full two feet of snow. I felt sorry for Tony. He insisted on maintaining his regular inspection of the filter in the river. Usually either I, Danny or Robbie went with him in case of accidents. It stayed bitterly cold for nearly a fortnight, though the days were bright and sunny.

The sight of endless falling snow meant that Hogmanay celebrations were muted, though Margaret and her helpers came up with a traditional steak pie meal for us just after midnight on New Year's morning. For the first time that evening one or two of the group became the worse for drink. Sian was the worst offender, having to be carried up to bed on Paul's shoulder. Duncan, too hit the whisky bottle hard and became maudlin and tearful. Esme decided to match his intake and she eventually fell asleep in her chair. As far as I was aware she spent the night there. Tony and Lily reached the giggling stage, but luckily were able to make it to their room under their own steam. With more bad weather to come I prayed that this would be an isolated incident. Thankfully my prayers were answered and there was no repeat. There were a few sheepish faces at breakfast next morning though!

It wasn't only Tony that suffered from the weather. A lessening in the heating and dimming lights warned us that the snow was affecting the solar panels. The original mansion had a sloping roof, so the heat beneath enabled the snow to slide off. The annexes, however, had been constructed with flat roofs and the snow just lay on them. At midday on New Year's Day therefore it was all hands to the pump, or in this case the roof. It took us nearly five hours to make a partial clearance, hampered as we were by the continuing snowfall. For the next couple of days we kept clearing the snow as it fell, but it wasn't until the third day when the skies cleared that the heating came back to something like normal and the lights stopped fading and flickering. Snowfall for the succeeding days was light and patchy, but we made a point of clearing each one promptly.

Needless to say the mood was gloomy. Only Lewis seemed happy. Apart from his shifts on the rooftop and brief breaks for meals he was glued to the radio. He brought us regular reports each day on conditions elsewhere. Our friends in Ireland had escaped the worst of the blizzard but were suffering from heavy rainfall. The Ayrshire communities had come off fairly lightly with only a few inches of snow, as had a newly contacted community living in caravans on the coast just south of Arbroath. Groups elsewhere were in a similar predicament to ourselves, two in the Highlands reporting close to six feet drifts. The snow lay for three full weeks, often icing over as temperatures plummeted during the night and stayed below freezing most days. Then a gentle thaw set in and by the first day of February the countryside was looking green again. I'd have liked to have made a start on ploughing and planting, but the volume of melted snow had left the ground sodden and unworkable.

The second Thursday in February brought sunshine and an unexpectedly high temperature of eleven degrees at eleven o'clock in the morning. I was studying the barometer just inside the front door when Lewis appeared from the stairway. He announced that he was going to get a breath of fresh air, so I joined him outside. We'd been chatting in a desultory manner for several minutes when the sound of a car engine broke the silence. We looked at each other in surprise. In a matter of seconds a rather battered looking Fiat Punto came round the final bend and pulled into the car park. Nothing happened for a good half minute, then the driver's door opened and a woman stepped out. At first I thought I was hallucinating, but a gasp from Lewis assured me that my eyes were not deceiving me. When I stole a quick glance at him I noticed that his mouth was wide open in amazement.

The woman, whom I judged to be about twenty-five, looked as if she'd just stepped out of the pages of a fashion magazine. Her brown shoulder length hair was neatly waved and shining in the wan winter sunshine. She was wearing a lemon yellow sweater and short pleated royal blue skirt, both of which looked as though they'd just come off the peg at Harrod's. Nylon stockings and royal blue matching shoes with four inch heels completed the outfit. As she came to a halt a couple of yards from us I also noticed that she was carefully made up, the first time I'd seen anyone wearing make-up since the disaster. Her fingernails were long and painted red. For once I was struck dumb and waited for her to speak.

"I'm sorry to trouble you," she began in what I can only describe as an upper class English accent. "Could you possibly give me something to eat please? I've had nothing except three small chocolate bars for the last forty-eight hours and I'm famished."

I pulled myself together and put on my best speaking voice. "Certainly. Lewis, would you take our guest to the kitchen, please, and ask Margaret if she can rustle something up." I turned back to the new arrival. "If you'll go with Lewis here we'll have some food inside you in no time. Once you've eaten I'd like to have a chat if that's all right with you. I'm curious to learn where you've been and how you got here." She thanked me and tip-tapped off after Lewis, who'd turned and was leading the way indoors.

I didn't want my chat with our guest to seem too much like an inquisition, so I bustled around trying to find one or two others to sit in. Robbie and Duncan among others were out checking rabbit traps but I managed to round up Danny, Lindsay and Esme. Some forty minutes later we were sitting at a table in the bar with the new arrival. Her name was Hester Whitley-Farningham; I noticed she stressed the double-barrelled surname. She had lived with her parents in Bloomsbury in London and her father had been a director of one of the leading banks.

"My boy friend and I were on a touring holiday in the Highlands," she explained as she warmed to her narrative. "We'd spent a week going up the east coast and along the north coast and were planning to continue down the west. We arrived in Kinlochbervie about four o'clock in the afternoon preceding the gas cloud. We drove into the car park of the hotel and he went off to the general store for some postcards. I was tired and thought we were going to stay the night there, so I lifted my suitcases out of the boot. When he came back he told me brusquely we weren't stopping and that he wanted to go on to Scourie. There was a blazing row and in the end the swine drove off and left me standing there. Silly me, I was sure he'd see sense and come back later, so I booked into the hotel in a double room. He never showed up."

"By way of consolation I had one or two vodkas too many in the bar after dinner. I should have known better: over indulgence always gives me indigestion. It was nearly midnight when I went to bed. For an hour or so I dozed before waking in some pain just after one. My ipod had been on the back seat of the car when it drove off, but I had a transistor with me, so I put the headphones on and listened to the radio. That's how I heard the first warnings of the gas cloud. To be frank I didn't take it too seriously, but on the better safe than sorry principal I locked myself in the bathroom and stuffed up all the cracks with sheets and blankets. It was only when the radio went off the air just after three that I got really frightened. I stayed in the bathroom all that day until eight o'clock at night. Even then it was only hunger that forced me to come out."

"You'll know what I found, of course. Dead bodies were everywhere, though thankfully not in the kitchen or dining room. The place was well stocked with food, so I stayed there for over a month until it ran out. Early on I broke into the general store across the road and stocked up with condensed and evaporated milk and a few other essentials so I lacked nothing."

"How did you cope with all the bodies?" Lindsay asked.

"I made sure I kept clear of them. The only places I used were the kitchen, dining room and my bedroom. The only thing that bothered me was the smell in the last couple of weeks I was there. Once the food had run out I realised it was time to move on. Luckily my older brother was a bit of a tearaway in his teens and when I was about fifteen he'd shown me how to start a car without the ignition key. I stole one of the cars in the car park and headed south. Each time I came to a hotel or restaurant I broke in and stayed for as long as the food held out. There was a length of rubber tubing in the car I stole, so whenever I needed petrol I just siphoned some off from someone's tank. All the time I expected to bump into other people, but as the weeks wore on I began to think I was the only person left in the world. I often thought seriously about committing suicide but something kept driving me on."

"When the snow came I was just south of Pitlochry on the A9 and had found a hotel. I stayed there until three days ago until the food there ran out. All that was left was half a dozen bars of chocolate. The last two nights I slept in the car. I was planning to head into Stirling today, but a short way from your turning I saw what looked like steam or smoke rising from this direction so I turned in and well, here I am."

It was a remarkable story. My estimation of Hester went up considerably. Very few people in her position would have been so resourceful. I came out of a reverie and realised that my companions were all looking at me.

"What are your future plans?" It was the obvious question to ask.

For once she was slow to reply. "I suppose I want to head to London eventually," she said.

"I don't think that would be very advisable," I told her. "For a start all towns and cities, especially London, will be disease ridden by now. Secondly there's no knowing what hardships and obstacles may be on the roads. You were lucky to get this far. If you do go on you'll have to make a wide detour past Stirling. There's an unsavoury crowd in occupation there. Your best bet would be to join up with a group, here or elsewhere. We know where many communities like ours are situated as Lewis has probably told you."

She didn't need much time for thought on this occasion. "You seem to be well set up. I'd like to stay here if you'll have me."

"With the greatest of pleasure," I responded warmly. "But I wouldn't be doing my job if I didn't give you a few words of warning. This is no place for nail varnish and high heels. We're well set up because we all work damned hard. It's long hours and physical work, too. For instance, for most of the spring, summer and autumn we'll be out in the fields, growing as much food as we can. That means getting dirty and being out in all weathers. When our animals are bigger there'll be cows and goats to milk. Even the indoor jobs aren't pretty and ladylike. There'll be rabbits to skin, toilets to clean and many more unpleasant tasks."

"I'll do my share," she insisted with a toss of her head. "I'm not afraid of hard work."

"In that case, welcome aboard. The first things you'll need to do are to get yourself settled in a room and then to see our doctors for a thorough check-up. Then you can get some more sensible working clothes." I turned to Esme. "Would you take care of Hester for the rest of the day, please. Danny and I will bring in her luggage. After she's seen the doctors and changed into something more suitable show her around and introduce her to everyone. We won't ask her to do any work today." I delivered the last sentence with a smile.

When they'd gone I turned to Danny and Lindsay. "What do you think?" I asked.

"She's quite a vision," Danny mused. "Not my type, though. She's much too la-di-da for me."

Lindsay was more forthright. "I doubt if she's ever done a proper day's work in her life," she said with a sniff. "She'll bear watching."

Danny gave a huge grin. "I can think of worse things to do than watching her all day." Lindsay gave him a look of pure scorn but said nothing as she walked away.

CHAPTER ELEVEN

After a snack lunch of beans on toast I called Duncan and started up one of the lorries. I wanted to check out a farm where we'd reaped a rich harvest of vegetables before the snow descended. At the last minute Kirsty asked if she could come with us. I didn't particularly want her along but I hadn't the heart to refuse her. We waited while she went to put on wellingtons and set out just after quarter past one. The farm in question was almost fifteen miles away, up near the village of Findo Gask. I was forced to drive slowly due to the pools of surface water on the roads. With no maintenance available many of the drains had become blocked and the melting of the snow had caused real problems. When we arrived it was to find several of the fields still under water.

A large percentage of the carrots and parsnips had rotted in the ground and we only got a couple of pounds of each after more than forty minutes' efforts. We had more luck with the turnips, swedes, winter cabbage and Brussels sprouts and another hour and a half saw the lorry filled to capacity. I was just about to get into the driver's seat for the return journey when Duncan put a hand on my arm.

"Are you in any hurry to get back, Dean?" he asked.

"Not really, as long as we're back before dark. Why?"

He gave a sigh. "It's so pleasant out here in the fresh air. I'd like to stay a little longer."

I remembered then that he hadn't been out of the hotel since before Christmas. Dr. Ling had diagnosed him with high blood pressure and we hadn't let him take a share of the roof clearances for fear of a heart attack.

"By all means," I agreed. "We'll stay for half an hour."

Duncan beamed and began to fill his pipe, while Kirsty took out her cigarettes. We seated ourselves on a low stone wall with our faces turned towards the sun and sat in companionable silence for two or three minutes. It was Duncan who spoke first.

"What would you both be doing right now if the gas cloud hadn't happened?"

"One of three things," I replied without hesitation. "I might be interviewing potential recruits, lecturing new arrivals or sitting at a VDU making out schedules. What about you, Kirsty?"

"Me? I'd prob'ly be at school unless I'd decided to play hookey for the day."

"Did you do that often?" I asked with a smile.

"Couple of times a month," came the reply. "Usually if it was history. I didn't like history and I didn't like the teacher. He didn't like me either. He was always picking on me."

Duncan then asked about our new arrival. I gave a summary of her story. "Poor little rich girl," he commented. "She's not going to find it easy fitting in."

I laughed. "I've a feeling that Lewis will look after her. He was obviously smitten."

"I don't like her," Kirsty announced firmly.

I turned towards her. "How can you say that? You haven't even met her."

"I don't need to meet her," she said defiantly. "All those fancy clothes and make-up and the finger nails and hairdo are enough to make my mind up about her."

The half hour was quickly up and we got back into the lorry. Before starting up I had another quick look at the map. When I'd planned the trip earlier in the day I'd worked out a different way of returning and wanted to refresh my memory. There were binoculars beneath the seat and I told Duncan, who was sitting in the passenger seat next to the window, to scan the countryside on the off chance of spotting something that might be of future use to us. My strategy soon paid rich dividends. We'd only gone some five miles when Duncan cried out to me to stop.

"Over there, Dean," he said and pointed. "To the side of that cottage. Those are beehives. I'm sure of it."

All three of us got out and went to look. Duncan wasn't wrong. To the side and rear of the cottage we counted ten beehives. All were covered. Cautiously I put my ear to the side of each one. I couldn't hear any buzzing, but I had a vague idea at the back of my mind that bees hibernated in the winter.

"The lorry's full, so we can't take them now," I said after some reflection.

"Couldn't we just take the tops off and set the bees free?" asked Kirsty.

I shook my head. "If we set them free here they'll stay in this vicinity. We need bees back at base, so the sensible thing to do is take them back there before opening the hives. Someone can come out tomorrow and lift them. Well spotted, Duncan. This is a godsend. We'll get our crops pollinated and have a supply of honey as a bonus, provided some of the inmates are still alive."

Back at base I arranged with Lewis and Gary to go out and pick up the beehives the following morning and site them in a field adjacent to the hotel grounds. I would have undertaken the task myself but I had another project to set in motion.

I next saw Hester at the evening meal and she looked very different. The designer clothes and high heels had been replaced by a blue track suit and stout trainers. Most of the make-up had disappeared and her fingernails, while still red, had been cut back to a workable size. She was seated at the far end of the table from me between Lewis and Esme and I noticed she chattered away freely to both of them. After the meal as most drifted off to play games or watch films I called Robbie, Danny, Tony and Ross into the bar for a meeting. These four were the most able among us when it came to DIY.

Our chickens were now almost grown to full size and it had become a matter of urgency to get them shifted outdoors. Accordingly I'd drawn up specifications for a sizeable and substantial enclosure for them. For the first time Robbie and I came close to falling out.

"We'll site it just outside the back door from the kitchens. First off I want concrete foundations about fifteen inches deep," I told the group. "If we can get them I'd like metal rods driven down deeper through the concrete and less than nine inches apart. On top of the concrete I want a brick or stone wall at least two feet six inches high, this surmounted by heavy duty wire netting to a height of seven feet. The whole to be fifty feet long by forty wide. We'll need two large wooden huts inside for nesting purposes."

Robbie's face had grown longer and longer as I spoke. At last he could contain himself no longer. "For Christ's sake, Dean. It's a hen house we're building, not Fort Knox."

"I'm glad you mentioned Fort Knox, Robbie," I came back. "It's appropriate. Those chickens are worth their weight in gold to us. If we lose them it's long odds against us getting any more. Sooner or later foxes are going to appear and it only needs a couple of foxes to get in amongst the chickens and we've lost the lot. I don't know much about the habits of foxes, but I do know they're cunning and I also know they can make tunnels. That's why this building needs to be as strong as we can make it."

Robbie subsided, but with ill grace. Luckily the other three agreed with me. I couldn't resist a parting shot, though. "Just to make your day even more unbearable, Robbie, in a short while we'll be needing another three or four similar enclosures." He just scowled at me!

The five of us took a couple of big vans into Perth next morning to pick up all the materials we would need. We all took heavy protective clothing and face masks, stopping at the outskirts to put them on. It was my first visit to the city since we'd stopped stripping the supermarkets and I looked around with interest. Evidence of decay and destruction was all around us. A number of buildings were burnt out and in one area close to the centre a block of shops and houses had been reduced to rubble. It resembled bomb damage, but my conclusion was that there had been a gas explosion. Our first call was at the B&Q superstore. Ross and I were in the leading van and had just dismounted when there came a blast on the horn from Robbie in the second. He pointed to a spot behind us. We looked round and promptly dived back into the driving cab. Two dogs were advancing slowly towards us, looking hungry and distinctly ugly.

"Pit bull terriers," breathed Ross. A moment later we heard two gunshots from the second van and the dogs fell and lay still. Gingerly we got out for a second time and approached the bodies. There was no doubt that the dogs were dead: Robbie's aim had been perfect. Close up we could see that both were badly under nourished. Their ribs were sticking out clearly in emaciated bodies.

Ross mopped his forehead. "Phew, that was close," he said through the mask. "It's a good job Robbie was so close behind. Ten seconds later and we'd have been torn to pieces."

It took us until four in the afternoon and stops at two more stores before we had all we wanted. Our toil was made more than a little unpleasant by the presence of half a dozen or so rapidly decomposing bodies. Presumably they'd been night staff or security guards. Thankfully the masks saved us from the odours but the sight of maggots at work made me feel sick. To add to our discomfort the place was overrun with rats and mice. I think we all felt depressed for we laboured with little or no conversation. I for one was glad when we got back to the open country and we could shed the masks and breathe good fresh air.

That evening brought two minor problems. From the start James had taken his duties as storekeeper seriously. From time to time he made out an inventory of our food stocks and at meal time he handed me the latest figures. I'd taken them up to my room, but had barely started to study them when there was a knock on the door. I opened it and found Paul and

Sian standing holding hands. They came in and found seats and I asked what I could do for them.

"We want to get married but we don't know how to go about it," Paul stated. "Sian's pregnant," he added.

"My congratulations," I said. "As for marriage, while I'm all in favour of it I don't see how you can. There are no churches and no registry offices any more. Really all you can do is to tell everybody you're married. At one time I believe there used to be marriage by cohabitation which was lawful. For the foreseeable future I suspect that will be the fashion."

Sian spoke for the first time. "Isn't it true that in the old days you could be married at sea by the ship's captain? You're our leader, so why can't you perform the ceremony?"

"I wouldn't have a clue how to go about it," I protested. "I've never been a churchgoer and I'm not even sure there's a bible on the premises. Tell you what. Give me a couple of days to think about it and talk it over with some of the others. If it's at all feasible we'll work something out for you." They seemed happy enough with that and left, still hand in hand.

Barely had I got back to studying the stock sheets when there was another knock on the door. Without waiting for an invitation Hester walked in. The working clothes had been cast off and she was dressed in a silver satin blouse and a short, very short, black skirt. The make-up and the nylons were back on too. I gestured her to a chair.

"Settling in O.K. and making friends?" I asked.

"Yes, thank you. Most of the people are very nice and this is luxury after all I've been through in the last few months." I didn't ask which ones hadn't been nice, being able to make a pretty good guess.

"So what can I do for you?"

To her credit she didn't beat about the bush. "Esme tells me you don't have a girl friend. I'd like to fill the vacancy."

I had had a vague idea of what she was after, based on the way she was dressed, but I hadn't expected a frontal attack. It took me twenty seconds or more to frame my reply. I wanted to be firm but not rude or uncomplimentary.

"I'm very flattered," I said at last, "but I'm not in the market. I'm sorry."

She wasn't prepared to give up easily. "You should have a girl friend, you know, if only for relaxation. There's not a lot of choice around and I'm available, so why not?"

I knew then that I was going to have to be firm. I've always believed that it's better to come straight out with the truth in dealings with other people.

"I'm going to be honest with you, Hester," I said, trying to sound as convincing as possible. "I don't mean this to be hurtful but it has to be said. You're just not my type. I've never been comfortable around ultra feminine women and that's just what you are. If and when I take a girl friend it will be someone down to earth and plain."

"You mean like that scruffy child that hangs around you all the time." She said it with a sneer in her voice and I felt my temper rising. I kept it in check as best I could.

"That scruffy child, as you call her, hasn't had a sheltered and comfortable upbringing like you," I said quietly. "She's been kicked around between care homes and foster parents since she was a baby. But she's worked as hard as anyone in this community and I respect her for it. For your information there's nothing sexual in our relationship. She looks on me purely as a father figure and I'm comfortable with that."

I thought that would be the end of it but Hester wasn't finished. "At least let me sleep with you tonight. I might make you change your mind."

"Full marks for persistence," I said with an edge of sarcasm to my voice, "but the answer's still no. In any case you've got a ready-made consort. Lewis is smitten with you and he's a good lad with no attachments. The way the world is now it's a case of taking what's available."

"But he's younger than me," she protested. "I prefer older men."

"In that case try your luck with Robbie or Duncan," I suggested. "Now if you'll excuse me I have to see Esme about a wedding." I stood up and opened the door for her. She finally took the hint and left.

I hadn't intended talking to Esme until the following day, but I didn't feel like carrying on with the stock sheets so I headed off to the library. She was sitting smoking in solitary splendour and I quickly sketched the request made by Paul and Sian. I asked if there was a bible among the books. She put out her cigarette and wandered over to the far corner. After a short scrutiny she pulled out a book and brought it over. It was the King James version of the bible. I asked her what her views were of me conducting a marriage ceremony.

"I think you should do it," she said decisively. "You're the nearest we have to any form of authority and it will seem just as real to Paul and Sian as a church wedding. I wouldn't be surprised if you get one or two more requests. While we're on the subject you'd better know you've got an admirer. Hester's been asking a lot of questions about you."

I made a face. "I've already been propositioned. I turned her down flat."

Esme smiled. "I rather thought you might. You could do a lot worse though."

"Maybe," I said shortly. "For the moment I'm quite happy as I am." I prepared to leave, but Esme put out her hand.

"Before you go there's something I want to say. I don't think any of us have ever thanked you properly for taking charge when you did. I want to do it now."

I laughed the compliment off. "If it hadn't been me it would have been someone else."

"No it wouldn't," came the reply. "Duncan went to pieces and Robbie wouldn't take the responsibility. If you hadn't got us organised we'd likely have perished in the cave. Even if we'd got out we'd all have split up and rushed off to our homes never to meet again. I certainly would have done. You realised straight away what was needed and kept us together."

I remembered I knew nothing about her family. "Did you lose many close to you?"

"Not especially close any more," she mused. "My daughter and son in law were in America and my younger son in Saudi Arabia. My ex husband was somewhere in the north of England with his new wife but we certainly weren't close by then."

I spent the rest of the evening trying to compose some sort of marriage service for Paul and Sian. I'd been at a colleague's wedding some eighteen months previously and vaguely remembered the vows that were taken. One disappointment was that there were no musicians among our company, amazing really given that we had nearly thirty people. In the end I picked 'The Lord's my Shepherd' as the hymn most likely to be known. It would have been nice to have had someone to play the wedding march, if only on a mouth organ. The following morning I took Paul aside and told him we'd go ahead with the wedding. He was overjoyed.

"You'll need to make a trip into Perth for a wedding ring and a dress for Sian," I told him. "I'll get Robbie and Tony to go with you. I don't want any of the women to go. Bring back seven or eight dresses of approximately the right size and while you're at it get plenty of rings. I doubt you'll not be the first to take the plunge."

The three of them took a Land Rover and of course wore full protective clothing. Remembering my previous brush with the pit bulls I warned them to be extra careful. They came back safely with over two dozen dresses and a large cardboard box of jewellery, not to mention heaps of artificial flowers.

CHAPTER TWELVE

I was determined to take my full share in the building of the enclosure for the chickens. Although I was hopeless at DIY I could still dig trenches and mix and carry cement. The project seemed to catch the attention of most of the others and before we'd been at work ten minutes we were joined by another eight willing volunteers. Lindsay and Selma were among them, both it seemed anxious to prove that they were as good as the men when it came to heavy work. In the end we had to settle for eight inches of concrete foundation. Our attempts to go deeper simply saw the trench start to fill up with water. Luckily we'd been able to get a large quantity of thick metal rods some two feet long. When we'd poured in three to four inches of cement we drove these rods in to the hilt at four inch intervals all the way round. It took us five full days to complete the structure but when finished even I was satisfied that it was as fox proof as we could possibly make it. Robbie and a couple of the other men went out the next day and came back with two large wooden sheds which we placed at opposite ends of the compound. The whole group turned out to watch the chickens being introduced to their new quarters.

We chose the following Sunday for the wedding. On the Friday Tony drew me aside after lunch. "Can you make it a double wedding?" he asked. "Lily and I have talked it over and we'd like to follow Sian and Paul's example." I asked Kirsty to find Paul for me and he joined us after five minutes. I gathered in the meantime that Tony had already discussed the matter with him.

"There are no problems," I assured them both, "though you'll have to accept it will be somewhat rough and ready. The question is do you want a joint wedding or one after the other?"

They looked at each other and nodded. "A joint wedding's all right by us. We'll talk to the girls and let you know." In the end, however, the girls were insistent that they preferred two separate ceremonies.

I'd roughed out what I was going to say but there were two things left to do. First I copied out the twenty-third psalm and printed off thirty hymn sheets with the order of service on them. These would do for both weddings. Then I went to see Margaret and Rowena. I asked if they could prepare something special in the way of a meal.

They looked at each other before Margaret replied. "The best we can do is something along the lines of the Christmas dinner. There are still plenty of frozen turkeys left. I'm reluctant to make anything with pastry in it, like a steak pie. We need to conserve all the flour for making bread. For dessert it will be a trifle or a fruit salad-tinned fruit of course."

"I can put together some sort of wedding cake," Rowena offered. She was the expert when it came to baking. "It won't take up too much flour. There'll be no marzipan or icing though, but I'll make it extra special by putting plenty of dried fruit in."

The kitchen arrangements were working well. Margaret and Rowena were both excellent cooks; the former a dab hand with meat and fish and the plainer stuff; the latter more into exotic dishes. To our surprise young Kirsty proved capable though only with plain cooking. She'd turned out some excellent stews, mince and casserole dishes. When I asked her where she'd learned she just shrugged her shoulders and said she'd 'picked it up along the way'.

Though I'd got used to public speaking in recent months I found that I was very nervous and self conscious when it came to the weddings. For a start I wasn't sure if the 'ceremony' I'd put together was appropriate. In addition I felt like an impostor even attempting the task. I was no minister or priest. Somehow I got through it, though I almost dried up at the point where the vows were taken. Robbie told me afterwards that I swallowed at least four times while asking the groom to repeat after me: 'I, Paul, take thee, Sian, to be my lawful wedded wife'. I thought the second ceremony would have been easier, but it wasn't. I was thankful when it was all over and we sat down to the joint wedding meal. I was asked to make a speech, but refused point blank. Instead James, as the oldest person present, said a few words wishing the two couples long life, health and happiness. While he was doing so I prayed inwardly that no-one else would want to get married!

By the last few days of February the ground had dried out sufficiently for us to get to work outside in earnest. We ploughed four fields within the hotel grounds and for good measure two more on the other side of the main A9. On the first day of March we planted our first lot of potatoes. Brian had been bringing on trays of seedlings of a variety of vegetables in the conservatory. I wanted to plant some of them outside at the same time, but Duncan, who'd been a keen gardener in his younger days, advised against it. With the outdoor work falling away to occasional weeding the DIY team elected to set up the second of the chicken runs, even though it would be at least a year before it would be needed. That necessitated another depressing trip into Perth.

All this time I'd been keeping an unobtrusive eye on Hester. I was pleased to see that she was making an effort to blend in, knowing that it wasn't easy for her. She'd kept well clear of me after I'd turned her down so unceremoniously but I'd expected that. The other men naturally liked her but her own sex showed mixed emotions. The married women apart from Margaret regarded her with suspicion, which I suppose was only to be expected. Lily largely ignored her. Lindsay and Kirsty were openly hostile. Apart from Lewis, who was still under her spell, she spent most of her time in the company of Esme and surprisingly Selma. One day when I was working outside next to the latter I asked her about the unlikely friendship.

"I suppose it's down to fellow feeling," Selma admitted. "We're each in our own way the odd one out. Apart from Sian she's the only non Scot and I'm the only black. No matter how nice everyone is there's always the thought of not really belonging."

I was shocked. "Surely you can't think that you don't belong. If you do I can put your mind at rest right now. You're one of the most important members of our community. You're strong, you're attractive, you work harder than most others and you're a professional. I doubt if anyone even notices the colour of your skin. I know if I had to describe you in fifty words the very last one I'd use is 'black', if I used it at all. But I'm glad you're on good terms with Hester. She needs the friendship."

One Thursday evening a few days after that conversation Lewis came into the evening meal with a message for me. "Captain Phillips would like to speak to you at eight o'clock and asked if you could be by the radio. Can I call back and say you'll be there?" I said he could, wondering what was in the wind. I went up to the radio room at about five to the hour and put on the headphones. Promptly at eight the good captain's voice echoed in my ear. Having ascertained that it was indeed me at the other end he launched straight into his message.

"We're starting our survey of the country tomorrow," he reported. "We've had a stroke of luck which will cut down the time it will take. There's a group of about forty people who've taken up residence at the old RAF base at Lossiemouth. They have three helicopters with pilots available for use and have ample fuel. They're going to cover the area north of the Great Glen, plus the Western and Northern Isles. One of our two craft will cover the land south of the Forth-Clyde valley while the second will do the central section. That will be the one that will drop in on you. The pilot is Graham Sinclair and he'll have a radio operator with him. Because we know exactly where you are you'll be one of the last on his list, so it will be three or four days at least before he gets to you. Any questions?"

"None, sir," I replied. "You can tell the two men they can be sure of a meal when they do arrive. Oh, is there anything you're short of at Turnberry that we might be able to help out with?"

"Nothing that I can think of at the moment unless you can rustle up a few dozen women from somewhere," he came back. "But thanks for the offer. Goodbye." I wandered round the building for the next half hour or so spreading the news.

I kept a watchful eye on the skies on the following Sunday but nothing appeared. It was a miserable day of incessant rain and any outdoor work was impossible. At least it gave us a chance to have a thorough clean up inside. Domestic duties had been skimped while we were preparing the fields. On many days cleaning had been reduced to simply clearing up the dead mice that our cats continued to provide in large numbers. Monday morning dawned grey and overcast but by ten o'clock the clouds had started to disperse and a watery sun was peeping through. I was one of a group transplanting cabbages when the drone of an engine could be heard above the muted chatter of those at work. We all stopped and looked up as the helicopter appeared in the sky to the north. A ragged cheer went up. There was just sufficient space between the chicken run and the first of our fields for the pilot to make a landing. Calling Robbie and Danny to join me I went to meet it. The radio operator was first out and to my surprise it was a woman. As she took her helmet off I saw that she was about thirty-five, tall and with short jet black hair. She introduced herself as Susan Beckett in an accent that I placed as somewhere in the English midlands. Moments later the pilot scrambled down to join us. As promised this was Graham Sinclair, an east coast Scot. He was long and lanky with reddish hair, prominent teeth and a determined looking chin. He told us he came originally from Montrose, though he hadn't been back there since boyhood.

I turned to Susan. "If it's O.K. with you I'll hand you over to Lewis Miller, our radio operator. He can show you everything there is to see and you can talk shop with him. The three of us here are ignorant when it comes to radio." She laughed and said that would be fine. Danny went off to find Lewis while I asked Graham what he would like to do.

"Just a general look round and a check on the details we have of your group," he responded cheerfully. "The main thing is that I can give you some information. We've only the mob at Stirling to visit and then we're on our way home."

"Be careful in Stirling," Robbie warned and went on to explain why. "I suggest that you don't leave the plane and make sure when you get out that Susan is covering you. I wouldn't put it past them to try and grab the copter."

Graham looked serious. "Thanks for the advice," he said. "It's not altogether unexpected. One or two rumours about them have filtered through to us. If we had any sort of radio contact I wouldn't even land there, but for the moment I have to give them the benefit of the doubt. Now to business. If you have a map of Scotland inside I can mark in all the settlements we've discovered. We've been in close touch with the Lossiemouth crowd all the time so we've now got a detailed picture. Of course there are bound to be one or two places we've missed for one reason or another but I'm confident we've got all the larger groups located."

Susan went off with Lewis to the radio room and Danny and Robbie accompanied Graham and I into the bar. Since we'd given the old manager's office over to the smokers I'd been using one corner of the lounge as an office. That's probably too grand a word to describe it. There was just a desk, a chair, a filing cabinet and a cupboard. Taking out a large map of Scotland I pinned it on the wall behind the desk and handed Graham a red marker.

"I'll start in the far north," he said as he began marking crosses on the map. "There are no survivors on Orkney or Shetland. There were two on the latter and one on the former but the Lossie crowd airlifted them to join the most northerly group on the mainland. That's between Thurso and Melvich. For some unexplained reason over a hundred sheep and a dozen or more cows survived so they've been well supplied with food. There are three small groups on the Western Isles. The largest is on Skye, close to Broadfoot. There's about thirty in that camp. There's a dozen on Barra and fifteen on Lewis. The last named had an interesting story to tell. They were all members of a scuba diving club and were partying when the news of the gas cloud first broke. They simply climbed into their gear, went under water and stayed there until their gas cylinders began to run out."

He continued to mark crosses on the map as he spoke. "Altogether we've located fifty-four groups, plus a dozen or more singles and couples. All of those were living rough and were more than glad to be told of larger groups they could join. Our mob at Turnberry are the biggest single unit at just under two hundred. Second largest is a group just north of Arbroath. There's about a hundred and twenty of them and they're settled in a caravan park. Like yourselves they raided local supermarkets and shops up and down the coast and are well stocked up. They've got a couple of fishing boats and seem to have unlimited supplies of fish though they're running out of meat, tinned or otherwise. They haven't any livestock, though. The nearest groups to you are near Killin and Kinross. Those at Killin are also living in caravans and there's only eight of them, two married couples and four children. The Kinross bunch is on a remote farm a few miles from Crook of Devon. There's about a dozen of them, all from the one family. At a guess I'd estimate the total population of Scotland is between fifteen and eighteen hundred. That's including the seventy or so in Stirling. Even if we accept the possibility that we've missed some I'm sure it won't be more than two thousand."

I looked closely at the map as he laid down the marker. South of the Great Glen the crosses were spread out fairly evenly. To the north there were far fewer and well scattered. Most of the west coast apart from Turnberry was unmarked with only a cross just south of Aultbea. I was lost in thought for a moment, then realised that Graham was speaking again.

"It's really been a depressing few days," he was saying. "Wherever we went there was evidence of tragedy in one form or another. Crashed vehicles on and off the road, properties and whole blocks wrecked by gas explosions and fires here there and everywhere. That's not to mention thousands of dead animals in the fields. The Lossie lot told me they'd seen over a dozen boats that had crashed into rocks or run aground. The ferry from Aberdeen to Kirkwall had capsized and turned turtle just off the Orkney coast. My colleague doing the southern run reported that the ferry from Belfast had crashed into the pier at Cairnryan. Wreckage of three planes has been spotted. One of them was either taking off or landing at Glasgow and crashed into a housing estate in Clydebank. I suppose we're all lucky to have survived, but I'm afraid there's a bleak future ahead of us."

"Not just us," Robbie said quietly. "Think of the generations to come, having to rebuild the world from scratch. It will be at least a thousand years before Earth is anywhere near to getting back to what it was before the disaster."

"What are your immediate plans?" I asked Graham.

"We've just the Stirling mob to see and then it's back to base. After that Captain Phillips and his advisers will study all the data and decide on the next move. He's thinking along the lines of a meeting between as many group leaders as possible to discuss ways of helping each other. You'll be informed of that if and when it happens."

I looked at my watch. "Lunch will be ready in half an hour. I hope you'll stay for that, though it will only be rabbit stew. Before then let us show you around."

"We're well used to rabbit," Graham laughed. "It's our staple diet too, though we do manage to vary it with fish. Meantime I'd love to have the grand tour. The skipper will want to know how you're coping."

CHAPTER THIRTEEN

We collected Susan from the radio room before making a circuit of the building and the grounds. At the end I asked Graham how we compared with the other groups he'd visited.

"I'd say you're as well set up as anyone," was his reply. "Funnily enough it's the larger groups that seem best situated. Even though they've more mouths to feed they seem to be better organised and have a higher morale. Perhaps that's the way forward; to get the smaller communities to join up. However, the decision isn't up to me, for which I'm thankful. I'm quite happy to do what I'm told and leave others to run the show."

Our two visitors took off around a quarter to two, with everyone present to wave them goodbye. Then it was back to work. At four o'clock Lewis went indoors to check on the radio. Ten minutes later he returned and called me aside.

"I've just had Graham on the radio," he informed me. "He gave me a message for you, which I've written down." He handed me a sheet of paper. 'As we descended to land on the King's Park in Stirling we were fired on by at least four men on the ground. Needless to say I got the hell out of there as quickly as I could. Thankfully the copter wasn't too badly damaged apart from a few bullet holes. Unfortunately Susan suffered a minor wound—a bullet in the fleshy part of the arm. She's fine though. Thanks for the hospitality and no doubt I'll be seeing you again.'

I showed the message to Robbie. He'd reduced his night visits to his friend Tam to once a week. Though the last one had been a couple of days previously he determined to go again that night. As always he refused any offer of help. As on many previous nights I stayed up to await his return. It was close to three a.m. when I heard his footsteps in the entrance. I had hot coffee waiting for him, to which I added a generous tot of rum.

"Wistance was furious with the men who fired on the copter," Robbie reported. "He called them for everything, pointing out that they could have captured it if they'd waited for it to land. Just as well we warned Graham. Tam's also been able to give me a rundown on the situation in Stirling. As you know we cleaned out most of the food stocks in Stirling and Alloa. They've been drawing their supplies mainly from Falkirk, Larbert and Grangemouth and are now looking as far afield as Linlithgow and Livingston. They're doing nothing in the way of growing their own crops and the estimate is that they'll start experiencing shortages in the late spring or early summer. Wistance has said openly that when that happens they'll steal from other groups. As the nearest we'll be their first target so we can expect an attack from the end of May onwards. As far as Tam knows they don't know exactly where we are yet but even Wistance will have enough savvy to send someone to do a reconnaissance."

"At least that gives us a couple of months' grace," I commented. "Can I leave you to plan our defence?"

"Sure thing." Robbie sounded confident. "Wistance still trusts Tam and looks to him for tactical guidance. Providing that doesn't change we'll know exactly when and how they plan to attack. I've an idea already as to how we can deal with it."

It was another fortnight before Captain Phillips asked to speak to me again. Despite several wet days we'd managed to get most of the planting done outside. In the conservatory most of Brian's pots and other containers were coming along well and he had a constant stream of visitors charting their progress. Leaves were appearing on the fruit trees that we'd planted in the front. All our livestock stayed healthy. We'd put the sheep and goats into the area at the front to keep the grass there down. Although we'd amassed a fair stock of farm machinery we'd neglected to include any lawn mowers. The only grass cutting implements we had were a couple of scythes and three sickles, so the less we had to cut by hand the better. Best of all the mood in the camp was good. The scent of spring was in our nostrils and that gave everyone a boost.

It was a Wednesday evening when Lewis brought me the information that Captain Phillips wanted to speak to me. I went up to the radio room and put on the headphones. As always the captain spoke briskly and concisely.

"We've set up a meeting for next Monday of as many settlement leaders as can make it. The venue is the Pitlochry Hydro, chosen because it's about the most central point for everyone. We sent a team up yesterday to clean the place up and make it ready. There'll be overnight accommodation and tea and coffee available, but you'll need to bring your own food, enough for an overnight stay. The first conference will be at two o'clock on the Monday afternoon. Any questions so far?" I had none.

"Travel arrangements," he continued. "Can you get there by road?"

"No problem," I assured him. "We've a wide choice of vehicles and plenty of fuel."

"Good." He sounded relieved. "We've a troop carrying helicopter here and there are two at Lossiemouth but we want to use those for the far flung areas. The more people who can go by road the better. I look forward to meeting you. That's all." He broke the connection abruptly.

On Sunday morning I cornered Margaret in the kitchen after breakfast. Rowena and Kirsty were occupied in the far corner but I kept my voice low. I knew that if Kirsty heard I was going away she'd beg me to take her with me and that wouldn't have been productive in any way.

"There'll be two of us going away tomorrow to a meeting that will last two days. Can you fix us up with enough food to keep us going?"

"No problem," she assured me. "I'll make you a couple of large rabbit pies and add a loaf of bread and some cheese. That should last you."

My intention had been to take Danny with me. I still saw him as a future leader and I thought the experience would be good for him. However, the events of that Sunday morning caused me to change my mind. Over the past few months I'd come to know everyone in our little community pretty well. I had sorted out those who were grumpy in the morning, those who could be relied upon to be the same in fair weather or foul and so on. It had become automatic to me to notice changes in behaviour. Lindsay was one who was easy to assess. Most of the time she was good-natured; occasionally she displayed impatience or sudden temper, but these moods never lasted more than twenty minutes. That Sunday she kept clear of everyone as far as possible, snapped and scowled at anyone who came near her and disappeared for long periods. The fact that Claire avoided her gave a clue to what might be the trouble but I couldn't be sure. I considered a direct approach but rejected the idea almost immediately. Any attempt on my part to interfere would almost certainly lead to a blazing row. I decided to take her instead of Danny to Pitlochry with me so that we could talk in complete privacy. I ran her to earth in the late afternoon moodily gazing at the chickens.

"Ah, there you are Lindsay," I began, giving her a big smile. "I've been looking all over for you. I want you to come to the meeting with me tomorrow."

There was no answering smile. "Why me? I'd have thought Robbie or Danny would be the obvious choice."

"That was my first intention," I admitted. "But they really should be keeping an eye on things here and in any case I want someone who'll see things from a woman's point of view."

"What's wrong with Esme or Myra?"

"Esme would sit there, listen to everything and say nothing. Myra only sees things from the medical point of view. I need someone like you who's not afraid to say what's on her mind. I've a feeling that there'll mainly be men at the meeting." I essayed a grin. "Much as I'd like to think so we're not infallible and you're more likely to spot if we're going wrong than another man."

Lindsay didn't seem enthusiastic but after a pause she nodded. "All right then. At least it will be a change of scene."

"Good. Be ready to leave at ten in the morning. I've laid on food and transport, so all you'll need to take is a change of clothing." I instructed. She made no reply and I left it at that. Going to the car park I selected one of the two Land Rovers, checked the tyres and filled up with petrol. For good measure I put three full cans in the boot as well. The last thing I wanted was to break down halfway there and have to walk the rest.

Lindsay didn't appear at breakfast but was waiting outside for me when I emerged at two minutes to ten. She was carrying a small overnight bag. My cheery good morning went unanswered. She waited patiently while I unlocked the passenger door and climbed into her seat still without a word. I closed the door on her, dumped my own bag with the provisions that Margaret had supplied on the back seat and got behind the wheel. We passed up the drive and on to the A9 proper. It was Lindsay who broke the long silence.

"Do you mind if I smoke?" was all she said.

"Not in the least," I replied. "It's a free country—nowadays anyway." I thought that might draw a laugh. It didn't. I waited for a couple of minutes, partly to see if she would say anything else and partly to marshal my own thoughts. I still hadn't worked out the best way to approach the subject uppermost in my mind. In the meantime I was driving fairly slowly. The road was already beginning to show signs of wear and tear. Finally I decided that the best policy was directness.

"O.K. Lindsay, time for some plain speaking. What's the problem?"

I got the expected response. "It's no business of yours," she snapped back.

"On the contrary," I replied mildly. "It so happens that it is. For better or worse you all made me leader of our community. I didn't want the job and if I could find someone to take it off my hands I'd pass it over tomorrow. But as long as I am still leader I'm going to do the job to the best of my ability. It isn't just about making plans and giving orders, you know. I have to be a welfare officer too. No matter how private we try to keep our personal affairs we can't avoid them having an impact on others. So I'll ask you again. What's wrong?"

She threw the stub of her cigarette out of the window and promptly lit another. She was silent for so long I thought she was going to ignore my request completely. I kept my eyes on the road and forbore to look at her. Suddenly I felt her slump back into her seat.

"If you must know it's Claire." She spoke so softly I could only just make out the words. "She's dumped me. She told me on Saturday night that she's in love with Brian and she's moved in with him."

This was more serious than I'd expected. "Maybe it's just a temporary infatuation," I said, risking a sideways glance.

Lindsay shook her head. "I'm a hundred per cent sure it isn't. After three years together I know Claire as well as I know myself. She's calculating, methodical and cautious. She never makes a move without considering all the options. So now you know and I'd rather not talk about it anymore if you don't mind." Another glance showed me that she'd turned her head and was gazing out of the window.

In a way I was glad of the silence that ensued. Thoughts that I'd been suppressing for months were coming into my mind. Despite knowing that I might unleash a storm I decided to test the waters.

I continued to look straight ahead while I spoke. "Lindsay, I'm going to ask you a very personal question. It's more than likely you'll take exception to it and want to hit me. If you do will you please warn me and I'll stop the car. Nobody benefits if I drive us both into a tree. Promise?"

I thought I detected the hint of a giggle. "I promise," was all she said.

"On second thoughts I'm going to stop anyway," I rejoined. "I could do with a drink of water." I pulled into the next lay-by, stopped and took a bottle of water from the glove box. After I'd taken a couple of swallows I handed Lindsay the bottle. She drank in her turn and put the bottle back. I looked straight at her and swallowed nervously.

"Are you a hundred per cent lesbian or are you bisexual?" I asked.

Her nostrils flared and I braced myself for a broadside. Then the ghost of a smile appeared on her lips and she shrugged. "I suppose I'm bisexual. I slept with one or two men before I met Claire. I can't say I enjoyed the experience though. Guess I'm a control freak, always wanting to be the driving force. I don't like the feeling of a man's arms around me."

"There's an easy solution to that," I ventured, knowing full well I was treading on dangerous ground. "Tie the man's hands behind his back."

Lindsay gave a scornful laugh. "What man's going to let me do that?"

"I would," I said quietly.

She looked at me in amazement. "God, you must be desperate."

"Not in the least," I replied truthfully. "I learned how to control my sexual desires a long, long time ago. At the same time I've been celibate for more than a year and some relief wouldn't come amiss."

"But why me? You could have practically anyone you want. Hester would jump into your bed in two seconds flat."

"Hester doesn't move me in the slightest," I said. "She's beautiful, yes, but all she offers is on the surface. Under that flighty exterior there's little or no substance. I prefer someone like you who's got depth and character. If you really want to know why I've spoken I'll tell you. Apart possibly from Selma you're the only girl in that place that I find attractive. I would have spoken before but I thought you and Claire were solid. Now the situation has changed I feel free to say what I feel. So what do you say?"

Her eyes had remained on my face all the time I'd been speaking. The expression in them hadn't changed. I fully expected her to tell me to get lost. Surprisingly she didn't.

"This has been a bit of a shock," she confessed. "I'd no idea. I'll need to think about it."

"I won't press you," I said as I started the car and pulled back on to the road. "Take all the time you need. I don't know what the arrangements are concerning accommodation, but I'll leave it to you to fix it up for us. Depending on how you feel you can take one room or two. That way I'll know what conclusions you've come to."

I could feel the mood was much lighter as we ate up the remaining miles. If I'd done nothing else I'd taken her mind off Claire for a while. There was more life in her voice when she next spoke.

"What do you want me to do at this conference?" she asked presently.

"I'm not exactly sure what form it will take," I told her, "but I imagine there'll be some sort of general session to begin with followed by discussion groups. Don't be afraid to speak up if you have any views at the main meeting. Other than that I'd like you to drift around and speak to as many people as possible. Try and find out how they're organised, how they're coping and any other information that you think will be of use to us. I know we have quite a good set-up but we can always learn from others."

"How much do I tell them about ourselves and our own place?"

"Hide nothing," I instructed. "Everyone's in the same boat and we've nothing to fear from anyone. The Stirling mob won't be there and they're the only lot that could cause trouble for us."

A clock somewhere was striking twelve as we drove into the car park of the Pitlochry Hydro. I remember being amazed that any public clocks were still working. There were a number of cars already there and on the lawn in front of the building I noticed two large helicopters. At the same instant I became aware of the sound of engines overhead and a third helicopter appeared on the horizon. Taking our bags from the car we walked in silence through the foyer of the hotel and up to the reception desk. Behind the desk was a man in his early forties with dark hair and a welcoming smile.

"I'm Harry Jennings, one time submarine captain and now a sort of adjutant to Captain Phillips." He reached below the desk and produced a couple of name badges. "We're giving everyone one of these to make recognition easier. Just fill in your name and location and pin them on."

"Dean Barclay and Lindsay Stevenson," I replied.

"Ah, Dean. Good to meet you. I've a message for you. Captain Phillips would like to have a few words with you as soon as possible. He's in the conference room, down that corridor and first on the left. By the way, we've given names to all the settlements and called yours Muirton Grange. You can put that in below your names. If you're staying overnight Vicky Shaw is dealing with the allocation of rooms. You can't miss her. She's about thirty with black hair and wearing a green sweater and black trousers."

I took one of the two food parcels Margaret had given me from my bag and handed it to Lindsay. "Would you see to the accommodation while I find out what the captain wants." I kept my face expressionless as I spoke. She nodded and moved away without speaking.

The conference room was easy to find. It had been laid out with a table and three chairs at one end and rows of chairs filling the remaining space. The sole occupant had his back to me when I walked in. Knowing that my feet would make no sound on the thick carpet I coughed discreetly as I walked towards him. He turned. I saw a rather small man, probably not more than five feet seven, slim, with sandy hair just beginning to show signs of grey. A narrow moustache adorned his upper lip. He was dressed in a pepper and salt two piece suit with clean white shirt and plain navy blue tie. I felt rather shabby, despite having drawn a brand new track suit from our clothing store that morning.

"Dean Barclay, sir," I said quietly. "I understand you wanted to see me."

He came to meet me with hand extended. "Ah, yes, Dean. I'm delighted to meet you at last. Graham was loud in his praises of your set-up at Muirton Grange. You seem to have done a good job there."

"I can't take very much credit for that. We've a good crowd," I responded. "Everybody pulls their weight."

"Nevertheless, no matter how good the troops are they need to be well organised. However, that's not why I wished to see you so quickly. I wanted to talk about that bunch of ruffians at Stirling. Have you any further news?"

I gave him a quick summary of the report that Robbie had made to me. He listened intently and without interrupting.

"I'm going to make reference to them at the meeting this afternoon. It looks to me as though we need to take some concerted action against them before they cause too much trouble."

"With respect, sir, I think that would be inadvisable," I suggested. "With so few people left in the world an unprovoked attack on any group would draw adverse criticism. It's almost certain that we'll be the first to be in danger from them. Leave it to us to deal with. As long as we have our mole in their camp we'll have advance warning of their plans and we'll be able to meet the threat accordingly."

For a moment he looked disposed to argue. Then he nodded. "Maybe you're right, though there is a possibility they've already committed an act of aggression. Unfortunately we've no proof. We'll play it your way, but just remember I can have a hundred armed men and women on the scene within three hours if you need any help. Now I suggest you get something to eat before the meeting at two. There's tea and coffee available in the restaurant and we've even the luxury of fresh milk. One of the Highland groups has several cows and their representative brought a full churn down with him. I'll see you again later."

Thus dismissed I made my way to the restaurant. It was nearly full and it took me a couple of minutes to seek out Lindsay. I eventually found her in conversation with an older, grey-haired motherly looking woman. Lindsay introduced her as Muriel McVay from Arbroath. While we chatted I let my eyes travel round the room. As I'd forecast women were very much in the minority and I was more than ever glad that I'd brought Lindsay with me. Including our present companions I only counted seven in total, one of whom was obviously Vicky Shaw. The green sweater was a vivid splash of colour among mainly dark and sombre outfits.

CHAPTER FOURTEEN

At five to two there was a general exodus towards the conference room. Lindsay and I found seats three rows from the front. The two captains were seated at the table facing the audience, which I estimated numbered close to seventy. It all looked very formal. Carafes of water sat on the top table and both men had open files in front of them. When the last person was in and the doors had been closed Captain Phillips rose to his feet. The room fell silent.

He began to speak in a clear and carrying voice. "For those of you that I haven't so far had the pleasure of meeting my name is Jack Phillips, formerly a captain in the Royal Navy. I'm based at Turnberry with what we believe is the largest group of survivors. I'd first like to thank you all for coming here today and express the hope that we will all benefit. Before I get on to the main business there's one point I'd like to stress. I've been asked by more than one person if this is an attempt to form a government of some kind. I can assure you all that there is no such intention. In my opinion such a move would be pointless. The population of Scotland is less than two thousand and widely scattered. While transport just now is fairly easy it will become close to impossible within a very short time. We calculate that we can keep the helicopters flying for no more than three years. Roads are already beginning to deteriorate and the fuel supplies we have hoarded won't last forever. In any case national government of any kind could do little. Any laws passed could not be enforced. My aim in calling this meeting is simply to try and forge closer ties between all the communities so that any in difficulties can call on help if needed. I also have some suggestions to make, but before I do is there anyone who disagrees with what I've just said?" Silence greeted him. He picked up a sheet of paper.

"As you all know we have carried out a detailed survey of the whole of Scotland. In the past few days Captain Jennings and I have analysed all the data gained from that survey. One salient fact has emerged from our study. The larger communities are faring better and their future prospects are brighter than those of the smaller groups. At present there are fifty-four groups in total. My suggestion is that some of the smaller and less well situated groups should link up with larger ones and we have prepared a list of possibilities. Before I go any further, however, I must stress that there is absolutely no compulsion to follow our advice. It will be a matter for individual groups to decide for themselves. Once the meeting is over Harry and I will speak to the various group leaders and then it is up to you."

"Our plan is to reduce the total number of groups to thirty-six or less. Apart from the old saying that there is strength in numbers, there are many advantages to be gained. Because of the availability of oxygen tents and protective clothing the number of doctors and nurses who survived surpassed that of any other profession. I can tell you that there are forty-two doctors and sixty-one nurses; that figure includes students. By reducing the number of groups it means that every community can have a minimum of one doctor and one nurse. As you also know, very few animals survived. Fewer groups will mean that each can have at least a male and female of every farm animal and build from there. With larger groups and goodwill between them we can equalise resources across the country."

"I've two more points to make and then I'll invite questions. Firstly I know everyone is working long hours simply to produce enough food to live on. But I'd like you all, and your constituents, to give some thought to future development. There are two areas I think we should be concentrating on. One is education. What are we going to teach the children who have survived and those of the next generation? If we are not to descend into savagery we must start now to prepare those who follow us for the tasks that lie ahead of them. The second area for study is transport. As I've mentioned, air and road travel will become near impossible in three or four years. There are a small number of horses that have survived, so the horse and cart will surely make a comeback. The other possibility is rail. There is still a considerable amount of coal under the ground and a number of steam engines in museums and other places around the country. I don't think long distance rail travel will be feasible for a hundred years or more, but it might well be possible to get some short local lines running. Think about it and share your findings with others."

"My last point is a grave one. There is a large community not represented at these talks. They style themselves the republic of Stirling and they are mainly made up of former prisoners from the jail at Glenochil. When our pilot attempted to land in Stirling his plane was fired upon and his radio operator injured. Recently we discovered eight people dead in a camp in the Ochil Hills. They'd been shot. There is no direct evidence that the Stirling mob was responsible, but as there is no other group nearby it is highly likely that they were the aggressors. It may be that we will have to take some action against them in the future. For now we are keeping a close eye on the situation. That's all I have to say at the moment. Does anyone have any questions?"

A man somewhere behind me took up the invitation. I turned round but couldn't see him distinctly. He had an east coast accent. "Are we still a part of the United Kingdom?"

Captain Jennings fielded that one. "I suppose technically we are. We have had contact with groups down south and have learned that two MPs were among the survivors. They have set up some form of government based in the countryside north of London. We've spoken to them and emphasised that we owe them no allegiance and will make our own decisions and policy. As you'll appreciate there are a number of English, Welsh and Irish personnel among the submarine crews that survived, including myself. We've discussed this matter of sovereignty with them and they are quite happy to be part of an independent Scotland should that come about. Personally I suspect it will be close to two hundred years before there are sufficient people in the country to make an issue of this."

Another question came from a woman directly behind me with an Edinburgh accent. "We're based on the coast. Is there any danger from oil escaping from the rigs in the North Sea and if so what action can be taken to deal with it?"

The two captains looked at each other. Finally Captain Phillips replied. "In all honesty we just don't know. Our helicopters didn't fly more than a mile from the coastline. There's no evidence at present of leaks at sea or on land. Hopefully the problem won't arise. There were stringent safety precautions in force, including an automatic shutdown of all pumping equipment in the event of a spillage. As to what we can do if a leak does occur I'm afraid the answer is nothing. We simply do not have the expertise to deal with it."

The final query came from the back of the room. "Do we know what conditions are like in the rest of the world?"

Again it was Captain Phillips who answered. "We're in radio contact with countries in various parts of the world. All the indications are that there have been very few survivors anywhere. I suspect that the total population of the world is around the one million mark. Now if there are no more queries I suggest we repair to the restaurant for tea and coffee and individual discussions. We can all learn a lot from each other's experiences.

Captain Jennings and I will move around and talk to those groups that we think could benefit by merging."

As we stood up and prepared to exit the room Lindsay whispered in my ear. "I'll start to drift around as you told me. Muriel's keen to meet other people so I'll latch on to her." I nodded agreement.

As I left the room I found myself next to a giant of a man in full Highland dress. He must have stood about six feet four or five, broad shouldered and with flaming red hair and beard. We peered at each other's name tags. I discovered my companion was Archie MacKay from Thurso. We shook hands and once in the restaurant shared a table and exchanged biographies. My new friend came from Bettyhill on the north coast. He'd been a teacher, having graduated from Aberdeen University with a first class degree in maths. He had a soft voice with just the faintest trace of a Highland accent. I spent ten minutes or so telling him my own recent history from the day in the cave to the present position at Muirton Grange. Then he told me his story and a sad one it was.

"I'd driven across to see my fiancée in Tongue that Monday evening. It was about twenty to two in the morning when I left her house and started to drive home. I put the radio on to help me stay awake and that's when I heard the first word of the gas cloud. I carried on until the news came through that Ireland had gone silent. Then I parked in a passing place, shut all the windows and turned off all the vents. I listened to the radio until it went off the air. It was a moonlit night and I could see the countryside around me quite clearly, including a couple of dozen sheep in the middle distance. At the instant the radio went dead they keeled over and lay still. That's when I started to get frightened. I remained in the car until ten o'clock. By that time the air was stuffy and I was beginning to have difficulty breathing. My hands were shaking as I opened the door and stepped out. I almost couldn't believe that I hadn't been struck down."

"Once I'd taken a few deep breaths I got into the car and drove straight back to Tongue. Shona, her parents and younger brother were all dead. I made myself a meal from food in the house and then dug a large grave. Half the time I couldn't see what I was doing for the tears that poured out. We were due to get married at the end of October. I buried all four, filled in the grave and made a small wooden cross to put at its head. Then I drove back home to Bettyhill. Nowhere did I see any signs of life. The following day I buried my parents and my grandmother who lived with us. On the Thursday I drove along the coast road towards Thurso. I was almost at the outskirts when I saw three cars coming towards me. We all stopped and I discovered that the cars carried survivors from Thurso. They were intending to camp near the village of Reay, close to the site of the former nuclear reactor at Dounreay."

"I was overjoyed to find that I wasn't the only one alive and naturally I joined up with them. We spent two full days burning all the bodies in Reay. Then the mains water supply dried up and someone remembered that when the nuclear reactor at Dounreay was in operation there had been radiation in the surrounding rivers and burns. Luckily we'd found Geiger counters in three of the houses, leftovers from days gone by we presumed. For another two days we checked every open stretch of water. Thankfully they showed no signs of radioactive material. After that we carried on in a similar fashion to you, scavenging around a wide area for food and other supplies. During that time we came across more survivors and now we've over forty in our group."

"Someone mentioned that you'd found a hundred or more sheep alive," I commented when he stopped speaking.

"That's right. In fact it was nearer two hundred. How they survived is a mystery. The only theory I can come up with is that the poison gas was blown about by the wind and that here and there wee pockets of pure air remained. Certainly the sheep that we did find alive were close together in groups. They were a real godsend. Nearly half were rams and we've been killing off most of them for meat. Naturally being on the coast we've a decent supply of fish too so we're not too badly off. We've ploughed up Reay golf course and are planting potatoes and other crops. Our main shortage is bread. We don't see any point in growing wheat when there isn't any yeast available."

"Surely one of the other groups will be able to give you some dried yeast," I suggested. "We're looking at ways to produce a regular supply of fresh yeast. When we get properly organised I'll contact you and let you know. What about power?"

"We have some," Archie admitted. "One of the survivors we found in Wick is an engineer. Under his direction we moved a wind turbine we'd come across and he fitted it up for us. As long as there's movement in the air we get enough for our needs, but on still days we go without. Bruce, the engineer, is devising some kind of wave power turbine. If he can get that working we'll have all the power we need."

I could have gone on talking to Archie for longer, but at that moment Captain Phillips materialised at my side. "Sorry to interrupt, Dean," he apologised, "But there's two people I'm anxious for you to meet. They're in the manager's office just off reception."

I followed him out of the restaurant and along to the office where two men were seated in chairs at a coffee table. One was of medium height, round faced, with lightish hair and hazel eyes and wearing spectacles. I estimated he was about forty. The other was fiftyish, close to six feet, dark, heavily built and with a ruddy complexion. Jack introduced the smaller man as Charles Vaughan and his companion as Alec Geddes.

"These are your nearest neighbours," the captain explained as we shook hands. "As I see it there would be advantages in them joining up with you at Muirton Grange. I'll leave you all to discuss the possibilities." He went out quickly.

"Perhaps it would be best if I begin by telling you both something of our set-up," I suggested. They both nodded and I proceeded to do just that. When I'd finished I looked at them expectantly.

Charles Vaughan was the first to reply. I realised immediately that he was English and probably from Lancashire. "We'd welcome coming to join you," he said. "We're not in great shape. There's eight of us altogether; myself, my wife and our two children plus my wife's sister, her husband and their two children. The night of the disaster we four adults were playing bridge. We finished the last rubber about one thirty in the morning and switched on the TV. That's when we first heard about the gas cloud. Donald, my brother-in-law, lived next door, so he went in and woke his two children. We all got into my caravan and sealed it up as best we could. We stayed there until the following afternoon before we ventured out."

"Currently we're living in caravans in the woods a mile or so out of Killin. We're short of petrol and our food supplies won't last much beyond the summer. We're in the middle of planting some vegetables, but we're plagued with rabbits so I'm not optimistic of getting much from them. Neither Donald nor I are very practical. We've tried to make traps but with no success. We've no heating. On dry days we've been building bonfires to keep warm; on wet days we huddle together wrapped in blankets. The nights are almost unbearable."

I became businesslike. "Right. We'll discuss details later on and get you moved over within the next few days."

"There's not much that we can contribute, I'm afraid. Of course we'll bring what's left of our supplies. As I've said, none of us are much good at everyday tasks. Donald and I are both clerical workers and our wives were teachers."

"Don't worry," I assured him. "We're well staffed with practical people. Most of the work is pretty menial anyway. Your children will be good company for the two we have already and your wives will be worth their weight in gold. There are no teachers in our group and as Captain Phillips said in his speech we have to start thinking seriously about education."

CHAPTER FIFTEEN

I turned to Alec Geddes. "What's your situation?"

"Better than Charles's, at least as far as food is concerned," he said in a distinct Fife accent. "We're situated on a remote farm roughly between Crook of Devon and Kinross, not far from Balado where they have the annual music festival. There's ten of us: my wife and myself, our two sons and their wives, my daughter and her husband, one granddaughter and my mother. We were lucky to survive at all. Jamie, my oldest son, had toothache that Monday night. He got up in pain just before half past one and switched on the radio while he searched for painkillers. As soon as he heard the news about the gas cloud he woke everybody up. After a short argument we decided to take it seriously, got dressed and went to round up some of the animals. We'd just finished building a new barn which I knew was virtually airtight. Jamie kept a portable radio with him. We rounded up five cows and a young bullock plus a pig and four sows and two of our three cats. The two dogs couldn't be found—they had a habit of roaming the area at night and might have been anywhere. There were no sheep nearby and we'd no time to bring in the horses which were stabled some distance away. We were just about to go and get some chickens when the news about Ireland came through. I told everyone to get into the barn and sealed up the only door with layers of insulating tape. It was eleven in the morning before Jamie insisted on going out despite our arguments. I guess you know the rest."

"As to our present situation, food is not a problem. We grow enough to support ourselves and there are plenty of fish in nearby rivers. We'll even get a little meat from time to time. Two of the sows have produced litters and according to custom most of the male piglets will end up in the oven. The kitchen and living room of the farmhouse have big open fireplaces and there's an unlimited supply of wood within easy reach. We won't freeze. In other areas we're not so well off. My mother suffers from asthma and arthritis and has run out of medication. One daughter-in-law is pregnant and Jamie is still having trouble with his teeth. We're short on fuel and on clothes and medicines. As far as joining up with you is concerned I'd ask the same question as Charles here. Would it benefit you? It would be ten extra mouths to feed and we wouldn't be able to bring much with us."

"On the contrary," I argued. "You'd bring us expertise. None of us know the first thing about farming. We're ploughing and planting, but everything we do is hit or miss. With you and your family on board we can expand into surrounding fields of which there are quite a few. Beyond that Gleneagles is only about three miles away. I know it sounds like sacrilege, but we can plough the golf courses and grounds there if we need extra fields. As I mentioned we have two doctors and three nurses so your mother can get treatment and your daughter-in-law have her baby under proper conditions. We've stocks of clothes and fuel that will last for many years to come and we've nearly four dozen chickens, two goats and two sheep. Added to your own livestock that will give us a sound basis for the future."

Alec rubbed a hand across a stubbly chin. "I'll have to talk it over with the family," he said at last. "It'll be a wrench leaving the farm. My great grandfather started it way back in the 1800's and it's been in the family ever since. The boys and I are proud of the tradition. There's a lot of sense in what you've said though. We'll discuss it when I get back tomorrow and I'll contact you to let you know our decision. We've got a radio transmitter now." He stood up, shook hands and walked away.

I turned back to Charles Vaughan. "When do you want to make the move?"

"As soon as possible," came the reply. "Let's see. This is Monday. Would Thursday be too early for you? We're short on petrol. In fact we've probably just enough to get one car the whole journey."

"Don't worry about that," I said. "We'll come over and pick you up. Expect us between eleven and twelve on Thursday morning. Did you say you had two caravans?"

"No, we've four in all. Why?"

"I'm thinking they'll be useful," I replied. "If Alec Geddes and his family do come and join us we'll be expanding well beyond the grounds of the hotel. It'll be useful to have caravans placed at various points in the surrounding areas to act as rest rooms and shelter in bad weather. If you can batten down everything inside I'll make sure we send four vehicles suitable for towing. Now can we find a map so that you can show me exactly where you're situated."

It took us ten minutes or so to find someone with a suitable map. When we did so Charles pointed out the location of their camp and I made a rough sketch of the neighbourhood. I also worked out the route that we would need to take. Leaving my companion to his own devices I went in search of Captain Phillips. I found him deep in conversation with three others, including Archie from Thurso. I waited patiently until he was free and then gave him a summary of my previous meeting. He seemed pleased.

"The strategy of reducing the number of groups seems to be popular," he commented. "So far we've arranged nine link-ups and there are four or five more on hold while the leaders go back and confer. Negotiations are still going on all over the place. I'm very hopeful we can reach the target of thirty-six or less." He looked at his watch. "Good heavens. It's past five o'clock already. I suggest we have a meal break."

I was still carrying the bag with our provisions so I went in search of Lindsay. I eventually ran her to earth in the hotel's kitchen, drinking tea with her new found friend Muriel and two other women. I'd intended to ask her what she'd done about accommodation for the night but she showed no signs of wanting to talk privately. I gave her her share of the food and left her to it. In the dining room I joined a group containing Harry Jennings, Graham the pilot and two other men that I hadn't previously met. One turned out to be from the Skye base and the other from Ballantrae. We spent a pleasant hour or more comparing notes. By the end of the evening I was left with the impression that, with the possible exception of Turnberry, we at Muirton Grange were as well organised as anyone. One thing of interest that I did learn during the rest of the evening was that nearly every other group in the country was run by an elected committee. Only two other men that I spoke to were, like me, in sole charge.

By the time ten o'clock came people had started drifting off to bed. I spied Lindsay in the opposite corner of the bar and managed to catch her eye. I pointed significantly upwards. She seemed to understand the gesture and with a few words to her companions she got up and came over to me.

"I'm ready to retire," I told her. "What did you decide to do about rooms in the end?"

I can't be sure but I thought I saw a faint blush on her cheeks, though it may have been a trick of the light. "I just took one," she said in a low voice. "Follow me."

Our room was on the second floor. The first thing I noticed when I went in was that there was a double bed. My heart began to beat faster. Our two holdalls were in the far corner. Wordlessly Lindsay went over, took out hers and my night wear and dropped them on the bed. Somewhat self-consciously we undressed on opposite sides of the room. When we were both naked I walked slowly towards her and held out a piece of rope that I'd taken from the car earlier in the day. She looked at it.

"Maybe we can dispense with that," she murmured.

"I'd rather you used it," I replied, equally softly. "I want this to be a success and it won't be unless you're completely relaxed and comfortable. If my hands are free I can't guarantee that I have enough self control not to put my arms around you." I gave her the rope and lay face down on the bed with my hands behind my back. There was a short pause and then I felt her bend the rope around my wrists. One corner of my brain told me she hadn't tied it too tightly. As I turned over I heard her blow out the two candles on the bedside table. One second later she eased herself on top of me.

I fully expected her to be rough with me, if only to demonstrate to both of us that she was the boss. Much to my surprise I was wrong. Her kisses were insistent but soft and tender. When she finally came to me she was gentle in the extreme, even when we reached the height of our passion. I was left with a feeling of fulfilment and contentment. What Lindsay felt I never found out. When I turned towards her she was fast asleep, her long dark hair spread out like a fan on the pillow beneath her head. It took me less than three minutes to free my wrists. I debated whether to risk putting my arms around her but decided against it. Turning away from her I composed myself for sleep. It took a while for me to drop off. The one thought that kept running through my mind was that I'd finally found the partner I wanted. Whether she would want me was another matter.

A faint light was filtering into the room when I awoke. The luminous dial of my watch showed me it was six fifteen. For a moment I wondered why I'd wakened, then I realised Lindsay was stirring beside me. We turned towards each other simultaneously and began kissing. By a supreme effort of self control I kept my arms at my side. We made love once more. I'm sure my control would have broken but she held on to my forearms to prevent me putting my arms around her. But once it was over she came naturally into my arms and put her head on my chest. Neither of us spoke a single word and a minute or so later her regular breathing told me she was asleep again. I soon followed her example.

Broad daylight was streaming through the window when I next awoke. Sleepily I looked at my watch and found the time was half past eight. I sat up. Lindsay was standing by the window, a cigarette in her hand. She looked round as I climbed wearily out of bed.

"I've washed already," she said. "There's half a jug of water left for you." I slipped on my trousers and shoes and made a quick but thorough toilet. Then I finished dressing and got to work with my electric razor. All this time neither of us spoke. On my part it was by design: I didn't want to discuss the events of the night until we were on our way home. When I did eventually speak it was on more mundane matters.

"Is there any food left over?" I asked her.

"A bit of rabbit pie and one sandwich," she replied. "I've split them in half. If you're ready we can go down to breakfast." On the way I asked if she'd learned anything useful on the previous day.

"Not a lot," she confessed. "We seem to be better off than most of those I spoke to. A couple of points did come up though. I think we need to pay more attention to hygiene. Two or three people mentioned they'd had an outbreak of stomach ailments and they put it down to inadequate cleaning rather than food poisoning. Oh, and nearly everyone I spoke to asked if we'd an optician on our strength. It seems that there's none to be found anywhere."

That was something that hadn't crossed my mind since my early conversation with Ling. None of our group wore glasses on a regular basis, though Esme, Duncan and Myra used them for reading. I made a mental note to quiz our two doctors again when we got back. Maybe one of them had some optical knowledge.

Alec Geddes buttonholed me at breakfast. "We'll probably take a couple of days to come to a decision. I'll let you know as soon as we do."

"There's no great hurry, Alec," I told him. "It would be next week before we can do anything. We're picking up Charles and his lot on Thursday and we'll need a couple of days to get them settled in. Tell you what. Radio me on Friday at five o'clock and let me know then."

"Will do. If we do decide to come we'll need to work out how to drive the cattle over. There's also some machinery that will be useful. I'd want to bring the ploughs, the combine harvester, a couple of tractors and a couple of small milling machines. There's also a butter maker and a cheese maker. Even if we don't join up you may like them. They're electrically operated so they're no use to us."

"Don't worry about transport," I said. "We've got half a dozen of the big supermarket trucks and plenty of fuel. We'll bring three or four over, say two for the animals and two for the machinery. I'll look forward to hearing from you."

After the meal we gathered in the conference room once more. The two sea captains were at the top table again and it was Captain Phillips who spoke. "I know you're all anxious to get away home, so I'll keep this as brief as possible. Once again I'd like to thank you all for coming. I feel it's been a most productive couple of days. Agreements have already been made to reduce the number of groups to forty-two and another dozen negotiations may be completed once you've had a chance to report back and discuss it with your own people. I gather too that arrangements have been made to share medical staff and livestock with those who have none. I mentioned yesterday some items that we all need to give some thought to for the future. Now I'd like to add two more that were brought up frequently in the talks I had with everybody individually. At present there are ample supplies of salt and sugar. But the time will come when they run short. Seaside communities will have access to salt and we may be able to arrange some sort of trade to supply the inland areas. Sugar is a bigger problem and I'd like all of you to look around your areas for sugar beet plants or seeds. If you do find any please share them with others. Trading could then be straightforward—sugar in exchange for salt."

"One final point. Several people have asked if we can make this a regular event. There were even suggestions that we should meet every three months. While such a plan has its merits I don't think we would be justified in using our precious supplies of fuel in such a manner. We must aim to keep the helicopters flying for as long as possible to cope with emergencies and the same applies to our road transport. I know I touched lightly yesterday on the use of the horse for transport and eventually it will come down to that, but I'd like to think it will be a few years yet before that becomes our only means of transport. I would suggest that we have at least one more meeting, say in a year's time. Keep in touch by radio, all of you and for those who came by car drive safely going home. Remember, there are no emergency services to rescue you if you get into difficulties."

It was a good twenty minutes before we reached the car park. Lindsay rushed off to say goodbye to Muriel and one or two other new acquaintances while I went around shaking hands with a dozen or more people, including two I hadn't even spoken to before. My last farewell was to Archie from Thurso. With twinkling eyes he told me that when holidays became the vogue again I was to go and visit him. The last of the helicopters was just taking off and the car park nearly empty by the time I started the engine and set off. I drove in silence for a couple of miles waiting to see if Lindsay wanted to open the conversation. Finally I could contain myself no longer.

"Well?" I asked her.

"Well what?" she countered.

"Are we an item?"

She lit a cigarette before replying. "Let's not rush things. I admit I enjoyed last night but I need to think about things. It's a big step for me to go straight. Give me time."

"Take all the time you need," I rejoined. "I'll be waiting. Meantime you know where my room is. Come whenever you want to." There was more I would like to have added but I was content with the progress I'd made. I'd built a bridge between us; now it was up to Lindsay to decide whether to cross that bridge or not. It was entirely up to her and I knew that putting pressure on her would be counter-productive. I'd the suspicion too that she still harboured lingering hopes that Claire would tire of Brian and return to her. I knew that if it was a choice between Claire and me I'd be the loser.

"Do you think Mr. Geddes will come," she asked in a deliberate attempt to change the subject.

"I think he will but I'm not a hundred per cent sure. I suspect it will be the granny that makes the final decision. It's a case of family pride against practicality. On the one hand it will be like losing a limb to tear themselves away from a place that's been in the family for over a hundred years. On the other they're without medical care and electricity. If it was left to Alec himself I'm pretty sure they'd come. We'll just have to wait and see."

It was after twelve when we got back to the hotel. As I parked the car Kirsty came running out of the front door. "Guess what?" she shouted when still a full ten yards away. "We've seen a bird." Bit by bit we got the story from her. She'd been feeding the chickens the previous evening. As she closed the door of the pen behind her she heard a cheep. When she looked up there was a robin sitting on one of the windowsills. Quickly she went back into the kitchen, scooped up a couple of slices of bread and put them not far from where the robin was sitting. Without waiting for it to come down she went inside and called everyone she could find to come and look. By the time she got back the robin was on the ground feeding. It had come back in the morning and seemed quite tame.

This was good news indeed. If one bird had survived then the odds were that there would be more. The next person I saw was Danny, who met me in the reception area. He reported that all had been quiet while we were away and that Brian wanted to see me when I was free. I asked Danny to let everyone know there'd be a meeting after the evening meal, then I dumped my bag back in my room and headed for the conservatory. Both Brian and Claire were there and busying themselves with watering cans. I asked what they wanted to see me about.

"Nothing important," said Brian. "I just thought you might like to see the first orange and plum trees coming through." He led me proudly to the row of pots nearest the window. Sure enough five or six of them had green stems peeping through the soil. As my gaze wandered round the whole area I realised what an excellent job Brian had done. The whole place was spotlessly clean, the containers all neatly lined up in rows and every one labelled. I walked around reading the tabs. Tomatoes, lettuce, courgettes, beetroot and radishes filled the smaller vessels. The larger ones held things like apple, pear, plum, orange and other fruit seeds. Trays were devoted to vegetables such as cabbage, cauliflower, carrots, parsnips, broccoli and brussels sprouts, these to be transplanted outdoors when big enough.

I knew that Claire had spent a lot of time helping so I made sure I included both of them in my praise. "You've done a great job, the pair of you. Obviously you've got green fingers. I'm thinking of scouting round for some large outdoor greenhouses. Do you think you could take those on as well." Brian flushed with pride and they both nodded enthusiastically. I looked at them standing there. I'd never been much good at reading emotions but I got the impression that they were very much in love. Inwardly I rejoiced. It would be the making of Brian and more importantly it brought Lindsay one step closer to me.

CHAPTER SIXTEEN

After lunch I went to see Ling and Myra. I ran them to earth in the small laboratory they'd set up. Some sort of experiment was in progress. Beakers, test tubes and bottles of chemicals littered the desk they were working at. They asked me to give them five minutes and to wait in the makeshift office opposite. Once they came in and we were all seated I told them about the concerns that had been raised at the meeting about hygiene and the lack of opticians. I asked if either of them had had any optical training. Myra shook her head.

"I know something about it," Ling declared in his precise English. "During my surgical training we touched briefly on the structure and function of the eyes. I also still have my notes. But I would be loath to attempt any surgery except in a dire emergency."

"What about laser treatment," I asked. "Do you have the necessary equipment?"

"We have laser capability, yes. But the same applies. I am not really skilled in that aspect and I could easily do more harm than good. As to other eye defects, all I could do is make tests. We have no means of making glasses or contact lenses. I suppose we could raid all the opticians' shops within range and collect up all the materials, but I'm not sure if I have the skill to prescribe accurately what would be needed. It would be a case of trial and error."

"I think we should send a party into Perth to do just that," I said. "There must be thousands of pairs of glasses in the city and among them will surely be some close to what individuals may need." I moved to another topic. "I'm not casting any doubts on your ability, but how well could you cope with a major emergency of any description?"

"Almost as well as we could before the disaster," Myra replied with confidence. "We have all the gear necessary to carry out major surgery and for post operative care. Paul knows enough to act as our anaesthetist and both Selma and Lily are experienced nurses. Don't forget we all worked in the intensive care unit. Why? Are you expecting any emergencies?"

"Sooner or later we're likely to be attacked by that mob at Stirling," I replied. "There are certain to be casualties, perhaps a large number. I'd like to be sure we're as well prepared as we can be."

"We'll do our best, of course," said Ling. "But we can only carry out one operation at a time. We only have the one theatre and even if we set up a second one any serious operation would need both of us present."

That brought another thought to my mind. "Are you doing anything to train the nurses to become doctors?"

"Indeed we are." Myra sounded indignant. "We're coaching them on a regular basis, often up to three hours a day. They'll never be fully qualified like Ling and I, but in three years' time they'll be able to cope with most things. They're all very bright."

I left it there and went to seek out Danny. Finally I ran him to earth out in the fields, planting seeds with Selma alongside. I gave them a quick rundown of the arrangements made at the conference.

"If the Geddes family come, and I think they will, they'll take full control of all the farming. The rest of us will obviously still need to provide the labour force. In that case the best plan will be to set up daily or weekly rotas so that everyone gets a fair share of outside and inside duties. I'd like you two to take that on if you will. Leave out those that have full time duties. That means Margaret and Rowena in the kitchens, the medical staff, James and Duncan. Better leave out Robbie too. I want him free to concentrate on his spying missions."

"Do we include you, boss?" asked Selma with a cheeky grin.

"Indeed you do. I'll take my full share. But don't start doing anything until I hear from Alec Geddes. This is just an advance warning."

At the meeting after the evening meal I gave the whole company full details of the Pitlochry conference. I mentioned the Vaughans and the possible arrival of the Geddes family and outlined my proposal for Danny and Selma to set up work rotas. I asked if anyone had objections. The question was greeted with silence, so I assumed everyone approved. Next I referred to the troubles some units had experienced with internal illnesses.

"We're going to have to take more care with our cleaning, particularly food surfaces and toilets," I went on. "I'm afraid disinfectant wasn't high on my shopping list when we were scavenging in that first week, so our stock is low. Can I have two volunteers to take a truck into Perth and fill it with detergents and disinfectant?"

Tony and Ross put their hands up immediately, as did Dr. Ling. I looked towards him and nodded.

"There's a huge stock of these things at the infirmary," he announced. "If it's all right with you Paul and I will take another truck and bring that here too. At the same time we can follow up your suggestion about bringing in a stock of spectacles and contact lenses." I told him that would be O.K. and went on to talk about the arrival of Charles Vaughan and his followers two days later with four caravans. I asked if anyone had experience of towing a caravan. Only Gary put his hand up.

"In that case we'll take three cars only with Gary, Robbie and myself," I directed. "We've only got two vehicles with towing bars attached anyway. Presumably Charles and his brother-in-law have driven with caravans in the past and have the equipment available. We'll take some cans of petrol through with us to fill their cars. It's only a forty mile trip for them so six gallons should be ample. If by any chance we can't get all four caravans back here in one go then one of us can go out again on Friday."

The first person to buttonhole me after the meeting was Kirsty. She didn't look happy. "If the farmer's family comes will that mean I can't look after the chickens anymore?" she asked anxiously.

I patted her shoulder. "I'll have a word with Mr. Geddes about that if he comes," I reassured her. "I'm sure he'll be quite happy to let you carry on. On that subject you do know, don't you, that most of the cockerels will be killed off for food when they're big enough."

She sniffed. "Of course I know. It only takes one cockerel to help the hens make chicks."

I spent the whole day on Wednesday working in the fields. Having been away for two full days I didn't want to give the impression that I was dodging the hard work. It wasn't a pleasant day. A biting east wind accompanied by recurring spells of fine drizzle made conditions most uncomfortable. Many times during the day I wished we'd looked around for some sort of mechanical seed spreader. Eight hours of sowing by hand took it out of the muscles and even a hot bath afterwards didn't cure the aches and pains. On the credit side of the day we saw three or four more birds, sparrows and finches so I was told, plus a few bees from our hives venturing forth to sample the scattering of wild flowers in adjacent fields. Meantime the two trucks arrived back full of cleaning materials of all types plus the optical stores. We unloaded them after the evening meal.

Gary, Robbie and I set out for Killin just after nine fifteen on the Thursday morning. The wind had dropped considerably though there was still the hint of moisture in the air. We took a Land Rover and a Mercedes, the two cars we had with tow bars attached, plus a seven-seat people carrier. Perhaps carelessly I decided to dispense with armed guards as we weren't going to be anywhere near the Stirling crowd. The directions Charles Vaughan had given me were spot on and we found their camp in the forest without difficulty. It took less than half an hour to refuel the two cars on the site, both of which had tow bars on them and to hitch all the vehicles up. The two wives and four children packed into the people carrier with Robbie as chauffeur, Gary and I had a caravan each at our backs and Charles and his brother-in-law Hector towed the other two. I found it a bit tricky at first and lagged a few hundred yards behind the others. After four or five miles though I got the hang of it and closed up. We reached Muirton Grange on the stroke of one. After a quick bite to eat we settled the newcomers in their rooms and arranged for all of them to get a medical check. That done I went back and put in another four hours in the fields.

On Friday morning I had a long chat with the two newly arrived wives. The subject was education. At the end of our talk we'd reached broad agreement on setting up classes and on what should be taught. The fact that the six children were all of primary school age made the task easier. The main emphasis would be on reading, writing and arithmetic, the original 'three r's'. Charles's wife Christine spoke Gaelic fluently and we agreed that a start should be made on the children learning the language. We both felt the importance of our history and were unhappy at the possibility of the old tongue dying out. Then for me it was back to the fields and to the backache! Thankfully by the close of the day that Friday nearly all the planting that could be done had been done. Hopefully hoeing and weeding would be less strenuous. At five to five I made my way to the radio room to await the call from Alec Geddes.

He was ten minutes late in coming through. Reception wasn't very good at first, but Lewis twiddled a few knobs and at last we could hear each other clearly. I got the news that I wanted to hear.

"It's taken a lot of argument and discussion," the gruff voice at the other end of the line told me. "In the end we've decided to join up with you. It was the medical care that tipped the balance. My old lady is poorly, Jamie's still having trouble with his teeth and the wee one's not too great. Now I think you said something about sending trucks through to take the livestock and machinery."

"That's correct," I affirmed. "How many will you need? We've got half a dozen of the large supermarket carriers, plus three large lorries. If that's not enough we can always make a second trip. It's not all that far and we've ample fuel."

"Six trucks should do it," he reflected. "We'll need one for the cattle, at least one for the rest of the livestock and one for seed and stuff. I know you've got ploughs already but ours is a good one and I'd like to bring it with me. Then there's a couple of tractors, a combine harvester, a spreader and two small electrically operated milling machines."

A happy thought crossed my mind. "Does the spreader plant seeds?" I asked hopefully.

"That's exactly what it does," came the dry reply. "It spreads muck as well, with a separate attachment. Now I'd better give you directions on how to get here. Have you got pencil and paper handy. It's a bit tricky."

I took down the instructions as he dictated them and read them back over to make sure I'd written them correctly. Signing off I told him to expect us between ten thirty and eleven on the Monday morning. On the Saturday outside work was impossible. Rain, mixed with hail, sleet and even a few flakes of snow, persisted for the whole of the daylight hours. It gave us the opportunity to have a cleaning blitz throughout the hotel and to get rooms prepared for the Geddes family.

All this time I'd had no chance to speak to Lindsay alone. Every time we met there were other people around and private conversation was impossible. I wasn't sure if this was deliberate policy on her part or just an unfortunate coincidence. I suppose I could have made the effort to force a meeting but I reasoned that trying to rush her would probably be counter-productive. All the time conflicting old proverbs were chasing each other across my mind. One was 'faint hearts never won fair ladies' and the other 'fools rush in where angels fear to tread'. I was inclined to give more weight to the latter, if only on the grounds that Lindsay was dark and not fair! Several times I thought about asking Esme for advice but in the end I did nothing. Lindsay knew how I felt. It was up to her to make the move if she wanted to.

It was about eleven when I went to bed that Saturday evening. Like everyone else I was tired after a day spent cleaning and polishing and I'd had a few energetic games of table tennis after the evening meal. Inside five minutes I was asleep. Something wakened me some time later. I was facing the clock and saw by the luminous dial that it was a minute to midnight. The room was pitch dark. Then I heard a faint rustling. Seconds later I felt the bedclothes being pulled back and someone got in beside me.

"Lindsay?" I breathed.

"In person," a soft voice replied with a giggle. "Why? Were you expecting someone else?"

"I wasn't expecting anyone," I replied, equally softly. "And there was always a possibility somebody had mistaken the room. If it's not a stupid question, what brings you here?"

"What do you think?" she whispered. "On second thoughts, get those pyjamas off and I'll show you. You can put your arms around me if you want to." I realised then that she was naked.

Sometime later, as she lay unmoving in my arms I thought it safe enough to ask the question that I'd been wanting to ask. "Does this mean you're moving in permanently?"

"If you want me to," she answered simply.

"I want that more than anything else in the world," I murmured. "When do we tell everybody else?"

"Whenever you like." I could hardly hear her and seconds later her steady breathing told me she was asleep. It took me twenty minutes or more to follow her example. The disaster and all the subsequent events were forgotten in the feeling of contentment that swept over me.

In the end we didn't make any formal announcement. Instead we went into breakfast together hand in hand. There were many surprised faces initially, then a few whistles and somebody started clapping hands. Only Hester looked daggers at us. I couldn't have cared less. My only concern was how Kirsty would react to the news. I eventually found her in the smoking room. I needn't have worried. She greeted me with a big smile, then jumped up and hugged me.

"I'm so glad," she said. "I knew you'd have to get a girl friend some time and I was afraid you'd go for that horrid Hester. I like Lindsay. She always treats me like an equal, unlike some I could mention. She's just right for you, too."

It was another day of rain so outdoor work was impossible. I spent a couple of hours in the kitchen peeling potatoes under Margaret's eagle eye. Once I'd finished Lindsay appeared from nowhere and asked me to help her shift her belongings into my, or rather our room as it had become. I agreed willingly, though I wondered why she needed help. None of us had much in the way of personal possessions.

From the outset our rooms were considered private and like most I hadn't visited Lindsay or anyone else in their own quarters. When I walked into her room therefore I got the shock of my life. One wall was completely taken up by cartons of cigarettes, two deep and six high.

"Where the hell did all these come from," I gasped.

Lindsay giggled. "You remember you said that we could only bring what cigarettes we could carry in the driver's cab?" I nodded speechlessly and she giggled again. "I'm afraid we disobeyed you. We all did it,

Robbie, Esme, Kirsty and I. We stuck another half dozen or more cartons in the back of the truck whenever we could and unloaded them when you weren't around. You must admit you made it easy for us. Duncan and Esme were teamed up a lot of the time and Duncan was happy to turn a blind eye. Kirsty and Robbie were together fairly often and of course you left me with Claire all the time. She moaned about it of course, but she would never have given me away. You're not going to confiscate them, are you?"

I couldn't find it in my heart to blame her. Comforts and luxury would be in short supply in the post disaster world and anything that brightened the austerity was to be sought after. If this was some people's way of alleviating hardship then I was happy for them.

"I suppose you never thought of just quitting," I suggested. Lindsay looked horrified. I thought she was going to say something, but she just shook her head emphatically.

Cloudy skies and a light drizzle greeted us when we awoke on the Monday morning. The trip to collect the Geddes family required careful organising. We were taking six trucks and three cars altogether. That meant eighteen of us would need to go, nine drivers and nine armed guards. I wasn't taking any chances on this trip. By now I'd no doubt that the Stirling mob would be roving further afield in search of food. I led the way in the people carrier with Kirsty beside me. Surprisingly she had turned out to be one of the best shots in our community. Much of our way was along second class roads and the lack of maintenance was beginning to be evident. Even before the gas cloud many of the minor roads had been neglected and despite the lack of traffic were breaking up rapidly. Grass and weeds were forcing their way up through the cracks in the carriageway and potholes were numerous.

Luckily I only took one wrong turning, but even that held us up for nearly twenty minutes. The road at this point was narrow and the whole convoy had travelled nearly a mile before I realised my mistake. There was no room to turn the trucks and we had to back them up to the junction before we could resume the formation. It was exactly eleven o'clock when we turned on to the track leading to Auchmallie Farm. There was only room for the three cars in the farmyard itself; the trucks simply lined up on the track. Ideally I'd have liked to start loading right away but Mrs. Geddes, a plump and homely woman who looked like the typical farmer's wife, insisted we should take soup and cups of tea before we did anything else. In the end I was glad that we obeyed her. The soup was thick, hot, rich and swimming with vegetables and accompanied by bread that had obviously been baked that morning. While we ate various members of the family came up to be introduced.

When we did get down to the business in hand we loaded the animals first, starting with the cattle. I took one look at the bull's horns and from then on made sure there was always someone between me and it. Alec Geddes noticed my discomfiture and gave a faint smile.

"He's quite tame," he said to me quietly.

"That's as may be," I retorted. "But those horns look lethal and I'm not taking any chances." In the end the farmer and his two sons did all the necessary action to get bull and cows on board and locked up. Robbie was driving that particular truck and, there being room to turn, decided to head straight back to Muirton. He was confident that he knew the way back, but for good measure I gave Claire, his guard, the directions that I'd written down. One of the farmer's sons went with them to choose a suitable field in which to release the cattle. We wanted them to have the shortest time possible locked up in the truck.

The pigs, the two cats and some of the machinery went into the second truck, while numbers three and four took the rest of the machinery. Then we backed the two remaining vehicles up to the barn, the same one that had saved the family's lives. My eyes widened at the quantity stored therein. Sack after sack of wheat, corn, barley and oats were brought forth and filled one truck. The second took more sacks of potatoes, dried peas and beans, swedes and turnips. Smaller parcels contained seeds of all description. There was just enough room in the truck for some personal possessions of the family.

Finally it was all loaded and we formed up the convoy for the return journey. Alec and his wife plus his daughter and her husband travelled with Kirsty and I in the people carrier, along with his mother. Gran, as she insisted we all called her, was a small bird-like old lady, bent a little with arthritis but still chirpy and sharp witted. I had to smile inwardly as she admonished her son and granddaughter from time to time as if they were still ten years old. She didn't spare me either. I was instructed to drive carefully and not jolt the car too much, easier said than done on the farm track and adjoining roads. I saw a look of surprise cross Alec's face when Kirsty took her seat and laid the gun across her knees. He made no comment though. The run back to Muirton was uneventful and we pulled up in front of the hotel at a quarter to five.

CHAPTER SEVENTEEN

The next few days were hectic indeed. We'd offloaded the cattle, pigs and the cats on the Monday evening, but the rest of the stuff we left until that Tuesday afternoon. First I showed the Geddes family, Gran excepted, over the buildings and grounds. Then we walked over the surrounding area while Jamie, Alec's oldest son, took notes designating which fields we would use for grazing and which for ploughing. He also noted details of what we'd already planted. When we came to look at the chickens Kirsty was standing by with an anxious look on her face. Alec spent three or four minutes giving the birds a minute inspection. Then he turned to her.

"You've done a good job here, young lady," he praised. "I've rarely seen healthier looking birds. Just you carry on the way you've been doing." Kirsty blushed and mumbled something, but I could see the delight in her face.

One problem that needed to be solved was where to store the machinery. In the end the only solution we could come up with was to move some of the petrol tankers out of the stables and use them for the purpose. The dozen tankers we parked in a vacant area some one hundred yards from the nearest building and covered them with tarpaulins. One stable took the milking machine. It meant a long trek to bring the cows in for milking each day, but there was no other option. The machines for milling flour were set up in two vacant rooms on the first floor of the southern annex along with the cheese and butter makers. We brought in the seeds and personal possessions but the sacks of grain and vegetables we simply left in the trucks until required.

Meantime Danny and Selma had been busy making out the rotas and these came into effect on the Thursday morning. Alec announced that the labour he'd need would vary from day to day so we settled for daily rotas. Despite the addition of sixteen extra pairs of hands there was still plenty of work for all. We fixed the working day at eight thirty until five with morning, lunch and afternoon breaks of fifteen, thirty and fifteen minutes respectively. Any task that needed to be done outwith those hours was on a voluntary basis and I was pleased to see that there was never any shortage of willing volunteers. Even the five medical staff, though exempt from the rotas, were often to be seen in the fields weeding and hoeing. Ling declared that only those hours in the fresh air kept him going. But it wasn't all hard work. Several people opted to learn how to milk cows by hand and transferred their newly acquired skill to milking the female goat as well as the cows. One of the things that we'd never bothered to do was to sex the half dozen lambs that we'd taken in. Jamie Geddes did that for us and told me that we had three rams and three ewes. I asked whether we should kill one of the rams for food but he shook his head.

"I'd rather wait until we've got six or seven rams, just to be on the safe side," was his opinion. "Time enough then to think about slaughter." In truth there was no immediate need. The supply of rabbits showed no signs of petering out and while a change in the menu would have been welcome we had to take every possible precaution to safeguard the future.

Gran gravitated to the kitchen as soon as she was settled in and had seen the medical staff. I thought there might have been a conflict of personalities but she and Margaret soon became bosom friends. She had quite an influence on our daily diet and we began to notice subtle differences and more variety in the way soups and main dishes were put before us. There was, however, a small black cloud developing on the horizon. Our stock of dried yeast was starting to run low. I asked Alec if he had any advice on the subject.

"Not really," he replied. "In the old days we bought all our yeast fresh from a wholesaler. As far as I know he got it direct from one of the breweries or distilleries."

I recalled something that Lindsay had told me on the way back from Pitlochry. "The group down at Innerleithen have reactivated the old Traquair home brewery and get yeast as a side product. I'll maybe put one of our handymen into investigating the possibility of starting up our own brewery. Alternatively we could set up a small unit to make fresh yeast from the dried stuff we've got left, but that requires a steady supply of sugar and we haven't got all that much sugar left. Is there any chance you could grow some sugar beet?"

Alec took off his cap and scratched his head. "It's something we've never tried ourselves, but I think there were farms in North Fife where it was grown. If you like I'll take one of the boys and a car and see if there's any seed lying around."

"Yes, do that," I responded. "But take an armed guard with you, say Lewis or Tony. If you don't come up with anything there's no harm done and we can always use the honey and make mead instead of beer. That should give us a supply of yeast though I'm not sure whether it would be enough."

On the Friday evening of that week I had a long talk with Charles Vaughan's wife and her sister. We discussed in greater detail the education of the children. As far as subject matter was concerned I left the decisions entirely to them. School would be for two hours in the morning and an hour and a half in the afternoon five days a week and would take place in two vacant rooms on the top floor of one of the annexes. What had originally been set aside as the conference room for the hotel yielded a blackboard, chalk, pens, pencils and a large supply of blank paper. There were mixed reactions from the children when they learned their fate. All six had attended school before the disaster but not all had enjoyed the experience!

Lindsay and I had settled comfortably into our new relationship. From a personal point of view I found it a great relief to have someone different to discuss new ideas with, knowing that I'd get an honest reaction. Previously the only person that I felt easy with in that respect had been Robbie and he looked at everything from the point of view of a man and a soldier. Lindsay being such a strong character I'd steeled myself for the likelihood of the odd row or quarrel, but though there were times we disagreed we always managed to sort out our differences in a reasonably amicable fashion. I was happier than I'd been for a long time and I think she too was content.

In general morale remained high despite the hard work and monotonous diet. There were one or two moans from time to time and I was aware that, apart from Hester, Sophie Laird had often disapproved of decisions I'd made. For that reason I was all the more surprised at a conversation I had some three weeks after the arrival of the Geddes family. It was a Thursday evening. Lindsay and I were sitting in the bar with Esme and Ross McTear. Nobody else was present. We'd been talking generally about how our lives had been changed by the disaster. Esme had taken little part in the discussion until Ross speculated on where we'd all be in ten years' time.

"Do you ever wonder why we're here now?" Esme queried. "I often think we'd have been much better off if we'd died along with everybody else." We looked at her in surprise.

"Surely not," Lindsay sounded shocked. "All right, life isn't a bed of roses. But we've got a roof over our heads, we're healthy and we've enough to eat, boring though it may be. Better still we're masters of our own destiny. There are no politicians or petty officials to tell us what to do, only Dean," here she smiled at me fondly, "and we can always kick him into shape if we don't like what he's doing. There's no war, no taxes, no unemployment, no drugs, no rich and poor and no crime. Granted some of us miss the telly, but when I think of how much rubbish there was on that maybe it's not such a great loss either."

Esme looked contrite. "I didn't mean to criticise Dean. I think he's done a marvellous job in keeping us all together and organising things the way he has. Much of what you've said is true, but I still think the future looks bleak. Our diet is going to get even more boring once the food stocks are used up. All our time will be spent in growing enough to eat and then we'll only provide ourselves with the basics. Do you realise that we'll almost certainly never again see things like oranges, bananas, lobsters, tuna, chocolate, coffee and a host of other things we once took for granted. Once our stock of clothes is gone we'll be reduced to wearing animal skins like prehistoric savages."

"Surely it's not as bad as that," protested Ross. "Yes, there are a lot of things we're going to miss, but things are not as black as you've painted them. Take clothes for instance. We'll relearn the skills that our ancestors had. There'll soon be a constant supply of wool, so we'll learn to spin and to weave. I'm sure we've enough talent within this building to find a way of making leather and fashioning it into shoes. The way I see it is that we're pioneers, building a brave new world for our children and their children. As it did before, knowledge and skill will stride forward with each generation. It may take three or four hundred years for civilisation to get back to anywhere near what it was, but someday it will."

That was the longest speech I'd ever heard Ross make and he delivered it with considerable passion. Still Esme didn't look convinced, though she didn't reply or refer to the matter again that evening. I wondered if the outburst was due to it being that time of the month, though Lindsay told me later when we were alone that Esme had shown signs of depression for some time. I made a mental note to ask Ling to give her a check up. We went on to talk of other things, but Esme's outburst remained in my mind. When Lindsay and I retired to our room I brought the subject up again.

"Are there others that think the same way?" I asked her.

"One or two are moody and quiet occasionally, but only Hester and Sophie are permanently at odds with everybody else," she replied. "Other than those two it's not the same ones all the time and usually whoever it is gets back to normal in a couple of days."

"What about you?" I'd deliberately avoided asking the direct question up until that point. "How are you coping with your new lifestyle?"

She smiled rather ruefully. "Better than I expected. You've been so gentle with me and so understanding that it's made things easier than I thought they would be. But I think it's only fair you should know this. If Claire came back and wanted to start our affair again I'd leave you in a minute."

"I've known that all along," I told her bluntly, "and I wouldn't blame you if you did. But I pray every night and morning that Claire's love for Brian remains strong. Having you with me makes life worth living, no matter what hardships we have to face."

A couple of days later Alec Geddes, with Lewis for company, took a large van and headed out to find a possible source of sugar beet. They left around nine in the morning and didn't return until nearly five in the afternoon. I was at the front door talking to Kirsty when they drove back into the car park and went across to meet them.

"Any luck?" I asked as Alec climbed out of the driving seat.

"Yes and no," came the reply. "We couldn't find any trace of sugar beet, but we did manage to get something equally valuable. Come and look." He led me round to the back of the van and opened the doors. It was empty except for a dozen or more hedgehogs, most of them rolled into their natural protective ball. I looked at them blankly, then back at Alec.

"I don't get it," I admitted. "How are they worth having. Do we eat them or something?"

Alec smiled. "Let me explain one of the basic facts of farming to you. If you turn over fresh grassland the way we're doing now you find that underneath it's teeming with slugs and slugs are lethal to crops. I reckon we'll lose up to thirty per cent of the vegetables we grow this year to slugs alone. Now you can keep the numbers down by using chemical slug killers and we brought plenty with us but that doesn't entirely solve the problem. Hedgehogs do. They eat slugs in large numbers. Within three years there won't be a slug within two miles of our fields. I hoped to find one or two hedgehogs, but to get as many of this is a real stroke of luck."

I wasn't quite as enthusiastic. I'd rather have had the sugar beet. "Bang goes our hope of a supply of yeast," I remarked.

"Not necessarily," Alec replied. "I haven't mentioned it before, but one of the wife's hobbies is making homemade wine. She can do it with just about anything, fruit, vegetables, even flowers. Though she used yeast she can do it without through natural fermentation. That'll give us a small supply of fresh yeast from time to time. It won't be enough to last us all year round, but even then we'll still have bread. Gran makes a very passable loaf of unleavened bread. But going back to pests, I'm worried about foxes. Much as I hate to suggest it when so few animals have survived, I think we should shoot any we see. Otherwise they'll be forever after our poultry."

I'd been considering that myself, so I readily agreed with him. More and more as the days passed I gave thanks that Alec Geddes had joined us. His input and professionalism was invaluable. Where we were guessing as to what and how much to plant he knew for certain. We'd been putting seed into the ground willy-nilly. He instinctively knew what crops would grow best in which fields and how to look after them. Our food supply was in safe hands for the future years. Perhaps the only real concern would be possible drought, but I consoled myself with the thought that such a catastrophe was almost unknown in central Scotland.

A few days later Donald, Alec's younger son, came to see me after the evening meal. "Gary tells me you've put a few trout in the river," he began abruptly. I agreed that was so but that we'd seen no sign of them since. "I'm not surprised. According to Gary you only got around thirty and there's a hell of a lot of river for them to spread to. Now I used to do a lot of fishing myself and I know the rivers near our old farm well. If it's all right with you I'd like to take Gary now and again and bring back a lot more fish to add to the ones already in the river."

"Great idea," I approved. "Take Duncan with you as well. He's a keen angler and it will do him good to get an outing or two. Can your dad spare you, though?"

"No problem," he assured me. "I've spoken to him about it already. We're well on with the ploughing and sowing. He and Jamie can handle the rest and you're all giving him plenty of help."

Slowly but surely during the months of April and May the number of birds increased. In addition to the robins that were our first sightings we now saw a few other species. Other living forms began to appear too. An occasional butterfly or moth could be seen in the meadows. The odd spider, beetle and jenny long-legs popped up in the house. There was still a steady inflow of mice, but the cats dealt summarily with them. Several people reported seeing hares around the outer reaches of our property. The first fox showed itself near the end of the month. I shot it myself two days later. It went against the grain but we couldn't afford any threat to our precious chickens.

On the evening of the last Friday in April Lewis ran me to earth in the snooker room. Harry Jennings was on the line from Turnberry and wanted to speak to me. I followed Lewis up to the radio room and put on the earphones. After exchanging pleasantries Jennings got down to the reason for his call.

"What can you offer in exchange for a pair of ponies?" he asked me.

"I'd need to see what our head of farming says about that," I replied cautiously. "Can I get back to you in fifteen minutes? Oh, I take it they're male and female." He affirmed that they were. Alec and Jamie were in the bar when I went downstairs. They were enthusiastic about getting horses and had a quick discussion.

"Tell him we can offer either six chickens and a cockerel or four young sows and a young pig," was their verdict.

Back in the radio room I relayed the decision to Harry Jennings. Then it was his turn to keep me waiting as he conferred with the other party. Twenty minutes later he was back. "They've settled for the pigs. It's the colony on Skye by the way. We'll send a copter up from here on Sunday morning if that's O.K. with you. They'll pick up the pigs, take them up to Skye and bring the ponies back with them. There are another couple of exchanges in the pipeline so they'll likely do those at the same time. Can I put the chickens on the list for a possible future exchange deal?"

"Sure," I told him. "We could use some ducks, geese or turkeys if there's any going, not to mention sugar beet seed."

Our old friend Graham was the pilot who arrived as scheduled. He stopped for just five minutes for a cup of tea while Alec, Jamie and Donald loaded the pigs into the copter, which was one of the troop carrying variety. Graham mentioned there were dry goods on board also being delivered in a trade. He expected to be back with our horses in the late afternoon. He was as good as his word. The sound of the helicopter came through open windows at ten to five. The whole group rushed out to meet it and a cheer went up as Graham led the two ponies down the exit ramp. The mare was a chestnut and the stallion black with a white blaze on the forehead. Kirsty and Alec were standing beside me at the time and the former was more excited than I'd ever seen her.

"Will we be able to ride them?" she asked Alec.

"I don't see why not," he replied with a smile as Jamie led them away. "We'll need to see if we can find some saddles somewhere."

An unlikely friendship had sprung up between the two of them. Kirsty had been overwhelmed by the praise Alec had heaped on her over her stewardship of the chickens and had held him in high esteem ever since. For his part he treated her like a favourite daughter. In fact there were times when he treated her better than his own daughter, who often received the sharp edge of his tongue if she didn't do something the way he wanted it done.

CHAPTER EIGHTEEN

R obbie was still infiltrating the camp at Stirling once or twice a week to contact his friend Tam. How they managed to meet so often without being detected I never knew. When I asked him he simply laid a forefinger to the side of his nose and said they had ways and means. Often I waited up for him on these nights, much to Lindsay's displeasure. Usually he had nothing special to report, but one Thursday evening at the beginning of May he finally had some information.

"Wistance has been talking to Tam about a possible attack on us towards the end of June," he began. "I gather the rank and file are beginning to get restless about the monotony of the food they're getting. Tam and I have made tentative plans. They'll need amendment nearer the time but for the moment this is the timetable. Tam's suggested to Wistance that sometime in the next four weeks he'll take a couple of the tearaways and spy out the land here. Then he'll advise Wistance that a straightforward night attack will take us by surprise and suggest a date. He'll be able to give us a couple of days' notice so that we can make our preparations."

"Why does he need to bring anyone with him on the spying mission," I asked. "Surely he can just come up on his own and meet you and I."

Robbie shook his head. "For all he's not a good soldier Wistance isn't a fool. Tam coming by himself could well look suspicious. Don't worry. He'll make sure he and his companions will keep well out of our sight. He's a first class fieldsman."

"Does Wistance know exactly where we are yet?"

"No," Robbie replied. "Up to now he's ordered all his people not to cross the barricade on the A9. He wants any confrontation to be on his own terms and in his own time. To make it look natural Tam will lead his companions up a couple of blind alleys before they 'accidentally' stumble on the hotel. And now I'm tired and I'm off to bed. I must be getting older. Once upon a time I could go without sleep for two days no bother." I had to be content with that though I wasn't entirely happy. I trusted Robbie to the hilt but his friend Tam was an unknown quantity to me. If he was playing a double game I could see disaster looming.

Harry Jennings arranged another swap deal for us a few days later. In exchange for four hens and two cockerels we received three ducks and three geese. Alec was cock-a-hoop. "All we need now is a couple of turkeys and we've got the nucleus of a proper poultry farm." Our remaining chickens produced their first eggs in that same week, another cause for celebration. Even Esme seemed to have cheered up.

A spell of hot weather in the middle of the month following two days of heavy rain provided the stimulus for rapid growth. I almost had the feeling that if I stood still long enough I would be able to see the corn growing. In truth there was much to be thankful for. Our livestock looked healthy, nearby fields were prolific with spring flowers and our fruit trees in front of the hotel were in bloom. The supply of rabbits for food showed no signs of diminishing. Even the bees seemed to welcome the sunshine and thanks to the efforts of the anglers the occasional trout could be seen in the river. Gary estimated that the trips made with Donald and Duncan had brought in well over a hundred additional fish. There was a darker side to the stimulus we got from these benefits though.

James Tulloch had revelled in his job as storekeeper, despite his lack of mobility. Once it was possible to move around the cellars and storerooms he'd made a complete inventory of all our supplies. As soon as this was finished he made out stock sheets and deducted every item issued. Thus he could tell me at any time just how much remained of a particular item. Towards the end of May I spent an evening with him going over his records. They painted a gloomy picture.

My original calculations had been made on the assumption that we would be feeding less than twenty people. Now we had more than twice that number. Despite the constant supply of rabbits our cold store was down to a side of beef, a whole pig and ten frozen turkeys. The sell by date of the turkeys was the coming December, so I'd earmarked them for the anniversary of the disaster and Christmas. There was enough tea and coffee to last for possibly another six months. Thanks to the use of sandwiches for the evening meals tinned meat and fish were almost exhausted. At the current rate of consumption they'd be gone in less than two months. All the butter and margarine had been used up, though Alec had promised a small supply of fresh butter within the month. At least we still had plenty of dried yeast to ensure bread supplies and hopefully this could be supplemented by Alec's wife and her wine making. On the credit side we'd hardly touched the stock of rice and pasta and by careful use of sugar and salt we could make what we had last for at least another eighteen months. It was time to bring in a stricter diet for everybody.

The following evening I had a long talk with Margaret and Gran Geddes. Rowena, being near to giving birth, had been excused from all duties. Gran had proved a welcome addition to our ranks. In conjunction with Margaret she'd revolutionised the way the kitchens were organised. Previously bread had been made in the morning to be ready for the evening. Since Gran's arrival either she or Margaret made the dough between ten in the evening and midnight and left it to prove. The other rose at four a.m. and started the baking. It was a big job. We were getting through a dozen large loaves a day. We talked around the matter for an hour or more and eventually agreed on the new menu.

Breakfast would consist of porridge as before. We had plenty of oatmeal and there'd be more available come the harvest. Bread left over from the previous day could be used up at this meal either plain or toasted. There would be only one hot meal a day and that would be at lunch time. On weekdays it would consist of the inevitable rabbit stew with potatoes and vegetables. As a welcome change and while stocks of rice and pasta lasted Sunday's lunch would be either paella or some kind of pasta that included tinned fish and meat while we still had some. The evening meal would henceforth be soup of some kind or another with dry bread; there would be no more sandwiches.

There were plenty of moans when I made the announcement at lunchtime the next day, but as I emphasised, there was little else we could do. In an effort to soften the blow I pointed out that come summer and autumn there would be fresh fruit from our own grounds and from the trees and bushes that we'd marked down the previous year, plus a continuing supply of salad items from Brian's conservatory. Then I caused depression again with my closing remarks.

"I don't want to add to the doom and gloom," I said with a suitably stern face, "but things will get worse before they get better. When the tea and coffee is gone there'll only be milk and water to drink. The rice and pasta won't last forever, nor will our remaining supplies of other foodstuffs. By this time next year we will have to exist on what we produce ourselves and that means little variety in our diet. Alec tells me it will be at least five years before we can kill off any of our livestock, though on rare occasions he'll cull any surplus male pigs, sheep or chickens. Rabbit is going to be our only meat for a long time to come, and when that's not available lunch will be vegetables only. Worse still, if we can't find a source of salt we're very soon going to have our food unsalted."

Someone, I think it was Ross, asked if it would be worthwhile raiding the supermarkets and shops again. This was something I'd already discussed with Robbie and Danny and we'd decided in the end that there was little to be gained. In our initial week of scavenging and on subsequent visits in protective gear we'd just about cleaned out all sources within a twenty mile radius. What was left was hardly worth the effort of collecting and in any case the towns and cities had become dangerous places to go. Rats proliferated everywhere. What few dogs and cats there were had gone completely wild and would attack anything living. They fed on the rats and mice and on any foxes that ventured into built up areas and wouldn't have hesitated to attack humans.

Dr. Ling asked about the fish that we'd brought to the river. I pointed out that there were less than two hundred of them so far and that to provide just one meal we'd need nearly four dozen. "As with the animals," I concluded, "it will be four or five years before we get any sort of return for our efforts."

Needless to say I got an earful from Lindsay as we prepared for bed that night. "You're never going to win any prizes for diplomacy," she told me in scathing tones. "Do you realise that in one evening you've caused more depression than we've seen since the disaster."

"What else could I do?" I protested. "The outlook is bad, and there's no point in trying to pretend otherwise."

"You didn't have to hit us with every bit of bad news at once," she retorted.

"Better get it over with than try and spin it out," was my answer to that. "There's more bad news to come. Robbie's certain that the crowd at Stirling will attack us before the summer is out. That's almost certainly going to mean casualties."

Lindsay had to have the last word. "Thanks for telling me," she said with heavy sarcasm. "That's bound to make me sleep soundly."

A surprise was in store three mornings later. Around ten o'clock I was busy cleaning toilets on the second floor of the northern annex when Kirsty appeared. "There's someone to see you at the front door," she informed me.

"Who is it?"

She shrugged her shoulders. "Dunno. He's a stranger to me. All I know is that he speaks kind of funny. I think he's foreign."

I followed her downstairs and to the main entrance. A ragged figure was standing and looking ill at ease. He was of medium height, fair and unshaven and wearing a threadbare jacket and jeans. I reckoned he was anything between seventeen and twenty-five.

As we shook hands he bowed and clicked his heels German fashion. "You are Dean, yes? My name is Jan Lekovic," he announced with a distinct accent. "My parents came from Slovakia but I was born and raised in Poland. I came to Scotland two years ago to find work. Since the bad day I have been living rough and I think that I am the only person alive. Today I walk far to look for food and I see people working in fields. They are the first people I have seen. I speak to them and they tell me to come to find you. I would like to stay here. I have worked often on farms, I am strong and I will take my share of the hard work."

"You're very welcome to stay, Jan," I told him. "But how did you manage to survive the gas cloud?"

"This I do not know," he replied. "I received big pay that day for work I had done and I went to the pub in the evening. I must have got very drunk, because I remember nothing until I wake up next morning in a field. I go back to the pub, but everyone is dead. I have been drunk many times since that day but now I am among people again I will drink no more. It is bad for me to drink," he concluded solemnly.

I told Kirsty to fix Jan up with a room, then to get him some clean clothes and take him to the medics for a check-up. The thought did cross my mind that he might be a spy from Stirling come to reconnoitre but I thought it unlikely. According to Robbie Wistance still did not know exactly where we were located and I soon discovered that Jan had entered our 'territory' from the north and not the south. I did, however, keep a careful watch on him for the following days but every indication was that he was exactly what he said, an extremely lucky survivor who had somehow not managed to come across other people. Apart from his capacity for work which was soon proven his coming solved a problem that had been on my mind for a long time. He and Kirsty took to each other right away and romance soon blossomed. I'd always felt responsibility for Kirsty and had had visions of her becoming the new world's first 'old maid'. I was delighted that she'd finally found a boy friend. It meant we now had a perfectly balanced society with a partner for everyone except Robbie and he seemed more than content with the solitary life. The odds against such equality must have been quite high.

By the beginning of June all the planting had been completed. Most of the outside work consisted of hoeing and weeding and Alec came to see me one morning to discuss future plans.

"You mentioned Gleneagles to me some time ago. We've got some spare capacity now and I was thinking that we could make a start on ploughing up the golf courses there ready for planting next year. Even though we've enough growing now to take us through this winter it wouldn't do any harm to budget for a surplus in years to come. There's no knowing if bad weather will cut down our yield and if we get as much as I hope it'll give us something to trade with. What do you think?"

"It certainly won't do any harm," I replied cautiously. "It seems a sacrilege to do it, but nobody's going to be playing golf for a long time to come and there's no way we can keep the courses as they are. Anyway, I'm more than happy to leave all the farming decisions to you. You're the expert. All I'd suggest is that you relocate one of the caravans to Gleneagles to give you shelter in bad weather. Whatever you do don't go into any of the buildings. They'll be full of disease by now." Work started there the following week.

From the second week in June we began to benefit from Brian's sterling work in the conservatory turned greenhouse. Lettuces and a few early tomatoes appeared unheralded on the table one lunchtime. Though he had come some way out of his shell, since the early days Brian was still quite shy and blushed deeply when he got a round of applause.

CHAPTER NINETEEN

The last Wednesday in June was the hottest day of the year so far. In mid afternoon the thermometer was reading eighty-four degrees. Going in for the evening meal Robbie whispered to me that he intended to make another sortie into Stirling that night. Accordingly, as soon as I'd eaten, I went up to our room and lay down on the bed. Sleep was impossible in the heat but I dozed from time to time. At a quarter to eleven I rose, went into the bathroom and took a cold shower. It did little to refresh me. I slipped on a tee shirt and a pair of shorts. Back in the room I saw Lindsay lying naked on the bed with the sweat pouring off her. There was a look of invitation in her eyes. I bent down and kissed her gently on the lips.

"I'm sorry, love," I said. "I'm not in the mood tonight." She looked disappointed but murmured that she understood. Robbie was in the reception area, dressed all in black as usual and with a blackened face. As always I told him to be careful and that I'd be waiting for him when he returned. Going outside he mounted his bicycle and I watched him disappear down the drive. There wasn't a cloud in the sky and a myriad of stars were shining like diamonds on a cloth of dark blue velvet. I went into the kitchen, made up a flask of coffee against Robbie's return and a cold drink for myself. Then I went back outside and sat down on the bench at the side of the front entrance. The heat was still stifling, eighty-two degrees showing on the thermometer in reception.

After a quarter of an hour I heard footsteps. I looked round. It was Danny, barefoot and wearing nothing but a pair of shorts. "I couldn't sleep," he said quietly. "There's no point in trying so I thought I'd keep you company."

We sat gazing at the sky in companionable silence for ten minutes when we were joined by Duncan. He too confessed to being unable to sleep. "Between the heat and Esme's snoring I was going quietly crazy," he confessed. He and Esme had moved in together a few weeks previously. I asked if Esme always snored.

"Only when it's hot, thank heaven," Duncan replied.

From time to time through the night one or other of us brought up a subject, but the following discussions always petered out after a couple of comments. From time to time we dozed off and occasionally someone would go back into the hotel for a drink of water. I'd waited up for Robbie many times before but the nights had never seemed so long as this one did. It was twenty to four before we saw the light of his bicycle bobbing along the drive. He dismounted wearily, took the cup of coffee from me without a word and lit a cigarette. Only then did he speak.

"The attack will come in the early hours of Sunday morning," he reported grimly. "Wistance wanted to make it Friday morning but Tam talked him out of it. He persuaded Wistance that we'd likely live it up on Saturday night, as they usually do, and that we'd be less alert on Sunday. That's the bad news. The good news is that Tam and I have worked out a plan that will give us success at minimum risk to ourselves. I've a few more details to work out, so I'd rather not talk about it just now. Can you call a meeting of everyone for after lunch today Dean?"

"Sure thing, Robbie," I replied. "Go and get some sleep, if you can in this heat."

We gathered in the bar in serious mood after our midday meal. Robbie had set up an easel with a sketch on it in front of the bar. When everyone had settled down he took centre stage and began to speak.

"You all know by now that the Stirling crowd will attack us early on Sunday morning. Their plan is to set off at one a.m. in two covered lorries. They'll drive to within five miles of here, then dismount and march the rest. They expect to catch us all asleep and totally unprepared. Now we simply can't let them reach here. The plan is to ambush them before they leave their transport. As you can see on this sketch there's a perfect spot for an ambush about eight miles down the road. We'll block off the road and as their lorries slow down we open fire from both sides. The risk of casualties to ourselves will be minimal."

Before he could go any further there was a scuffle in the audience and Sophie Laird stood up. "You can't do that," she cried. "It's cold blooded murder." There was a low murmur of what sounded like agreement.

Robbie opened his mouth to reply but was forestalled by Dr. Myra. "I'm with Sophie. As a doctor my job is to save lives, not to take them wantonly. There must be another way. Why can't you simply stop the lorries, tell the occupants we're prepared for them and turn them back?"

"All that will accomplish is that they'll find a different way of attacking us, one that we can't defend against," Robbie retorted with contempt. "Get this into your heads. This place is indefensible. I could capture it easily with just half a dozen men: Wistance has fifty at his disposal. All he needs to do is station snipers around the place and pick us off one by one as we go out or appear at the windows. Similarly we can't just let them get here even if we're ready for them. That way we might win in the end, but it will cost the lives of many of us in this room. Do you want that? Let me tell you one more thing. The order that Wistance will give to his troops will be to kill all the men and take the women as slaves. How do you fancy being a slave to some young tearaway?"

"I still think there must be another way," Sophie persisted.

"Then please tell me now what it is," countered Robbie. I could see that he was beginning to lose his temper, so I jumped up and stood beside him.

"I don't like it any more than you do," I announced. "But Robbie's right. We have no choice. It's them or us, kill or be killed. Look around you. Do you really want to be burying some of the people here come Sunday afternoon? Yes, there is an alternative. We can take as much as we can and move away and start afresh somewhere else. Are we going to throw away all the hard work we've put in over the last nine months to placate a megalomaniac? I'll answer that question myself. No way, not even if it means Robbie and I have to meet them on our own, just the two of us."

There was an immediate response. Cries of 'you won't have to' and 'I'm with you' echoed all round the room. I held up a hand for silence. "I promise that nobody who opposes Robbie's plan will be forced to take part in it. It will be strictly volunteers only. Now would you please let Robbie continue without interruption." There were no further protests, though the look Sophie gave me would have killed a weaker man.

"Thank you," Robbie said. "Now I'm ninety-eight per cent certain that the attack will come in the way I've described. But Wistance is an unpredictable character and there's just a chance he might change his mind at the last minute. So we'll have to leave a majority of people on guard here. I'll discuss that with those concerned tomorrow. Ten picked men will form the ambush and they'll be picked by me."

That sparked off another interruption. This time it came from Hester. "That's sexual discrimination," she protested in that affected drawl of hers. "Most of the women here as just as good with a rifle as you men." Selma weighed in with a 'hear hear'.

"I won't dispute that." Robbie had regained his calm. "I'll go so far as saying that some of the women are better shots than most of the men.

But if we're going to rebuild this world we need children, lots of them. It's our duty to put the safety of women first and foremost and that's why it has to be men in the front line. We can afford to lose some of the men, tragic though it may be. We cannot afford to lose any women. Now back to business. The ten of us will leave here at eleven o'clock and drive to this point here." He pointed out a spot on the map. "From there it's a quarter of a mile to the ambush point. I'll go into more detail with those involved some time tomorrow. We'll be blocking both carriageways of the road with large trucks placed sideways. Dean, perhaps you'd arrange for two to be painted black before Saturday. At midnight an ambulance with medical staff on board, volunteers if you insist, will leave and drive to this point here a mile behind the battle zone. It will stay there without lights until required or dismissed. Any questions?" I expected more protests but none came.

"Good," Robbie said. "Now I'd like to brief the ambush party. That will be Dean, Danny, Alec, Jamie, Donald, Lewis, Ross, Tony and Jan. It's a dry day, guys, so let's go outside." So saying he took down the sketch, put it under his arm and marched out.

"Before you all go there's one more thing," I announced. "As Robbie has said Wistance is unpredictable. It's not beyond the bounds of possibility that he'll send two or three snipers along to try and pick some of us off before the attack proper. From tomorrow morning nobody leaves the building except for vital tasks. The only ones I can think of are milking and collecting eggs. Those who do this will be accompanied by an armed guard at all times. All other outside work is suspended. Do not show yourselves at windows. From tomorrow night we will mount a guard in selected spots outside: Robbie and I will make the necessary arrangements tomorrow after lunch."

Robbie had waited just outside the door to hear what I was saying. Now he led the way to a spot underneath the largest of the fruit trees. The day was just as warm as the previous one and that particular apple tree was the only one that afforded reasonable shade. I remembered when it had been planted. Danny and Lewis had brought it back from one of the foraging missions. It was about fifteen feet in height with long spreading branches and deep roots. I never did work out how they'd managed to dig it up and carry it to and from the lorry.

Robbie leaned with his back against the tree while the rest of us sat on the ground facing him. "We'll leave here at eleven o'clock as I said," he began. "We'll drive down to the point where the two trucks will be set up as a barricade. No boots, by the way, trainers or other stout shoes with soft soles. It's possible they might have scouts out before they send the main party and sound carries a long way at night. Once at the ambush scene we split into two groups. I'll be in the first group stationed here," he paused to point at the sketch map. "Danny and Lewis will be on one side of the road about twenty yards further down, with Ross and Tony on the opposite side. Dean will take the second group thirty yards more. He'll be on the other side of the road from me. Alec, Jamie, Donald and Jan will be with him, two on one side and two on the other, twenty or so yards from Dean. Once we get to our positions there will be no talking. We'll all be behind a ridge some eight feet high. Keep your heads below it until the action starts. I know we'll all have blackened faces and dark clothing but moonlight can play funny tricks and it's vital the enemy don't know we're there until we start firing."

My attention wandered for a moment or two as I concentrated more on the man than the words he was saying. This was Robbie as I'd never seen him before; decisive, authoritative and precise. At that moment I realised something I should have known all along. This was what he had been trained for and what he'd given most of his life to. He was a professional soldier from the top of his head to the soles of his feet. The problems of everyday life held no interest for him. But war was his metier and we were going to war, small though the scale might be. With an effort I focussed my attention once more on the instructions he was giving.

"Now there are one or two things we don't know and can't guess. We don't know whether the two lorries will be on the same carriageway or not. If they are we don't know how far apart they'll be. If they're not we don't know if they'll be abreast or one behind the other. We don't know if they'll be running with or without lights. If I was running the show I'd use sidelights only but Wistance may think differently. He's brash enough to travel on full headlights. If there are lights we'll have a good five minutes to see them coming. If not we'll have less than two to catch the sound of the vehicles. All this means that we may have to improvise at the last minute. It's a pity mobile phones don't work anymore or that we don't have some kind of walkie-talkie device. Then we could station someone a mile or so away to give us advance warning. But there's one order I'm going to give that's set in stone and must not be broken. Either Dean or I will be the first to fire. Only when you hear a burst from one of us do the rest of you open up."

"If the lorries are one behind the other on the same side I will wait until number one is about twenty yards from me and then fire at the windscreen. That will be the signal for the rest of you to open fire. If they're on opposite sides and abreast Dean will open the firing, also aiming at the windscreen. As soon as you hear that first burst start firing at the sides of the lorries. Rake them from end to end at between three and five feet from the ground. Don't go any higher than five feet or you risk hitting one of us. Use the whole magazine before you stop firing, then quickly replace it and hold fire unless you see someone leaving a lorry. Do not move from your positions until I give you the order. Is all that clear?" We all nodded without speaking. "Once we've accounted for all the enemy I'll fire a green light from a Verey pistol. That will be the signal for the ambulance to come and deal with any casualties. Hopefully there'll be none but if there are we need to get them treated as quickly as possible. Finally each of you will carry three two foot lengths of rope in your pocket. If there are any survivors among the enemy make sure they're disarmed and then tie their hands behind their backs, line them up at the side of the road and watch them until we can take them back to base. Now I'll repeat all this tomorrow and Saturday so think about it meantime and let me know if you're unsure about anything. That's all." The others dispersed quietly. I stayed behind while Robbie rolled up his sketch map.

"Just one question, Robbie. What about your friend Tam? Won't he be in one of the lorries?"

Robbie smiled. "He's an old soldier, Dean, and more experienced than I am. An hour before Wistance is due to set out Tam will be struck down with a severe illness, a heart attack or something like it, which will make it impossible for him to fight. The only risk he's taking is if we fail and they win. The very fact that we set the ambush will tell Wistance there's been a traitor in the camp and dumb as he is it won't take him long to figure out who. So for Tam's sake as well as ours we have to succeed. By the way, why have you confined everyone to barracks for the next few days? Do you think someone will slip away and tell the enemy what we're planning?"

"That was part of my thinking," I admitted. "I'd be surprised if it happened, but there were some strong feelings expressed in there and I don't want to take the slightest chance."

"Good thinking," Robbie approved. "We'll make a soldier of you yet."

I laughed. "No chance. I'm a lover, not a fighter."

The rest of the afternoon was spent painting. We took an Asda truck and a Tesco truck and painted them black on both sides. These trucks would serve a double purpose. If the enemy were travelling without lights they wouldn't see them until the last moment and probably crash into them. If they had lights then they'd start to slow down as soon as they spotted the trucks. Either way it would give us an additional advantage.

The mood was sombre that evening. Unusually there was little or no chatter during the evening meal. After we'd eaten I advised everyone of the roster for guard duty and suggested those on first call get some rest. Though most of those not involved headed for the games rooms afterwards the snooker, pool and table tennis players showed little enthusiasm in their games. I fully expected to have to face further questioning from Myra, Ling or Sophie but not one of the three came near me. I almost suspected that they were avoiding me on purpose. In what little conversation I had with Lindsay before we climbed into bed the subject was carefully avoided. Friday and Saturday brought no lightening of the tension.

On both days Robbie took the front liners, as he'd dubbed us, to the far end of the hotel grounds. After going over the orders again he drilled us in the positions we were to take up and without gunfire of any kind staged rehearsals of the battle. It all seemed unreal to me, more like some kind of game. As part of my firm's management training programme I'd once been on a paintball battle weekend. I'd enjoyed it in a macabre sort of way, but had treated the whole thing as a joke and spent most of the two days laughing. It was hard to convince myself that this time it was deadly serious. We were going into a life and death battle. I or any of the others could be dead or badly wounded by next Monday morning. Waiting was the worst part. I kept counting the hours and minutes, wishing that we could get on with it and get it over. The time seemed to drag.

Saturday's training session was in the morning. Leaving four people on guard the rest of us went to our rooms to sleep. For my part this wasn't easy. It was still hot outside and in and I did little more than doze for a few minutes at a time. Round about five o'clock I did drop off properly and the next thing I knew was Lindsay shaking me awake at seven. I dressed ready for battle; black track suit, black balaclava, and black trainers, while Lindsay watched. When I was ready to go downstairs to eat she put her arms round me and kissed me more tenderly than she'd ever done before.

"You will be careful, won't you and not take any risks," she pleaded. "I couldn't bear it if anything happened to you. I'll be counting the minutes until I see you back safe and sound."

I was deeply touched but made light of things. "We have to get the job done, but self-preservation will be top of my priority list," I reassured her.

I found I had little appetite, but I took a bowl of soup and some slices of bread. Then it was off to the kitchens, where Robbie had earlier burnt some wood to make soot. Solemnly the ten of us blacked our faces. We were prepared.

CHAPTER TWENTY

A t eleven o'clock precisely we climbed aboard the trucks. Robbie drove the lead vehicle and I drove the other with Alec Geddes in the cab beside me. The ambulance, with Paul driving would follow on in the rear and peel off at its appointed place. We drove slowly using only sidelights. Two miles from our destination a flick of Robbie's rear trafficator told me that he was turning off his lights and I followed suit. At a suitable point I took my truck across to the northbound carriageway. We crept towards the spot for the barricade and stopped. The passengers dismounted and Robbie and I turned our vehicles sideways. They comfortably blocked the whole road and the grass verges. Silently we moved to our designated positions on the ridge. As I settled down I sneaked a look at the luminous dial of my watch. It was fifteen minutes to midnight.

The next three hours were the longest of my life. After what seemed like a full sixty minutes had passed I looked at my watch again. It was two minutes past twelve! One or two midges were buzzing around threatening to make life unpleasant. I blessed the fact that all but my face was covered up. It was oppressively hot and the heat was exaggerated by the woollen track suit I was wearing. Sweat was pouring off me. I tried to focus my mind on other things but it was impossible. I kept returning to thoughts of Lindsay and the others back at the hotel, ready and waiting to fight for their lives if we should fail. I kept visualising the scene of the coming battle and trying to foretell how it would work out. At times my hands were trembling so badly I wondered if I'd even be able to hold the rifle when the moment came.

Thoughtfully Robbie had insisted that we each bring a litre bottle of drinking water with us. Long before one o'clock I was assailed by a raging thirst. I drank deeply and twenty minutes later regretted doing so. I had to creep as best I could to the bottom of the ridge and make a toilet.

All the time I pondered whether real soldiers had similar emotions and fears before they went into battle. Most of all I wondered what was going through Robbie's mind at that precise moment. Was he ice cool or were his nerves on edge too? At least his orders were being obeyed. Though my nearest neighbour, Jamie, was less than twenty yards away I never heard the slightest sound from him throughout those long hours nor any from anyone else. A touch of cramp around two o'clock forced me to turn over on my back and for a few minutes I lay there gazing at the sky. At first a myriad of stars speckled the deep blue expanse. Very soon, though, the clouds rolled in from the south. It was so peaceful at that moment that it was hard to think about the carnage that was to come. It wasn't long before the moon and most of the stars were obscured and the night became dark as pitch.

It was twenty minutes to three when we heard the first sounds of engines in the distance. The clouds were breaking up and a little diffused moonlight was filtering through. I shuffled myself into a more comfortable position and aimed my rifle in the general direction of the road. The butterflies in my stomach felt as big as eagles. It seemed ages, though was probably less than a minute before we had our first sight of the enemy. Diffused light crept round a bend in the road a quarter of a mile away. Then the lorries came into view. They were driving fairly slowly on dipped headlights and were both on the left hand carriageway some thirty yards apart. The distance between Robbie's group and mine was near perfect.

The first lorry had just passed me before the driver spotted the obstruction ahead. I saw the brake lights go on out of the corner of my eye. Immediately I heard the burst of fire as Robbie opened up, followed by a steady rain of bullets from the rest of his party. But my attention was now fully focused on the second vehicle. It too had started braking and I could see two indistinct figures in the driving cab as I squeezed the trigger, aiming at the lower part of the windscreen. Immediately my group started firing into the rear of the lorry. Suddenly I heard a massive explosion behind me. Still firing I stole a quick glance over my shoulder and realised that the first lorry had crashed into the hillock at the side of the road and caught fire. Pieces of red hot metal began to rain down over a radius of more than a hundred yards. One dropped just an inch or two from my face and I could feel the heat coming from it. I heard two or three cries above the noise of the fusillade. I shifted my aim slightly. The driver's foot must have been hard on the brake when my bullets caught him, because the lorry had come to a halt at an angle of forty-five degrees to the carriageway. This gave me a chance to pump bullets into the side of the lorry.

The guns behind me had fallen silent after the explosion. As my magazine expired those close to me followed suit within two or three seconds. All that could be heard was the crackle of flames from the blazing lorry. As per instructions I clamped a second magazine into place and waited. Thirty seconds or more went by and then I heard Robbie's voice calling my name. In the light of the fire I saw him walking down the road towards me. I shouted to the rest of my party to stay where they were and went to join him. He looked pale but composed in the eerie firelight.

"A job well done," he remarked quietly as he came level with me. "Nobody survived in the first lorry. Let's check this one and then I'll send for the ambulance. We've one or two minor casualties."

Rifles at the ready we approached the back of the second lorry and lifted the flaps. The sight that met our eyes will haunt me forever. Bodies lay in grotesque positions and there was blood everywhere. I think Robbie asked if anyone was alive, but all I could do was stagger to the side of the road and be violently sick. I wasn't a stranger to death by this time but the scale and nature of the massacre we'd just perpetrated was too much for me. I knew in my heart of hearts that there was nothing else we could have done but that didn't make the aftermath any less horrific. Wiping my mouth as best I could I made my way back to Robbie's side. Just as I was passing the driver's compartment I thought I heard a sound. I looked in, then called to Robbie.

"I think there's someone alive in here," I shouted. He came quickly to my side. The passenger door was locked from the inside but a blow from a rifle butt shattered the window and we were able to open the door. I recognised the form immediately. It was the lady captain I'd encountered at the blockade the first time we'd been prevented from going into Stirling. Robbie turned away and sent a green Verey light into the sky, the signal for the ambulance to set off towards us. At the same time he shouted for someone to shift the two lorries we'd used as a blockade. I suddenly remembered the woman's name: Louise Buckley. She looked in a bad way. Recalling my firing pattern I reckoned she must have been hit by at least half a dozen bullets. Her battledress blouse was soaked in blood, but as I watched her eyes flickered and she gave a faint moan. I didn't dare try to move her. There didn't seem to be any movement in the blood that covered her upper body so I reasoned it had probably stopped flowing.

"Bear up and hang in there," I whispered. "There's help on its way." I don't know whether she heard me or not. Her eyes closed again and all I could hear was the rattle of the breath in her throat. I took her left hand and held it, hoping that it might bring a little comfort.

The ambulance arrived some five minutes later. Robbie briefed the crew quickly and Paul and Lily were soon at my side bearing a stretcher. I let go the hand I was holding as Myra and Ling told me to stand aside. They made a lengthy inspection before telling the stretcher bearers to lift Louise gently on to the stretcher and take her to the ambulance. Ling joined them, Myra staying behind to make a brief report.

"I don't hold out much hope," she stated bluntly. "She's been hit several times and has lost a lot of blood. If there is no damage to any of the vital organs there's a slim chance, but I wouldn't put it at higher than one in ten."

As she turned away I touched her on the shoulder. "I'm group O," I told her. "You can take blood from me if you need a transfusion." Myra nodded and then was gone.

We'd suffered four casualties of whom Danny was the most serious. A piece of burning metal from the explosion had penetrated his right thigh. He was in great pain despite the morphine injection Selma had given him but managed a weak grin as he was carried off on a stretcher.

"Guess I won't be fit for duty for a while, boss," he said to me.

I patted his shoulder. "We'll just have to manage without you then. Main thing is that you get well again. At least you'll get personal nursing care. Now this is an order. You're to do exactly what Selma tells you or you'll have me to answer to."

Our other walking wounded were Jan with a burnt left shoulder, Tony with minor burns to arm and leg and Ross with a gashed forehead. They too went back in the ambulance. Once it had left Robbie and I looked at the wreck. The flames were dying down. There must have been intense heat generated as the bodies within resembled charcoal.

"It's a hell of a way to go, but at least it was quick and merciful," Robbie remarked reflectively. "Incidentally, Wistance was driving. He wasn't wearing a helmet and I saw him clearly for a split second before I opened fire."

"What are we going to do about the bodies?" I asked him.

"Nothing we can do," he said tersely. "It's too big a job to bury them, even if we did make a mass grave. We'll push the second lorry off the carriageway and leave it. I'm sorry if that sounds hard hearted, but remember they were coming to kill us. I've no sympathy to spare for any of them." He raised his voice to speak to all those remaining. "Once we've got that lorry shifted the rest of you take one of our trucks and head back to base. Ask everyone to prepare a couple of dozen rooms, then they can stand down and get some sleep. Dean and I will take the other truck into Stirling and liberate the women left there."

Within five minutes we were on the road south. After one look at me Robbie took the wheel. As I took my place beside him and as he started the engine I automatically laid my rifle across my knees. He gave a tight smile.

"I think you can relax. There shouldn't be any danger now."

"That doesn't mean we should be less careful," I retorted. He shrugged his shoulders and put his foot harder on the accelerator. The barricade on the road had been left open and we met no impediment as we drove into Stirling and up to the castle entrance. Turning the engine off, Robbie picked up his rifle and silently beckoned me to follow him. Instead of going into the castle we moved farther up the hill to a small terraced house. Robbie knocked softly on the door; two taps, a space, then three more taps. Quickly the door was opened and I saw the shadowy form of a woman standing with a pistol in her hand.

"It's all right Molly, it's me," Robbie said in a normal tone. "It's all over."

The woman relaxed and held the door for us to enter. As we crossed the threshold a thickset man appeared at the far end of the lobby. He came quickly forward and clasped hands with Robbie before leading us into a comfortable looking lounge. I was introduced and Tam produced a bottle of whisky. Though not normally a spirit drinker I welcomed the exceptionally large dram that was handed to me.

"Right, you old fox, how did you dodge the column?" Robbie asked after swallowing at least half of the tumbler he'd been given.

Tam grinned and winked. "I had a massive stroke forty-five minutes before zero hour. Molly manufactured some false tears and rushed off to tell Wistance. He came hotfoot to find me lying half conscious on the bed, one arm and leg stiff and mouthing unintelligible words."

"And gave me the fright of my life," Molly added indignantly. "He was so realistic I thought he really had had a stroke. It was only when Wistance went out and Tam winked at me that I stopped panicking."

Tam took up the tale again. "I knew Wistance would come back to check before setting off so I kept up the pose. Sure enough, I heard the lorries pull up outside and he came in again. I mouthed a few more words and managed to screw up my face to look like one side had fallen in. He turned to Molly and told her to keep me warm and promised to come back with a doctor when they'd captured your place. I take it all went well or you wouldn't be here now."

Robbie nodded. "They're all dead except the lady captain and she's so badly wounded she's unlikely to survive the night. We've come to take you to your new home and to pick up the women. Do you know where they are?"

"They'll be locked up somewhere, probably in the dungeons. I know where the key is."

Robbie turned to Molly. "Pack up anything you want to take with you. We'll head off as soon as we've got everybody rounded up."

Tam led the way to the castle. In the vast entrance hall he picked up a bunch of keys from a chair and led the way down. Sure enough the women, all twenty-seven of them, were locked in one dungeon. I judged their ages to be between fifteen and forty. It was a shocking sight. Most were in pitiful condition. There was barely enough room for them to sit down and many were standing. Their clothes were ragged and not very clean. One woman was holding a baby to her breast and four or five more were in the advanced stages of pregnancy. Three had black eyes and several others bore facial bruises. They showed little emotion as we opened the door and confronted them.

I swallowed hastily and spoke. "Don't be afraid. Your troubles are nearly over. Wistance and all the men except Tam here are dead. We're going to take you back to our place for the time being. There you'll be given food and drink, clean clothing and beds to sleep in. Tomorrow or the day after the doctors will give you complete health checks and then we'll discuss matters. We can't undo the past, but we will, I promise you, make sure that you have a much better future. Come with us now to the truck."

One woman in her thirties thrust forward. "What about that bitch of a captain?"

"Severely wounded and not expected to live," I replied shortly.

"Good. I hope she suffers for days before she dies and goes to rot in hell," the woman said viciously.

The women followed us meekly and began to board the truck. Before they were all in Tam spoke quietly to Robbie and I. "Hold on for just a minute. I want to check on Wistance's quarters." We left Molly with the women and followed Tam to a house a short way up the street. The front door was locked by a standard Yale. A short burst from Robbie's rifle blew the lock to pieces and we went in. Tam led us first to the front room.

"This is as far as I was ever allowed to go," he explained. "Wistance used this as an office. I've always wondered why he didn't let anybody further into the house apart from the captain." We soon found the reason. The two back bedrooms were stacked from floor to ceiling with tinned food, clothing and medicines. Tam swore quietly.

"The bastard," he said with venom. "He used to draw all his rations from the main store, even when we were short. Yet he had all this stocked up for the two of them."

I was impatient to get back home. "We'll send someone over to collect this stuff tomorrow. There isn't room in the truck to take it now and in any case those women are in need of food and clothing as quickly as possible." We left the house and went back to the truck.

"You and Molly go in front with Robbie," I said to Tam as we reached the driver's cab. Robbie was lighting a cigarette and that gave me an idea. "Give me the rest of the packet and your lighter," I said. "Some of the women might be glad of a smoke." He felt in his pocket and produced a full packet.

I climbed into the back. The women were squatting quietly on the floor, several with their eyes closed. "It won't be long now," I told them, raising my voice over the noise of the engine firing. "You'll soon be able to have a nice hot shower, a change of clothes and a meal. Meantime do any of you smoke?" Some half a dozen hands went up. I handed Robbie's packet and lighter to the nearest with instructions to pass it round. The truck started off with a bump and I sat down more suddenly than I'd intended. Sitting next to me was a woman in her late twenties. She told me her name was Tricia and that she came originally from Falkirk. I asked her how bad life had been in the castle.

"You can see for yourself," she answered, pointing at a livid bruise on her forehead. "We've been treated like slaves from the moment we arrived. Wistance himself and that bitch of a captain kept their distance but the young ones just did what they liked with us. There was never enough to eat, only water to drink and no clean clothes. What we're wearing now is mostly what we had on when the disaster happened. We were forced to do all the cleaning and washing for the men. Anyone that rebelled got beaten. It's a wonder that we've survived. I hope to God you meant what you said about things being better. I'm pretty tough and can take it, but some of the younger girls are vulnerable and have suffered more than enough."

"You have my solemn word," I assured her. "From now on you'll get the best of treatment and you'll take your place in the new world as partners and not servants."

CHAPTER TWENTY-ONE

It was half past five when we got back to Muirton Grange. I climbed out of the truck and looked across to the entrance. Half a dozen people were gathered at the front and as I watched Lindsay and Kirsty came running towards me. Telling Robbie to help the women out I moved forward. Kirsty almost threw herself into my arms.

"I'm so glad you're safe," she crooned as she hugged me tight. Lindsay was less demonstrative, but she gave me a warm smile. "That goes for me too," she said.

"I'm rather pleased about it myself," I said, making light of the situation. "Now there's work to be done. Take these ladies to the clothing store first and fix them up with new clothes from the skin out. Then take them to their rooms so that they can get a shower, by which time hopefully there'll be a meal ready for them."

"Margaret and Gran are in the kitchen now," Kirsty informed me. "They said to tell you that something will be on the table within the hour."

"Good. Off you go. Lindsay, a moment please."

I waited until Kirsty was out of hearing and then started walking towards the entrance. "As soon as the women are in the shower collect up all their old clothes and take them away and burn them. Also several of the women are smokers. I'd like you, Esme and Kirsty to give up some of your precious cigarettes to them. I'll see you later." She nodded and hurried to catch up with Kirsty. I turned to Robbie.

"Will you get Tam and Molly settled. I'm going to check on the casualties." He gave me a thumbs up. As I reached the reception area I saw Sophie standing with a shocked look on her face. I should probably have kept my mouth shut, but I couldn't resist the jibe. "Do you still think we were wrong to do what we did?" She gave me a searing look and turned away without speaking.

As I entered the medical suite the first person I saw was Myra, just divesting herself of face mask and gown. She looked tired and drawn. "How are they?" I asked.

She went over to a wash basin and started to rinse her hands, speaking over her shoulder. "We've taken seven bullets out of the woman. By a miracle none hit a vital organ. I took blood from half a dozen of our people and we've given her a transfusion. We've done everything we can, but I still don't rate her chances better than one in five."

"Do you want blood from me?" I asked.

She looked at me critically. "Come and see me after you've had some sleep. You're in no state to give blood just now."

"What about Danny?" was my next question.

"Ling and Lily are getting the theatre ready just now," came the reply. "We've given him another shot of morphine to ease the pain and we'll operate under local anaesthetic. He'll be walking around on crutches for a while but there shouldn't be any lasting damage. He's on a stretcher next door if you want to see him."

Danny was looking white and drawn and obviously still in some pain, but he managed a smile from somewhere as I walked in. Selma was beside him, looking anxious and holding his hand. I asked him how he felt.

"I've been better," he admitted. "They're going to get at me with their scalpels any moment now."

I patted his shoulder. "You'll be running around like a two-year-old in no time. I'll see you later today. Look after him well, Selma."

Back on the ground floor the first person I saw was Robbie. He asked me about the wounded and I repeated what Myra had told me. He looked thoughtful.

"What are you going to do about the woman if she does recover?" he asked me.

"To be honest Robbie I haven't a clue. As far as we know she hasn't killed anyone, so we can't accuse her of any crime. Let's just wait and see if she survives. Then I'll talk to her and make a decision on what's to be done. One thing's for sure. We can't let any of the other women get near her or there'll be murder done. Now I suggest you do what I'm about to do—get a bite to eat and go to bed for a few hours.

I headed for the kitchens, where I found Margaret and Gran and a few other helpers hard at work. There was a cauldron of porridge on the go. I helped myself to a large plateful and ate it standing up. Tiredness was washing over me in waves and I was afraid that if I sat down I'd fall asleep on the spot. Having checked that everything was in hand I finished my meal and headed upstairs. It was hot in the room so I simply stripped,

143

lay down on the bed and knew no more. I had a dim memory of Lindsay coming in some time later and putting a sheet over me; the next thing I knew she was shaking me awake.

"What's the time?" I asked her, still only half conscious.

"Half past two," she said with a smile. "How are you feeling?"

"Better than I was, though I could have slept the clock round. Is everything all right?"

She nodded. "The refugees are all sound asleep as are the rest of those who were on the battlefront with you. Most of the others are back at their normal duties. Gran Geddes has kept a bowl of stew for you in case you're hungry. Anything you want me to do?"

"Not for the moment, thanks. Keep an eye open when the refugees wake up and look after them. Check with Ling and Myra to see when it will be convenient for the women to get their medical checks." I suddenly realised that I was feeling hungry. "I'm going to chase up that stew and then I'll need to contact Captain Phillips at Turnberry and bring him up to date. If you can find Lewis ask him to meet me in the radio room in half an hour." Lindsay gave a mock salute and left the room.

I had a quick wash and shave, put on a clean shirt and shorts and went down to the kitchen. Margaret was there on her own and within three minutes a steaming bowl of rabbit stew and half a loaf of bread was placed in front of me. While I ate Margaret told me the refugees, as Lindsay had dubbed them, had all had a full breakfast of porridge and beans on toast.

Lewis was waiting for me in the radio room when I made my way there. "I haven't contacted Turnberry yet," he reported. "I wasn't sure how long you'd be and I didn't want to keep them hanging around. Lindsay said you wanted to talk to Captain Phillips." I nodded.

In less than thirty seconds he was speaking to someone at the other end and passing on my request. "You're in luck," he told me as he handed over the headphones. "The captain is in his office close by and will be with you in a few seconds." Sure enough, in less than a minute I heard the dry voice announcing itself in my ears.

"Dean Barclay, Muirton Grange," I announced briefly and formally. "I'm reporting to inform you that the Stirling problem has been solved once and for all." I went on to give him a summary of our night's work. "It wasn't pleasant," I concluded, "but I don't see what else we could have done." He was quick to agree. I went quickly on to my next topic: the twenty-seven women we'd rescued from the castle dungeons.

"You've mentioned more than once that men outnumber women at Turnberry by three to one. I suggest we bring the whole lot down to you later in the week after they've had medical checks. We'd have difficulty feeding them through the winter anyway. Do you agree and if so can you feed and house them?"

"We'd welcome them," Captain Phillips replied with some enthusiasm. "As you say, we're badly in need of extra women to redress the imbalance. Housing is no problem. Most of our people have moved into the village, so we've at least thirty bedrooms vacant in the hotel itself. Our reserves of tinned food are high and our crops are doing well. Like everyone else we rely on rabbits for our meat, but we get plenty of fish. There are two boats in service and they go out daily except in bad weather."

"It won't interfere with your marriage laws I hope. I remember you telling me when we first talked that you were planning on every woman having three husbands."

He laughed. "We never went ahead with that in the end. By a large majority we voted to keep the one to one relationship but with every woman having to accommodate one or two extra, er, let us call them men friends. A couple of dozen extra women will ease the burden. Some of the women are looking very tired in the mornings!" I wasn't sure if this was meant as a joke or not so I forced myself not to laugh.

I did a swift calculation. "In that case we'll bring them to you on Thursday morning. It'll take a couple of days for the doctors to give them the once over."

"I've a better idea," came the voice in my headphones. "From somewhere or other we've acquired three buses, including a luxury coach. I'll send that up to you now that there's no problem travelling through Stirling. Expect it to arrive around eleven o'clock in the morning." He signed off.

After the evening meal I called the new arrivals together and told them of the arrangement I'd made with Captain Phillips. Many of them looked doubtful and I hastened to reassure them. "The simple truth is that we'll not have enough food this winter to feed you all. There's nothing to worry about. Turnberry is properly run and you'll be well treated. Captain Phillips is an ex Royal Navy man, nothing like Wistance who was a jumped up Pay Corps corporal. You'll have rooms of your own in the former Turnberry Hotel, a good varied diet far better than we can offer you and you'll be nobody's slaves or servants. You'll be expected to take your share of the daily work, of course, but in this new world we've been landed with you'd have to do that wherever you are." Some of my audience looked relieved, though the majority bore an 'I'll believe it when I see it' expression.

Before retiring for the night I checked with the medical staff. Ling and Myra had gone off duty for a well-earned rest, leaving Paul and Lily in charge. Danny had responded well to his operation but was sleeping when I looked in to see him, the faithful Selma at his bedside. She whispered that the operation had gone well and showed me the piece of metal that had been removed from his thigh. It was small and flat, not more than an inch across and an eighth of an inch thick, but the edges were jagged and apparently it had penetrated quite deep. Luckily the wound was clean. If it hadn't been there would have been an ever present risk of gangrene and the possibility of Danny losing his leg.

Paul showed me into the cubicle where Louise Buckley lay, still in a coma. There'd been no change in her condition since the operation, though it hadn't worsened. She was breathing on her own through an oxygen mask and drip feeds of saline and blood were attached to her arms. She looked somehow childlike lying there and it was difficult to imagine that she could incur such hatred as she obviously had among the other women. Before I headed for my own room I got Paul to take blood from me.

If I'd had any thoughts that the next couple of days would see things back to normal they were quickly dashed. Shortly after breakfast Sian unexpectedly went into labour and provided extra work for our already hard-pressed medical section. Despite Danny's indisposition and her own nursing duties Selma had made out rotas for the day and shortly after breakfast I reported to Jamie Geddes. The first of the potato crop was ready for lifting and I spent a back breaking morning alongside the other dozen in the field. In some ways it was a relief: a return to normal after the daunting weekend. Even then administration matters weren't far away. We'd brought lunch with us in the form of the inevitable sandwiches and barely had I sat down to mine when Jan Lekovic came and joined me. He looked serious.

"Dean, there is something I have to come and ask you," he opened. "Kirsty wants me to move in with her and I am wanting to do that too. But she tells me she is only fifteen and I think that the law is that she must be sixteen, yes?"

"I don't think you need worry too much about that, Jan," I assured him. "The old laws don't apply anymore. We make our own now. I think it would be good for you both to be together but there is one thing I want you to remember."

"What is that?" he asked, looking relieved and happy.

"I'm very fond of Kirsty," I replied. "She's had a very hard childhood and I've vowed that she should have happier times in the future. I think you can give her those, but I'm warning you here and now that if you hurt her in any way I will personally break every bone in your body."

"I would never hurt her. I love her," Jan protested indignantly. "I will look after her and treat her with, how you say, the velvet hand. That is a promise most solemn." He went away smiling happily.

Danny was awake and cheerful when I went to visit him before the evening meal. He insisted on hearing all about the aftermath of the battle, saying that Selma had told him little or nothing. I gave him quick rundown including the arrangement with Turnberry. "I'm going back to our own room tomorrow. Ling says I'll be able to walk there with crutches, so I can get back to making out the duty roster. They say it'll be a month at least before I'm fit for normal duties though."

"Count yourself lucky," I told him, feeling the ache in my muscles. "Lifting tatties isn't a bundle of fun I can assure you."

Our conversation was interrupted by a thin cry from the room next door. "Looks like the population has just increased by one," I said to Danny. Moments later Paul emerged with shining eyes. "It's a girl," he announced. "She's a month premature, but healthy at six pounds two ounces.

I put in a couple of hours in the fields on Thursday morning before going back to the hotel to meet the bus from Turnberry. It arrived at five minutes past eleven and I was surprised to see Captain Phillips himself emerge. We shook hands.

"Thought I'd come along myself," he stated. "I haven't had a day out for ages and I wanted to see at first hand how you were getting on. Incidentally, I've brought you a couple of sacks of salt. I reckoned you might be running short." I thanked him warmly and asked if he could spare them.

"Oh, salt's no problem for us," he responded airily. "Don't forget we're by the sea. I've got three people working full time on making salt from seawater. Some of my old crew are pretty bright when it comes to mechanical matters. They've rigged up an extraction plant to make the salt by evaporation. It looks like something a madman put together but it works. We can produce ten kilograms of salt a day working full out. Now can I meet our new friends."

Before we went into the bar where the women were assembled I briefed the captain on the state in which we'd found them and the indignities they'd had to suffer at the hands of Wistance's followers. He listened intently. Once inside I introduced him to his audience.

"Good morning, ladies," he began. "My name is Jack Phillips and I'm part of the committee that runs our settlement at Turnberry on the Ayrshire coast. Now I hope to talk to you all individually over the next few days, but I've heard from Dean here of the awful time you had at the hands of Wistance and his thugs. I want to assure you here and now that those days are past and that we will do everything in our power to make up for them. I can't promise that you'll have a life of leisure; I wish I could. But at least I can promise you reasonable comfort, the privacy of your own rooms and that you can live the rest of your lives with dignity and without fear. That's all I want to say just now. Please follow me out to the bus. You'll find sweets, chocolates and cigarettes near to your seats. Help yourselves to whatever you want." He led the way out.

I stood by the front entrance to say goodbye as they filed past. Most of them thanked me as they did so and to my embarrassment two or three insisted on kissing me. I watched and waved as the bus drove off, then went back to the fields.

After that life returned to something approaching normality. There were the usual moans about the monotony of our diet. Rabbits were still plentiful and formed the meat content. Like everyone else I wouldn't have wept if I never saw another bowl of rabbit stew. But as July came to an end the increasing supply of fresh vegetables made meals a bit more bearable. Brian's conservatory was producing large quantities of tomatoes and lettuce, these mainly used for the filling of the sandwiches that were back on the menu. But supplies of yeast were rapidly running out and by mid August we were condemned to unleavened bread for most of the time. This was unpalatable to say the least but very filling. Mrs. Geddes had commandeered some of the early fresh fruit for wine making and once in a while had yeast to spare, but from then on we were lucky if we had fresh bread once a fortnight. Sophie and Hester still avoided me whenever possible and ignored me if ever our paths crossed.

By popular vote we decided to make Tuesday the third of August a holiday, with only essential tasks being carried out. I wasn't altogether sold on the idea of celebrating, if that's the right word, the disaster that had changed the world forever, but I gave in to the majority. As Esme put it to me, we had much to be thankful for. We had food and shelter, comradeship and health. I could have pointed out all the things and the loved ones that we had lost, but for once I held my tongue. The day being fine and warm we opted for a barbeque lunch. Alec had slaughtered two of the male pigs, the first of our livestock to be killed for food. Led by Ross and Jamie half a dozen of the men built a spit while others gathered wood for the fire. To give the kitchen crew a break we didn't bother with cooked vegetables. Brian provided bowls of tomatoes and lettuce and there was cold pasta prepared by Margaret the night before. It was a double celebration for Danny, who that morning abandoned his crutches and walked, or rather limped, for the first time since his injury. I wished we could have filmed that meal. Jamie Geddes appointed himself head chef and expertly handed out large thick slices of meat. It was like some feast from the dark ages as we all sat around eating chunks of pork out of our hands. Much to my dismay everyone insisted that I made a speech at the end of the meal. I didn't think it was appropriate and said so but they were all relentless. I got to my feet reluctantly.

"This won't be a long speech," I began. A voice from the back, which I suspected belonged to Lindsay, interrupted. "Thank heaven for that." I waited for the laughter to subside. "In many ways this should be a sad day, but I prefer to think of our blessings. We are alive, healthy and have enough food and creature comforts to make life bearable if boring. This has been brought about by the hard work and dedication by every single one of you here. I just want to thank you for the support you've all given me and beg that it will continue. I won't deny there are hard times ahead, but if we continue to work as a team then we'll get through them too. I can't promise a return to pre disaster days, but we can make a bearable future for ourselves and our children." I sat down to applause, which embarrassed me even more. After that most people lay and gossiped or slept in the unbroken sunshine. In the end I had to agree that the break had been good for us all. We went back to work on the Wednesday morning with renewed energy.

CHAPTER TWENTY-TWO

All this time Louise Buckley had remained in a coma. Ling or Myra gave me daily bulletins on her condition, but they both emphasised that with every passing day her chances of survival were marginally increased. Three days after the anniversary Myra met me coming in from the fields at five thirty to report that Louise had regained consciousness.

"If you want to talk to her you can have ten minutes, no more," I was told. "She's still very weak. She's had some soup to eat and I'm taking her off the drip tomorrow morning if she has a peaceful night. All being well she'll be on solid food in a couple of days or so. The danger's not completely passed, but her chances are now very good. She must have the constitution of an ox to come through what she's done."

When I went into the sickroom I found Louise propped up in the bed with just a sheet covering her. She still looked deathly pale and her blue eyes were sunk far back in her face. She managed a weak smile, which vanished as quickly as it appeared. In its place came a wary look.

I tried to sound light hearted. "I know it's a silly question, but how do you feel?"

"I've been better," she admitted in a surprisingly strong voice. "I've seen you before somewhere, haven't I?"

"At the barrier on the A9 last year," I replied. "The sentry called you out and we spoke briefly."

Recognition dawned. "I remember now, though I've forgotten your name." I enlightened her and asked if she'd any questions.

She hesitated for a moment. "I suppose the main one is: why did you bother to help me? You'd no reason to. You could have left me to die. If the positions had been reversed that's what I would have done. The next question is: what are you going to do with me?"

"The answer to your first query is simple," I said gently. "We didn't seek a fight with you or with anyone else. When there are so few survivors it seemed wrong to us to reduce the population further. But you forced us into defending ourselves. However, we are still humane enough to give you every chance of recovery. As to what we're going to do with you, we'll leave that question until you're fully fit and then discuss it. We won't hurt you, that I can promise. Now the doctor says no more than ten minutes, then you must rest. Is there anything I can get you?"

"You don't have a cigarette on you by any chance?" she asked hopefully.

"Sorry, I'm afraid I don't smoke. In any case I'm not sure you should either in your condition. Tell you what I'll do. I'll ask the doctor what she thinks. If she says it's O.K. I'll get some for you."

I expected Myra to veto the idea out of hand, but to my surprise she gave the matter some thought. "Her lungs are undamaged, so three or four a day won't harm her. Her main problem as she gets better is psychological. If she's used to smoking it might actually do her good." She must have seen my reaction to her words, for she laughed. "I know as a doctor I shouldn't say things like that, but I'm a human being too. But don't give them to her. Leave them with me and I'll ration them as I think appropriate." I went and sneaked a packet from Lindsay's supply and a spare lighter and handed them over as instructed.

The following Monday, after the evening meal, Alec Geddes came across to speak to me. "Have you got an hour or so to spare?" he asked me. "If so Jamie and I would like to have a chat about some ideas we've been mulling over."

"By all means," I replied. "Do you mind if I bring Danny along. I'm always wanting to give him more responsibility. I had it in mind that he'd take over from me one day, though now you've arrived the honour will likely devolve on you."

"Forget it," he said gruffly. "I'm a farmer, nothing more. I agree with you about Danny. He's a good lad and will make a good leader in time. Bring him along by all means."

Thus began a series of meetings which we came to call either our five year plan or our blueprint for the future. Alec kicked things off at that first meeting. "I think I can safely say that as far as basic food supply is concerned we're heading for a reasonable surplus this year. That's allowing for a thirty per cent loss due to slugs, rabbits or other natural causes. With the Gleneagles golf courses coming into production next spring we'll be in an even better position. What Jamie and I have been discussing is a move towards more ambitious produce. It occurs to us that there must be hundreds of greenhouses scattered around within a thirty mile radius. How about putting a team to work tracking them down, dismantling them and bringing them back here for us to use? The field across the river is an ideal location. I actually thought about that as soon as we arrived, which is why I haven't tried to cultivate that area. I've spoken briefly to Tony and he tells me that we have a surplus of power most of the time and that it would be an easy matter to run a cable across the river and heat a few greenhouses the year round. That means we can look at growing semi-tropical fruit. Bananas and pineapples may be out of the question, but there's no reason why we shouldn't grow oranges, lemons, grapes, peaches, melons and figs. It would add a touch of luxury to the diet."

I didn't need any time to consider. "I like it," I said warmly. "Two problems, though. Where are we going to get the seed to start these extra crops and can we spare anyone to find and move the greenhouses? It's not a one man job."

Alec was ahead of me. "Young Brian has two or three orange and lemon trees and some melons growing in the conservatory. For the rest, in the few days after the disaster I collected seed from all manner of fruit and vegetables as insurance against a future shortage. As to manpower I can get along with fewer people for the next few months. Danny and I can liaise on that and on another couple of projects I've got in mind."

"In that case," I agreed, "we can make a start this week. I'd suggest Tony, Robbie, Duncan and Ross for the job. They're the leading handymen, unless they're needed for your other suggestions."

"Duncan might be useful on the second idea I've had," Alec responded. "I'd like to see the anglers among us go full time and stock the river with as many fish as we can."

"Isn't that a waste of time," Danny broke in. "We've put well over a hundred trout in already but there's not been a sign of them ever since."

"All the more reason for putting more in," Jamie spoke for the first time. "Sooner or later they'll spread across the whole length of the river. But Dad's even more ambitious than that."

"So far we've concentrated on trout," his father continued. "But there's plenty of perch around and they're edible too. Also there's no reason why we can't transfer some salmon from the Tay. With no fishing in the last year or more the river should be teeming with them."

"Wait a minute," I protested. "I love the idea, but something occurs to me. I know little or nothing about fishing, but don't salmon have to go back to where they were spawned at some point in their lives? There'd be no point in bringing them here if they're simply going to swim away again."

"Donald's got a plan to cover that," Alec pointed out patiently. "The river isn't too wide and he proposes putting down a couple of barriers about four to five miles apart. He's had a look at possible places and reckons he can do the job himself with a little help. The barriers would be metal grilles so as not to impede the flow of the water. If we bring salmon in over the next few months they'll lay their spawn here in the spring and the offspring will always return to spawn. We can lift the barrier at any time thereafter. The added benefit is that it will keep the trout we add in this part of the river."

"In that case let's do it." I had an immediate vision of a juicy salmon fillet sizzling in the pan. "More changes to your duty rosters, Danny."

"One more idea for tonight, then," Alec smiled. "I think we can solve the yeast problem."

"You'll earn everybody's undying gratitude if you do," I spoke with feeling. "Unleavened bread is even less popular with the masses than vegetable stew. Expound."

"It was something you mentioned months ago that gave me the idea. Why don't we set up our own brewery? There were four or five small private brewing companies in the vicinity before the disaster. We can bring back the equipment from one of them and set it up here. We've no hops, but there's plenty of barley. We can make our own malt, mash and ferment it. The result may not be top quality ale but it should be just about drinkable. Jamie knows more about that than I do. He had a spell a few years back brewing his own."

"Don't you need sugar to start the fermentation?" Danny asked.

"There's sugar in the malt," Jamie explained. "Boiling the malt in water releases that sugar. Incidentally, I've checked with James. There's just enough dried yeast left over to kick start the first two brews if we need to. From there on we'll have enough and plenty to spare for baking. The yeast multiplies as it ferments."

The more I thought about this last suggestion the more I liked it. Though all our people had been sparing in their alcohol consumption the stocks that we'd had in the bar were all but exhausted. A regular supply of home brew would be a comfort to many. I suppose we could have organised a foraging expedition to collect up any bottled beer and spirits still left intact but I was reluctant to waste petrol for what I considered a frivolous purpose.

Before we broke up that evening I made one final plea to Alec. "We've covered a lot of ground this evening, but two basic problems remain, sugar and salt. If you can find a way of providing those you'll be a hero for evermore."

"Salt is beyond me, I'm afraid," Alec grinned. "But I'm going to do another tour of the northern half of Fife. There must be sugar beet seeds somewhere." The four of us had further meetings over the next three days and our plans went into operation the following week.

I got into the habit of visiting Louise once a day. Gradually some colour returned to her face and each day she seemed a little stronger. Robbie too spent a lot of his free time with her. When I thought she could stand a serious talk I asked her why she had thrown in her lot with such an obvious megalomaniac as Wistance.

"I didn't have much choice, did I?" she responded with some heat. "He picked me as his partner as soon as I arrived. It was that or be dumped in with the rest of the women and you saw how they were treated." She sighed. "I suppose, too, I was dazzled by him at first. He had such grand plans. His army, as he called them, were going to conquer the whole of Scotland in time and he would proclaim himself king. I would be his queen. He kept boasting about his master plan and about all he'd learned fighting in Afghanistan."

"He was a corporal in the Pay Corps," I interjected. "The nearest he got to Afghanistan was Salisbury Plain."

"I suspected something like that," she admitted. "But I was living on the fat of the land and I wasn't going to burst the bubble. To change the subject, Myra says I can leave this room and go for a walk. Just a short distance at first, then I can build up to going outside. Will it be all right for me to meet others?"

"Yes, of course. Nearly everyone here is ready to forgive and forget; in fact most of our people here feel sorry for you. One or two might give you the cold shoulder but no more than that. The only ones left from Stirling are Tam and Molly and I've spoken to them. They don't bear any grudges either."

It was a week before Louise was strong enough to venture outside. In the meantime she explored the hotel, nearly always accompanied by Robbie, and joined us for the evening meal. As I'd forecast, she met very little animosity. Predictably the only ones not to welcome her were Hester and Sophie, though some others were cool in their attitude towards her. Esme in particular went out of her way to make her feel part of the community. Before another week had passed Robbie cornered me in the bar one evening.

"Have you made up your mind what we're to do about Louise?" he asked me bluntly.

"My original idea was to send her up to Arbroath," I replied. "Obviously we couldn't let her go to Turnberry. The other women would have lynched her. But she's settled in so well here and has been accepted by most of us so I'm quite happy for her to stay permanently. Forgive the curiosity, but are you keen on her?"

Robbie nodded. "I'm not much of a ladies' man but I think the attraction's mutual. I'll talk to her. I just didn't want to make any advances if you were going to send her away." Louise moved in with him the following day.

The blueprint for the future began to take shape. Jamie took a team down to a small brewery in Dunblane and transferred all the necessary equipment to the stables. All the remaining full fuel tankers had been removed and we shifted the empty ones into the car park. Brewing started almost immediately. The anglers were excused all other duties and spent day after day trawling rivers around the area and as far afield as the river Tay for trout and salmon. In between times Donald foraged Perth for materials and made a start on planning his barriers. Greenhouses of all shapes and sizes started to appear in the field across the river that formed our northern boundary. The best prize was a forty yard long hothouse, lifted from a former tomato growing concern somewhere near Larbert. Alec and Tony together laid on heating and this would house our more exotic crops like oranges, figs and peaches.

CHAPTER TWENTY-THREE

A ugust ended in a heat wave. A survey of the surrounding countryside revealed that the fruit trees we'd mapped the previous year were ready for harvesting. After consulting with Alec Danny organised four teams of two daily to take on this task. I well remember the tenth of September. For the first time ever Lindsay and I were paired together and allocated an area around Bridge of Earn, coincidentally one that I'd visited the year before. We set off in a lorry at half past eight of a glorious morning. The sun shone in a cloudless sky and gave warning of another hot day. The first few gardens that we visited had apple and pear trees, all mature and quite high. Scorning the ladders that I discovered in nearby outhouses Lindsay insisted on climbing every tree. We soon developed a routine. I would stand underneath the tree with an open sack or basket into which she would drop the fruit as she picked it.

After a half hour lunch break we moved on to a large mansion house standing in lonely splendour some three miles from the next nearest habitation. I remembered it well from twelve months before. There was a small orchard at the back with a dozen or so trees, apples, pears, cherries and plums. The plums in particular had been plentiful the previous year but this time the trees were groaning with the weight of fruit. We worked with a will, filling sack after sack. Shortly after three I called a halt, suggesting a fifteen minute break. We sat on a seat just outside the back door.

Lindsay lit a cigarette, sat back and sighed. "This is the happiest day I've spent for a long, long time. Up in those trees I felt like I was ten years old again. I wish every day could be like this."

"Me too," I agreed. "Though a lot of my pleasure has been because you're here with me. I sometimes think I'm beginning to fall in love with you." As soon as I'd uttered the sentence I could have bitten my tongue out. The word love had never been used by either of us during our relationship. That had been based on companionship and physical needs. I fully expected to get a verbal broadside or a hoot of laughter in response. I was due for a shock.

"I'm not in love with you," she said seriously, "and I wouldn't pretend that I was. Sometimes I think I'm simply incapable of really loving anyone. But I do like you. I like being with you and I like living with you."

"Yet if Claire crooked her finger you'd run back to her in less than a minute." I couldn't hold back the jibe.

Again Lindsay surprised me. "This may come as a shock to you, but no, I wouldn't. All right, if she invited me to a romp between the sheets I wouldn't say no, but being with Claire on a permanent basis was far too stressful. It's so much easier living with you. You're the most tolerant person I've ever met. You don't nag me when I leave my underwear strewn all over the floor, you don't yell at me for opening a window or leaving the toothpaste with the cap off and you don't complain about me smoking in the room. The only way I'll leave now is if you throw me out."

"I'll never do that, "I told her. "So it looks like we're stuck with each other. Now before we get too sentimental we'd better get back to work."

As we stood up and started to go back to the orchard Lindsay put a hand to her head. "I almost forgot to tell you. I'm pregnant."

I gaped at her, then burst out laughing. "Lindsay, you're priceless. The most important piece of news since World War Two and," I mimicked her voice, "you almost forgot to tell me!"

She looked sheepish. "How do you feel about being a mother?" I asked in a more serious tone.

"Kind of half and half. Part of me is excited and part dreading the actual birth. I've never really envisaged myself in childbirth. From all I've heard it's pretty painful."

"Don't worry," I comforted. "There are ways of dealing with the pain. Myra and Ling will look after you. Hey, and no more climbing trees. If I'd known about this sooner I'd have stopped you even if I'd had to tie you up."

We spent another two hours stripping the orchard. Much to my surprise Lindsay stayed meekly on the ground while I used the ladder to pick. We spoke little. I was still assessing my own feelings about becoming a father. Like Lindsay I was split between two emotions. In a way I welcomed the thought, but it would mean even more responsibility than I was carrying already. I wondered if I'd be able to handle it.

Mid September saw the announcement of two more pregnancies, not including Lindsay's. Sophie and Selma were the new candidates for motherhood. We'd laid in a small supply of tinned and dried baby food in that first week after the disaster but it was now obvious that our stock would be exhausted very quickly. Tony, Lewis and I decided to make another trip into Perth to see if we could scavenge some more.

One of the first things I noticed as we entered the city limits was the acceleration of decay. Roads were showing signs of cracking and weeds were appearing on them and on the pavement wherever we went. Gardens and verges were overgrown with grass, plants and weeds shooting up out of control. I didn't spot any evidence of more explosions, but in several places fire had ravaged whole areas. Rats were everywhere. All the ones we saw looked lean and hungry and there was evidence that they were feeding on each other. Three times we came across a full scale battle between what appeared to be organised gangs of the beasts. Thankfully they didn't attack us. I think the noise of the truck's engine gave them pause for thought. We were armed, of course, and if any group ventured too close we fired on them and any that weren't killed fled as fast as they could. Though we were in the city for over two hours we saw no signs of any other animals.

"Have you thought what a problem those rats will be if they move out into the country?" Lewis observed on the way back. "They could put us all at risk."

"It's a worrying thought," I admitted. "Hopefully the dogs will deal with them, though I suspect that those we saw have disposed of any dogs that survived in the city. It's something we'll need to consider, but my hope is that the coming winter and the lack of food will kill most of them off."

By the end of October the bulk of the harvest was in and the workload was eased. Our planning committee gave itself a silent pat on the back. Alec's calculations suggested that we had more than enough food preserved or still in the ground to see us through the coming winter. Milk, eggs, cheese and butter all covered daily requirements. Jamie's brewery had started supplying satisfactory quantities of yeast and we were back to eating proper fresh bread once more. The beer that resulted was thin and a little flavourless but just about drinkable. In a flight of fancy Jamie suggested we should expand, bring in a pot still and start our own distillery! He was voted down, but the gleam in his eye suggested that he wasn't prepared to abandon the idea completely. The best news of all came from Alec. His wanderings in Fife had finally led him to a small quantity of sugar beet seed. That left salt as the only vital commodity that we had no access to.

Alec, Jamie, Danny and I continued to meet at least once a week and exchange ideas. At one such discussion Alec came up with a new suggestion.

"It's obvious the number of people here is going to go up over the next ten years as more babies are born. Sooner or later we're going to run out of space. Now that we'll be starting to farm Gleneagles it might be an idea to clean up the hotel and make it fit for living in again. I don't say we do it all at once, but as spare capacity comes up we can use it to do a wee bit at a time. I've spoken to Dr. Ling about disposing of the bodies and fumigating the place and there are no major problems there, just an unpleasant day or two. I've also had a word with Tony. Given time he thinks he can lay on power and provide some sort of water supply." The idea was approved with the proviso that it be given a low priority.

All was not sweetness and light on the domestic front, however. It was Selma who warned me that my popularity wasn't universal. For some weeks there had been a whispering campaign trying to persuade people to push for a properly elected committee. I had a pretty fair idea of where it had started. Hester hadn't spoken more than a dozen words to me since the night I'd rejected her advances and Sophie had been at pains to avoid me since the night of the battle. I talked matters over with Alec and Danny. They told me I had their full support and armed with that knowledge I decided to meet the challenge head on. Accordingly I called a meeting of the whole community one evening.

I'd decided on my line of approach, so when everyone was seated I got up to speak. "I understand that there's a feeling among you that the time has come to form an elected committee to run affairs here. Personally I'm all in favour. As most of you know I've suggested this myself more than once in the past and been voted down. It looks as though the time has come to put it to the vote once more. Would all those in favour please raise their hands."

Eleven hands went up. Without making it obvious I identified all. Gary and Sophie, Ross and Rowena, Lewis and Hester and Charles Vaughan and his three companions from Killin made ten of them. The only surprise was that Sian was number eleven.

"Eleven in favour," I said. "Make it twelve. I'm voting for. Now can I have a show of hands for the status quo." All our original group except Sian raised hands, plus the entire Geddes family, Jan and Selma. The rest of the medical team abstained.

I made a quick count. "Twenty-three. Regrettably the motion is defeated. But can I say two things. Firstly this is an issue that won't go away. I still think it is the way ahead and if nobody else brings the matter up I will do so myself at regular intervals. My second point is this. All major decisions nowadays are in fact taken by a committee. Admittedly it is unelected but I do nothing without first consulting Alec, Jamie and Danny. Anyone who'd like to join that committee is more than welcome to do so and we'd certainly like to have one or two ladies on it to put the woman's point of view." Sophie and Hester were sitting together in one corner and I deliberately looked straight at them and smiled. They didn't respond, but sat looking ahead with stony faces. "Additionally our meetings are not held in secret. Everyone can come and listen to our discussion and make any contribution they'd like."

"There's one other matter I'd like to mention briefly while we're all together. We're planning on making Gleneagles Hotel habitable again. This is a long term project which could take two or three years to complete but we feel it is necessary. Our numbers will increase as time goes by and sooner or later will outgrow the space available here. We will, of course, continue to work as one community and any move to Gleneagles would be on a voluntary basis."

Our day gathering fruit had brought Lindsay and I even closer together and we had developed a new routine at bedtime. Instead of hitting the sheets immediately we sat and talked for ten minutes while Lindsay had her last cigarette of the day. On that evening it was she who opened the conversation.

"You know, you're cleverer than I thought you were," she said.

I looked at her suspiciously. "I'm not sure whether to take that as a compliment or an insult."

"It's a compliment, you clown," she asserted.

"So what have I done to deserve it?"

"The way you took the wind out of their sails by saying you were in favour of their proposal. That was a smart piece of diplomacy."

"It wasn't diplomacy at all," I retorted. "I've never wanted to be in sole charge as you well know. I really would welcome a properly constituted committee of management."

"Which would spend all its time talking and getting nowhere," she fired back as she ground out her cigarette. "Now come to bed before we freeze to death."

It was during these night time talks that I finally learned something of Lindsay's background. It was an all too familiar story. Her parents were in their forties when she was born, both professional people and unashamed social climbers. They'd wanted a daughter who would enhance their image, accompanying them demurely on their search for culture. Instead they got a tomboy more interested in climbing trees and playing football with the boys. As she got into her teens she scorned the fashionable outfits her mother bought her in favour of tee shirts, jeans and trainers. The final rift came when she was fifteen. At a family gathering, in response to an aunt's question about boy friends, she announced loudly that she was a lesbian. From then on her parents washed their hands of her. Though she hadn't any particular desire to go to university she accepted a place at St. Andrews simply to get away from home, supplementing her student loan with evening work in a fast food outlet. On arrival at the university she'd been allocated Claire as a roommate. Within forty-eight hours they were emotionally involved, though as she'd mentioned previously their relationship was often stormy.

"I think that's why I'm so comfortable with you," she concluded. "You accepted me as I was, warts and all. You've never tried to change me."

"That's because I don't want to change you," I said gently. "I like you exactly the way you are. I suppose I'd like to see you stop smoking; not because I object or disapprove, simply to safeguard your health."

"Maybe I will one of these days." The she gave an impish smile. "Don't hold your breath though. I will make you one promise. I won't smoke around the baby once he's born."

"You think it will be a boy then?" I enquired.

"It had better be," she snorted. "I'm hardly a role model for a daughter, am I?"

"On the contrary," I responded. "You're the perfect role model. In the world of the future girls will need to be strong and resilient, able to work side by side with men in the fields. It will be hundreds of years before there's a place for those who are merely decorative."

A couple of days later I was leaving the radio room when I bumped into Tony coming down from the roof. "Just the man I want to see," he said. "Can we talk?"

"Sure. Go ahead," I replied as we headed for the stairs together.

"I'm worried about the power supply," he confessed. "As you know the solar panels only work in daylight. Remember last winter there were quite a few near blackouts at night? Well this year it'll be worse. We're consuming more electricity than before with the extra people that have arrived, plus there's the big greenhouse to heat. Unless it's a very mild winter we're going to be left without power on most nights. I've been worrying about it for some time, but I think I've come up with a solution, if you want to hear it."

"I certainly do. Fire away."

"There were small wind turbines on the market before the disaster, specially made for domestic use. Singly they didn't deliver a great deal of power, but if we get enough of them they can make the difference and provide the extra electricity that we'll need. I've been watching the weather over the last couple of weeks and there's only been one night when there's been no wind at all. Now there was a firm on the outskirts of Stirling that specialised in these turbines and another one in Dundee. There were ones that can be mounted on a roof and free standing ones on pillars for setting into the ground. I'm not an expert by any means, but I'm confident I have enough know-how to wire them into our main system. If you approve and can give me Danny and Ross full time for a couple of weeks we can bring in the gear and get it all set up. By my calculations twenty on the roof and a dozen on the ground will meet all our needs and to spare."

"Start tomorrow," I told him. "I'll see Danny right away and get him to alter his duty rosters accordingly. You brief Ross." In truth the electricity supply was something I'd not thought about. We'd been so used to having unlimited power at our disposal through that spring and summer none of us apart from Tony had bothered to consider it.

There was still one problem that weighed heavily on my mind, the lack of salt. The gift from Turnberry would, used sparingly, last us up to Christmas and a bit beyond and I supposed that if we sent transport down there Captain Phillips would let us have more. While we'd all got used to unsalted or lightly salted food I was only too aware that the human body needed a certain amount of salt to maintain good health. In fact I wasn't allowed to forget the fact: Ling and Myra reminded me at frequent intervals. I brought the matter up once again at a meeting of our committee early in November.

"After next year will you be able to grow a reasonable surplus of sugar?" Danny asked Alec.

"No problem," came the reply.

Danny turned to me. "There you are then. It's more than likely we'll be the only settlement producing sugar. We can swap our surplus for salt from Turnberry or Arbroath, sack for sack."

"You're forgetting something," I pointed out. "Our fuel won't last for ever. At the rate we've been using it I reckon we'll run out in three to four years' time and that'll be the end of transport."

"And you're forgetting something," Danny retorted. "In three or four years' time we'll have horses. We'll go back to the middle ages and have the horse and cart as our main transport. I'm sure we can find or make suitable carts. It's what, seventy or eighty miles to both places. That's a day's journey. Whoever goes can stay overnight and come back the following day."

Jamie broke in. "That won't be necessary. They'll be as keen to get our sugar as we will to get their salt. They'll meet us halfway. That's forty miles—four hours' travelling time at most."

I turned to Alec. "What do you think?"

"It's a good idea," he said cautiously. "There's just one wee fly in the ointment. I'm duty bound to pass sugar beet seeds on to other communities after our first crop next year. It wouldn't be fair to hold them back just so we can barter for salt."

Danny looked crestfallen, then brightened up. "Maybe we could come to an agreement with one of the other places. They take our sugar and not bother growing any of their own. It's worth a try, anyway," he ended defiantly. I promised him I'd raise the matter with both places when next I spoke to them on the radio. Privately I thought that by donating seeds to either or both they'd be grateful enough to supply us regularly with salt and not look for an exchange deal.

"Talking of transport," Alec said, "didn't you tell me that yon captain from Turnberry mentioned getting the railways up and running again. The main line runs close to here and connects with Arbroath. Trains would be quicker than a horse and cart."

"I've thought quite a lot about that since last March," I told him. "I've come to the conclusion that it's just not practicable. Finding a steam engine is easy enough. They ran on the Bo'ness to Kinneil private railway, so I presume there'll be at least one at the Bo'ness depot. There should also be a stock of coal there. It's after that the problems start to pile up. Someone would need to learn to drive the thing. We'd need to link up carriages by hand. Although the private route has a junction with the main line from Edinburgh to Perth we'd need to adjust the points along the way. As far as I'm aware points and junctions in Scotland were computer controlled so we'd have to change the points manually with hammers, risking damage. Even if we overcame all that and got an engine and a couple of trucks or carriages to Gleneagles we'd need a supply of coal."

"They say there's still plenty of coal left in the old mines around here," Danny observed.

"They're all sealed up, "Alec broke in, "and what coal there is will be deep down."

"Exactly," I said. "It would be far too dangerous to try and dig it out. With so few people left we simply can't afford to risk anyone's life for something that will only have marginal benefits." And that's how we left it.

CHAPTER TWENTY-FOUR

The weather remained mild and mainly dry through November. This gave us the chance to push ahead with the various projects we had in hand. Donald Geddes, Ross and Robbie went off one day in one of the supermarket trucks, returning hours later with half a dozen lengths of wire mesh stainless steel grille and oxy-acetylene cutting equipment. Where they'd unearthed it I never did find out. Donald had chosen the two points in the river for the barriers. Half a dozen of us turned out to help him fix them, though my contribution was confined to holding things when I was told to do so. As I've indicated before, I'm no handyman. We first went upstream for a couple of miles to a point where the river narrowed slightly and where trees grew close to the banks on both sides.

The method of securing the grilles was simple. On the river bed they were held in place by boulders large enough for one man to carry. The top corners were attached by thin, strong wire cable to adjacent trees. I must admit I was doubtful whether they would hold firm, but a concerted effort to shift them by three of us failed to move them an inch. The river was a good ten to twelve feet deep, but Donald made light of it. An experienced scuba diver, he did all the underwater work himself in a wet suit, despite the water being freezing cold. The second barrier went up downstream some five miles distant from the first. The whole task took six of us two full days to complete.

Thereafter Donald, Gary and Duncan spent every day fishing on the Tay and surrounding rivers and lochs. They left the hotel at daybreak with a packed lunch, returning after dark. By the end of November around fifty salmon were reposing in our improvised pen, along with nearly twice that number of trout and more than a couple of dozen perch. With the barriers in place we could see fish swimming about in the river close to the hotel for almost the first time. While all this was going on Tony had recruited Danny and Ross and was busy setting up wind turbines on the roof and in the grounds. He'd managed to locate about thirty of the rooftop models and a dozen pedestal-mounted ones. The latter he placed at the highest points in the half mile surrounding the hotel. By the end of the month he professed himself satisfied.

"The only time we'll run short of power if it's completely windless throughout the hours of darkness and that doesn't happen very often round here," he informed me.

The first real frost of the winter arrived on the last day of November, to be followed two days later by snow. Some six inches blanketed the countryside and all outside work came to a halt. The supply of rabbits promptly dried up and we were back to the basic diet of porridge for breakfast, vegetable stew for lunch and sandwiches, usually cheese or lettuce and tomato, for dinner. To lift the ensuing gloom, Alec slaughtered some of the surplus cockerels from our first batch of chicks on two successive Sundays. Roast chicken had never tasted so good. The snow lay for nearly three weeks before a thaw and milder weather set in.

I spent much of that time on the radio to other communities, including some based in England, Wales and Ireland. The number in Scotland had reduced to thirty-two over the year. Two of the smaller units had given up the struggle and moved in with bigger and better equipped groups. At the end of a fortnight I came to the conclusion that we were still in much better shape than most. Turnberry, Arbroath and ourselves were the only sites with a near constant power supply. The wave power experiments at Thurso were going well, Archie MacKay told me, but it would be another nine months before they could expect to have round the clock supplies. Half a dozen other places had partial systems up and running. In a couple of cases wind turbines had been moved from existing sites and set up close to the groups; in the others nearby wind farms had been connected by means of long cables. The remaining settlements relied on wood fires for heat and cooking. Supplying the wood was generally a full time job for teams of four or five, reducing the manpower available for other tasks. The future for them looked brighter, however, as I discovered when I contacted Turnberry towards the end of my radio marathon.

One interesting item that I learned during my talks with other places was that people in ones and twos were still arriving in the way that Hester and Jan had joined us. In all cases they'd wandered around the countryside, scavenging food and clothing and believing that they were the only ones left alive. In total some seventeen or eighteen had been added to Scotland's estimated population since our meeting at Pitlochry. Two stories in particular deserve mention. A fifty-year-old man, alone on Orkney, crossed to the mainland in a rowing boat. His first landfall had been Scrabster, from whence he'd rowed along the coast until he saw smoke rising from the camp at Thurso. Even more remarkable was the story of a Norwegian married couple in their mid twenties. After months of wandering round their homeland without meeting any other survivors they arrived in Bergen. There they commandeered a luxury yacht, packed it with food, clothing and fuel and set out to sail to America. Their reasoning was that if any country in the world had come through the disaster it was likely to be the U.S.A. In the North Sea they had to run the gauntlet of a severe storm which blew them many miles off course. The yacht developed a minor leak and in desperation they made for the Scottish coast. Beaching the boat just north of Aberdeen they broke into a superstore and took two bicycles, after which they cycled south before arriving at Arbroath.

In an hour long conversation with the redoubtable Captain Phillips I learned that he had a master plan taking shape regarding the power situation. Three of the former submarine engineers had a working knowledge of renewable energy systems and their operation. They would be taken by helicopter to all the disadvantaged communities in turn to install the most suitable type of power system for each group. In some cases this would be by solar panels similar to ours; in others it would involve transporting wind turbines from the nearest available location.

"I estimate it will take us a year at least to get round everybody," he concluded. "By that time we'll be running short of fuel for the copters, so it's imperative we get on to it as quickly as possible."

While in contact with him I mentioned our ongoing shortage of salt. "We can soon sort that," he came back cheerfully. "When the weather improves send somebody down here. We're producing far more than we need, so we can let you have a dozen sacks or more. Better still, come yourself, stay overnight and have a look around. We can exchange thoughts and ideas. There's always something new to learn and outsiders can often spot something that we've overlooked. The roads around here aren't too bad if you drive carefully. Let me know when you're coming and we'll kill the fatted calf for you." He chuckled. "I mean that figuratively and not literally."

I decided there and then that I'd take up his invitation. It was four days short of Christmas before the snow finally disappeared and milder weather set in. I took Alec along with me. He was keen to talk to fellow farmers from another location. We chose a medium sized van in the optimistic hope that we might be given more than the promised salt for the return trip. As I mentioned to Alec Ayrshire was by the sea and there was always the possibility that they'd have a surplus of fish while we were there. I filled up with petrol before leaving and as an added precaution put four one gallon cans of fuel in the back. I also made sure there was a full set of tools and two spare wheels. The prospect of breaking down halfway to and from our destination was one that didn't bear thinking about. As a gesture of thanks Alec had brought along a small quantity of the precious sugar beet seed to give to his opposite number.

I drove slowly. While the roads weren't too bad there were a fair number of potholes and occasional large cracks to be avoided. I felt a great wave of nostalgia as we came up to the Raith interchange at Strathclyde Park, remembering how often I'd circumnavigated that huge roundabout in happier days. Here we had to go carefully to avoid a number of wrecked vehicles. Out of the corner of an eye I noticed that the former Toby Inn at the corner of the park had been gutted by fire. Going through East Kilbride on the way to the orbital road that would lead us on to the M77 we saw plenty of rats and as in Perth several pitched battles between rival gangs of the beasts. We stopped at noon on the far side of Ayr to eat the food we'd brought with us. There were fields close to the layby we'd chosen and they were teeming with rabbits.

"If we ever run short at home we can always come down here," Alec remarked. "We could get a week's supply within just two or three hours."

It was half past one when we drove up to the entrance of the old Turnberry Hotel. Harry Jennings was waiting for us on the doorstep and promptly suggested a cup of coffee before getting down to business. I was surprised to find they still had coffee, given the fact that their community numbered over two hundred, but Harry assured me their stocks were sufficient for at least another year. As soon as we'd finished Alec was whisked away by one of his fellow farmers and Harry took me down for a tour of inspection of the village. This was a real eye opener. For a moment I imagined I'd been transported back in time. Houses looked freshly painted, gardens and verges were neatly tended and the streets clean and free of rubbish. There was even a village shop open.

"We have a rationing system in operation for meat, fish and clothing," Harry explained. "Everything is delivered to the shop either from our stores at the hotel or direct from the farms. The manager of the shop keeps a tally of all that's issued to make sure everybody gets their fair share. Vegetables are plentiful and not rationed. We've three separate farms, one for livestock, one for cereals and one for vegetables. The soil around here is extremely fertile and there don't seem to be many pests, so our crops have been large. Now let's go and see the salt factory. We'll go back to the hotel first and pick up your van, then you can load up and save yourself time in the morning."

The salt factory was another eye-opener. Housed in a long low single storey building close to the shore, it had three chimneys belching smoke as we drove up. Inside it was divided into three compartments. Three quarters of the space housed eight huge boilers. The heat was intense, as it was in the smaller adjoining room. Harry explained the system.

"This is one of the benefits we've had from having engineers around. The four from the two subs designed and built this place on their own. Sea water is pumped into the boilers and heated until all the water has evaporated. You see these trapdoors at the base of each boiler? There are six to each unit. Once all the water has gone we shovel the wet salt out through them and take it to the kilns in the next room. The heat from the boilers is used to blow a stream of warm air through the kilns, thus drying off the salt. Once it's dry we bag it and store it in the third room. We're already producing fifty per cent more than we need and that's with only one eight hour shift on duty. If the demand increases, as I'm sure it will, we'll go over to a two shift rota, possibly even a twenty-four hour, three shift system. If we had unlimited transport we could easily supply the whole of Scotland."

Captain Phillips had been overseeing some work at the far end of the complex and joined us for the evening meal. Yet another surprise awaited us. The original hotel restaurant had been converted to a self service arrangement. When Alec and I went up to the counter we were offered a choice of grilled mackerel, fried herring or baked cod steak. To add to our pleasure there were real chips to go with the fish. As we took our seats at the table with the two captains Alec whispered to me that he was glad he came. Like myself he'd never expected to sit down to a fish supper again!

Over the meal I mentioned the doubts that I often felt about locating where we had and not at the seaside. Jack Phillips sympathised, but insisted we'd done the right thing. "You had to make an instant decision and personally I think you made the right one. I agree that there are many advantages in a coastal location, but just think about it. Say you'd headed for Tayport or somewhere along that coast. Would you have had the quality of accommodation that you have at Muirton Grange? Would you have found somewhere equipped with solar panels to give you electricity? Would you have had enough land available for farming?" Put like that I had to agree with him. He laid a hand on my arm. "If in the future you do decide to move we can easily accommodate you here. There are plenty of houses still empty in the village and plenty of land still capable of being cultivated. But I think it would be a shame to move after all the work you've put in to your present site."

After the meal the two captains excused themselves saying they had work to do and Alec was hauled off for more talks with his opposite numbers. I was happy just to wander around the hotel and meet people. I spent a lot of the evening talking to many of the women we'd rescued from Stirling Castle. The difference in them was there for all to see. The scars and bruises had disappeared; all had put on weight and glowed with health. Seven or eight had babies in their arms or by their side. All were voluble in their thanks at being sent to Turnberry after leaving Stirling. I spoke at length to one sitting alone in a corner and busy knitting baby clothes. She was in her early forties and introduced herself as Maisie.

"Everyone here was so kind to us when we arrived," she reported. "For days I thought I was dreaming and I'd wake up back in yon castle. You know, you came just in time. More than a few of us were thinking about suicide. One girl did take her own life about ten days before you freed us. We found her in the morning, huddled in a corner in a pool of blood with her wrists slashed. She'd picked up a piece of broken glass during the day and hidden it in her clothing. We never could find out what those young savages did with her body. Probably they burned it. I didn't have a sheltered upbringing by any means, but I never realised that there were so many evil people in the world. Tam and Molly did what little they could to help us, but there wasn't a lot they could do. Talking of evil people, what happened to that bitch of a lady captain?"

I had to tell her that Louise had recovered and that we'd let her stay with us. By way of explanation I told Maisie what Louise had said about having no choice. She sighed.

"I suppose in her position I'd have done the same," she said at last. "But she could still have used her influence on our behalf. That's all in the past though and I'm not as bitter as I was six months ago. Don't bring the bitch down here though. There's plenty who'd be only too happy to scratch her eyes out."

We left Turnberry at half past nine next morning after a mouth watering breakfast of porridge, bacon and eggs. Jack Phillips saw us off with a warm invitation to return whenever we wished. Not only that, he gladdened our hearts by handing us a large box of assorted fish packed in ice, enough to feed all our group for one meal. Away from the coast the weather had turned colder again. There was no frost, but frequent bursts of drizzle made driving unpleasant and I was forced to keep the speed down to around the thirty mark. For the first half hour we discussed all that we had seen the previous day. At the start of the M77 at Fenwick Alec took over in the driver's seat. We travelled in silence for some ten minutes thereafter. Then Alec gave a cough and changed the subject.

"I've been giving more thought to our blueprint for the future," he said over the noise of the engine. "I took a long look at the clothing store last week. You stocked up well. I reckon we've enough of nearly everything for the next ten years at least. But sooner or later we're going to have to make our own and the sooner we start to learn the better. The only raw material we'll have is wool, so I suggest we scout around for spinning and weaving machines. The most likely place to find them is in museums, I guess. Gran knows how to use them, so if we can get two or three she can instruct others. Incidentally, I didn't see any knitting needles anywhere. If you haven't got any hidden away it'd be a no' bad idea to get some."

"I thought about that last night when I saw Maisie, the woman from Stirling, clicking away," I responded. "It's a good idea. By the look of things babies are going to be arriving on a regular basis from now on and we haven't all that much in the way of clothes for them. There must be plenty of wool still in the stores in Perth, Stirling or Dundee if the rats haven't eaten it all. I'll get Danny to organise a gang to scout around. They can check the museums at the same time."

We arrived back some time after one, hungry and damp. The drizzle had intensified and by the time we'd transferred the sacks of salt and the box of fish from the van to the kitchens we were both soaked.

CHAPTER TWENTY-FIVE

Christmas came and went. We dined well on the day itself off the last six turkeys remaining in the cold store. Somehow I felt that the last link with the world we once knew had been severed, despite Alec's assurance that by the following Christmas we'd have chicken, pork and possibly even lamb on the menu. The cold store itself was still more than three-quarters full, but now it held frozen vegetables and fruit instead of meat. Our tinned meat was also close to finished, though Margaret and Gran found enough tinned steak and cooking fat to serve us the traditional steak pie on New Year's Day. The weather stayed wet and miserable throughout the period, but at least there were no night frosts and our enhanced power system gave us an uninterrupted supply of electricity. The rain was followed by snow, thankfully just a few light falls.

It was the middle of January before the weather was settled enough to start on Alec's latest plan. Three parties of four were despatched to Perth, Dundee and Stirling to stock up on wool and knitting needles and to trawl museums and other likely places for machines to spin and to weave. I joined Tony, Lewis and Jan on the Dundee trip. Though others had been to the jute city in the past year it was a first visit for me. Sadly it was just as depressing as Perth. Large areas had been gutted by fire or explosions. There were fewer rats to be seen than I expected and I wondered if cold or hunger or both had decimated their numbers. We also saw two or three foxes in the distance but they ran in fright as we drove near to them. Knowing that the Arbroath crowd would have taken everything worth having in Dundee I expected little from our foray but in the end I was pleasantly surprised.

We soon found two wool shops, one on Albert Street and one on Gray Street. Though there were a few mice scurrying around the floor of the first one the stock was largely undamaged and we piled everything we could lay hands on into our truck. The second shop was bigger and contained every conceivable aid for the home needlewoman. Apart from wool, cotton and silk there were materials for crochet and rug making. Included in the latter were fifty or sixty canvases. I was all for ignoring the rug items but Lewis protested loud and long.

"My grandmother used to make her own rugs," he declaimed. "When I was nine or ten I used to help her and I loved it. It's the perfect way to relax. I'm sure it will be popular and it will add some colour to our rooms." I gave way gracefully. From the wool shops we toured the museums but came up with nothing useful. Museums in Dundee seem to have concentrated on maritime affairs and local history.

We were the last party to return to base and when we put all our gains together we had a vast stock of wool, knitting needles and other things. Unfortunately none of us had come across the machines that we wanted and needed.

"There's nothing else for it," Alec said with a sigh. "We'll have to go further afield. One place I know we'll find what we're looking for is the agricultural museum in East Kilbride. The boys and I will head off there tomorrow."

They returned triumphant with half a dozen strange looking contraptions which they declared were either exactly what we needed or could be adapted for our use. Gran Geddes fell on them with great glee and demanded that one of the sheep be sheared next day so that she could demonstrate their use. Alec had a hard job persuading her that it was far too early in the year for shearing.

The pregnancies began to mount up during January. Claire and Rowena, again, were the first to announce their news, followed surprisingly by Hester and Myra. It surprised me at any rate. I'd always thought Hester was too preoccupied with her figure to risk having a baby and somehow I'd never envisioned Myra as a mother. Knowing I could speak frankly to her at any time I broached the subject the next time we were alone.

"From the moment I qualified I was determined to concentrate on my career," she said quite frankly. "Even if I'd married someone it would have been on condition that we didn't have a family. Even in our first few months here I kept to that decision. Then Ling and I talked it over and I realised that I could have both. We've agreed that we'll see how the first baby pans out and then maybe go for one or two more."

"There's no reason to suppose the one coming won't be healthy is there?" I said with some alarm.

"Nothing tangible. But I'm thirty-eight, and the older a woman gets the more risk there is of a child not being one hundred per cent. It's only a slight risk, admittedly, but it's there. If there's anything at all wrong with junior inside me then he or she will be an only child. Ling and I are both agreed on that."

Ploughing and seeding started during a fine dry spell in the third week in February. I think we were all glad to get out in the open again after what had seemed a long winter. On the second day of operations I was paired with Claire. This was only the second time we'd worked together. The first occasion was shortly after her breakup with Lindsay, when she'd been uncommunicative and replied to comments of mine in monosyllables. This time round she was bright and talkative. We discussed a number of things before she brought the subject round to her former lover.

"I take my hat off to you," she said with a smile. "I just don't know how you can live with Lindsay. She used to drive me up the wall."

"I don't have any problems," I replied lightly. "It's a matter of tolerance, I suppose. We recognise each other's faults and we simply accept them and get on with the job of living. Yes, we disagree on many things and argue quite a lot but we never get heated. I think she's happy with me and I know I'm happy with her. If you ever try and take her back you'll have a fight on your hands, I warn you."

"No chance." Claire sounded emphatic. "Brian may have his faults but I can correct those. He's really quite a sweet person when you get to know him."

"I do know one thing," I said. "You've been the making of him. He needed someone strong for a partner and you've done wonders with him. He's so much more confident and practical than he used to be."

"I'm sure I've helped, but the greenhouse has to take a lot of the credit. When you put him in charge of that it was a tremendous boost to his ego. It was the first time in his life he'd ever been given any responsibility and he was determined not to let you down. Thankfully he has a gift for growing things, so he's been able to make a success of it. That's made him even more confident."

From the beginning of the year I'd made a point of spending at least an hour every evening on the radio talking to other communities. I'd developed a number of long distance friends in that way and we were all keen to keep in touch. For my part I found it interesting and informative to find out how other groups were coping and it was useful to all of us to exchange views and ideas. One call that I made faithfully every week was to Archie MacKay at Thurso. He was always the most cheerful of my contacts, even though things weren't going too smoothly in the far north.

"The wave power installation is going well," he told me one evening in early February. "Our worries are in other directions. We're running short of fuel for a start. Short journeys now have to be by horse and cart. We've had to ration vegetables as we didn't grow enough last year to see us through the winter. Being so far north our growing season is shorter than yours. We're living mainly on fish and rabbits. I suppose in a way we're lucky. Being close to the sea we don't get the snowfall that you get inland, so the boats can go out most days. There's a body of opinion wanting to move further south, though they're in the minority at the moment."

I told him about our efforts to make Gleneagles habitable. "It'll take us the best part of a year to get a power supply and water into the place, but when it's done we'll have room for another fifty or sixty people. You'd be more than welcome to move in."

"Thanks for the offer, Dean, I'll bear that in mind," came the response. "Personally I'm in favour of staying here, but as I'm sure you do I have to go with the majority."

My contact at Turnberry was usually Harry Jennings and from him I learned that work on the plan to bring power to those without it had started. One of the teams, as he called them, was currently in Skye, where the installation was nearly complete. From there they would move on to Lairg. Jack Phillips had decided that the more northerly outposts had the most urgent needs. Fuel for the helicopters was running out faster than petrol and diesel for road transport and his reasoning was that more southerly sites could be reached by road. Another team was at work in the Borders and a third on the Mull of Kintyre, where a group of around forty was situated at Machrahanish. It was from Harry that I learned another meeting of all communities at Pitlochry was to be held on the first Monday in April.

Most of March was wet and windy. We worked outside as much as we could, often in pouring rain. When it got too bad Alec had us toiling in the greenhouses. I took the trouble to count them one day during a break. Apart from the big centrally heated one we had forty-eight others of varying sizes. Under Alec's direction we planted most of them with tomatoes, courgettes and lettuce. Three were reserved for bringing on seeds and young plants. Jamie took charge of those and only members of the Geddes family were recruited to help. This was a sensible idea. Of all the rest of us only Brian really knew much about seed germination. At break times on dry days there was always a group on the river bank watching the fish.

"They say it's restful to stand and watch fish," Esme remarked to me one day. "I'm beginning to think they're right. I could stand here all day just watching them. They're so graceful."

"I haven't got a poetic nature," I retorted. "I'd rather see them grilled and on a plate with chips and mushy peas!"

"You've got no soul," she protested.

I'd wanted to take Lindsay with me to Pitlochry again, but she was far advanced and the baby was likely to arrive any time in the following few days. I was getting excited and worried in equal measures, far more so than Lindsay, and I didn't want to take the slightest risk. My second choice was Alex, but he cried off on the grounds of having too much to do. It was the start of the lambing season and our ewes were due any day. In the end I took Danny. I still saw him as my natural successor and I felt it would do him good to meet and learn from other group leaders. We set off on a grey and overcast Monday morning. The roads were still passable with care but speed was out of the question. More potholes and cracks had appeared and at a couple of spots there'd been minor landslides that partially blocked the main road. Thankfully we didn't have to make any detours, but even so it took us nearly three hours to do a journey that in happier times could have been done in an hour.

The first person that I met as we entered the Hydro was Muriel McVay from Arbroath. After the initial greeting she asked after Lindsay. I told her of the impending birth of our first child and she looked at me shrewdly.

"The two of you got together after all then," she remarked. "I rather thought you would. She spoke very warmly of you last year and I saw the way you looked at her. I'm pleased for you both."

A cold lunch, mainly the inevitable sandwiches, awaited us in the hotel's main restaurant. As in the previous year Jack Phillips had sent a squad up a day or two in advance to get everything ready for the meeting, but on this occasion he'd laid on food as well. Here we were joined by the newly arrived Archie MacKay, accompanied this time by his partner Morag. We talked mainly of trivialities, knowing that more serious business was to follow. Muriel reported that things at Arbroath were going well. Food, especially fish, was plentiful and they were extending their area of cultivation that year. The Norwegian couple were more than proving their worth. The husband had been a civil engineer in his native land while his wife was a first class chef. Like all the other communities babies were being born there on a regular basis and Arbroath currently boasted eight children under one year old.

Archie told me that they'd had a long discussion the week before on whether to stay in Thurso or take up my offer to come to Muirton Grange. At the end of the day they'd decided on the former. The general opinion was that they'd worked so hard to build the site up to what it was that it would be a retrograde step to move on. They had some power and they had fish in plenty, their livestock was multiplying at a satisfactory rate and by simply extending the land under cultivation they could make up the shortfall in fruit and vegetables. As Archie explained, everyone in their community had been born and bred on or around the north coast and they all felt an affinity to their surroundings.

All too soon it was two o'clock and we filed into the conference room for the meeting. Jack Phillips and Harry Jennings were our hosts once again and the former gave the opening address.

"Firstly I'd like to thank you all for coming. A few of the people I spoke to by radio questioned whether another full meeting was really necessary and whether it would simply be a waste of valuable fuel. The fact that every one of Scotland's thirty-two townships is represented here is, I think, testimony to the fact that you all see the value of getting together once more and continuing to exchange ideas and experiences. We can learn from one another and so improve the standard of living of all who have survived. Personally I believe last year's meeting has brought great benefits to everyone. Through our exchange system each community now has the basis of a full farmyard. We all have at least one mating pair of horses, cattle, sheep, pigs and goats, plus chickens, ducks, geese and turkeys. Managed properly, as I'm sure they will be, they will, in five or six years' time, provide us with all the dairy products we need. The horses are perhaps the most valuable of all our assets, for they will give us our transport in the future. On that subject, if any of you should find your stallions infertile, contact your nearest neighbours and arrange for a short loan of a suitable animal."

"Harry will tell you in a moment of the projects we have in hand. Before he does I'd just like to say a word or two about a couple of major worries. All the inland communities are short of salt and everyone is short of sugar. In the case of the latter there is good news. The folk at Muirton Grange have managed to get hold of a small quantity of sugar beet seed. Grown this year it will provide enough new seed to give every community a small amount. Once it's ready to pass around we'll make arrangements for it to be distributed. As far as salt is concerned the seaside groups have enough and to spare, so it's just a case of finding transport to go and collect it. I would suggest as part of your informal conversations this afternoon and evening you all try and work out some sort of system for doing so. I've studied the map and apart from Muirton Grange and Lairg no community is more than sixty miles from a seaside group, so it should be possible to make the necessary journey. We'll meet again briefly before we leave tomorrow, but now I'll pass you over to Harry."

Captain Jennings wasn't as good a public speaker as his counterpart. He hummed and hawed from time to time and spoke from notes. A couple of times a voice from the back had to ask him to speak up. "Most of you will know from the radio of the initiatives that are in hand. The most important one is the provision of electricity to those communities that have little or none. We made a start on this during February and work is progressing well. Three installations have been completed already and we hope to finish the whole project by the end of this year. Our three engineers are working flat out and I can promise you that even if we don't meet that target you will all have at least some form of heating by next winter. Now we've heard already that the problem regarding sugar is likely to be solved within a couple of years. Forgive me if I'm stating the obvious, but growing the sugar beet plants is only part of the process. After that the beet has to be boiled and the sugar extracted and dried from the resultant liquid. It can be done on a small scale in the kitchen, but it would be much more efficient to set up specific apparatus for the process. When our engineers are working on the power supply they will give you the instructions on how to build and use such an apparatus. While with the coastal communities they will also take a look at your means of extracting salt from sea water and advise you on how it can be improved or modified."

"I was intending to say a few words on use of the radio network, but in talking to many of you recently I think we are already using it to its best advantage. What I would suggest is that you all keep in regular contact with your nearest neighbours. Isolated we may all be, but there's no need for anyone to feel that they have to deal with problems and disasters on their own. If anyone is in difficulty call for help right away. I know we all tend to think of our own areas as some sort of independent personal kingdom, but we're still Scotland and we're still all one country. Yes, we'll each make and abide by our own rules, but that doesn't preclude us from helping each other when the need arises."

Harry sat down abruptly and Jack Phillips stood up once more. "I've just one more thing to tell you before we split up. Most of you probably know this already but in case anyone doesn't I'll mention it briefly. There is no longer any danger from the outlaw crowd that called itself the republic of Stirling. They were foolish enough to mount an attack on Muirton Grange and, not to put too fine a point on it, were annihilated. We can now all build our future in peace."

I didn't see any point in asking Danny to do as Lindsay had done the previous year and mix and meet with others. For one thing he was the youngest person present by far and for another I didn't think there'd be all that much to be gained. Regular radio contact in the past year had made most of those present familiar names to me and it was just a question of fitting the faces to those names. Danny himself showed no inclination to wander. "I'm here to listen and learn," he confided to me later in the afternoon.

CHAPTER TWENTY-SIX

U nlike the previous year when the ensuing conversations were mainly on a one to one basis, this time we split into groups of between five and eight. From time to time some would leave one group and drift on to the next. I found this a much better way of meeting people and exchanging information. The talk was nearly all about producing food, power and adding to the amenities of the spartan life that we were all consigned to. Comparisons were made on things like crop yields, milk surpluses, excess power, shortage of water and many other day to day concerns. By the end of the afternoon I was even more convinced that we at Muirton Grange were in a better position than most and possibly even second best behind Turnberry. I learned little that was new or helpful. A certain amount of more technical talk emerged from time to time, but that went way over my head. Farmers must have been well represented, for much of the conversation centred on that aspect. There was a great deal of discussion of things like crop rotation, soil erosion and yield per acre. Most of that was beyond me also.

Our brewery and that at Traquair were the subject of many questions and much envy. We hadn't been the only group to suffer from a shortage of yeast. Again the technical aspect was all Greek to me, but the Traquair representative, one Andrew Crawford, was able to pass on instructions on how to get started. As he pointed out, there had been any number of small private breweries in Scotland prior to the disaster and it was a simple matter to remove all the equipment and reassemble it.

Just before we broke up for the evening meal I was buttonholed by Jack Phillips. Taking me by the arm he led me away to a private corner. "Just a quick private word, Dean. The wife of one of our engineers is due to give birth any day now and he wants to be within reach. I've agreed to let him work near home so that he can get back to her every night. Now I know you've got a good electricity system, but I'd like to send him to have a quick look over it and maybe advise on possible improvements. Can you receive him on Thursday?"

"Certainly," I replied. "I know little or nothing about that side of it myself but I'll make sure Tony, he's the one that has set up the whole thing, is available to spend the day with him."

Jack rubbed his hands together in a characteristic gesture. "Good. His name is Barton Phelps, by the way, and he's from Yorkshire. He'll drive up and be with you sometime between nine-thirty and ten."

"While you've got a minute Jack, there's one thing I'd like to mention. We looked into the possibility that you suggested last year about getting the railways running. We're fairly certain we can get hold of one or two steam engines and with a bit of luck get them back to Gleneagles. The problem will be getting coal to run them. The feeling is that it would take too much time and labour to search for any open cast mine sites. There are a number of disused pits within reach but it would be far too dangerous to reopen and try and work them."

"That seems to be the general view," Jack admitted with a nod. "We've managed to get an engine down to Girvan. It was lying in a shed in Springburn. Luckily one of our group had worked on the railways at one time and knew how to operate the points manually, so we hitched up a diesel engine and pulled the steamer, a couple of carriages and a truck down to Girvan. We haven't made any attempt to use it yet. There are one or two open cast mines in Dumfriesshire, so maybe later this year we'll go down and load up." He gave a laugh. "Who knows? Maybe your next consignment of salt will come by rail."

During supper Danny got into conversation with a retired postman from the Isle of Bute community. They had a common interest in sailing and were soon oblivious to their surroundings. Once the meal was over I felt like some fresh air and exercise so I headed outside intending to take a short walk. It was unusually warm for an evening in April, though dusk was beginning to fall. I'd barely gone ten yards from the front entrance when I heard my name called. Muriel McVay was sitting on a nearby bench. Somewhat reluctantly I abandoned any idea of a stroll and sat down beside her.

"Do you think of the past much?" she asked me abruptly.

"Now and again," I admitted. "Most of the time I'm too busy. Why?"

"I do, often. I keep asking myself what I'd be doing now at any given moment if there'd been no cloud of gas."

"So what would you be doing at this time?" I asked.

"We never had children. Probably I'd be slumped in a chair in front of the telly watching Coronation Street," she replied. "My old man would have gone off to the pub to play darts or snooker and sup a few pints of beer and I'd have been glued to the box until he came in at closing time. What a worthless existence it all was. This is maybe a horrible thing to say, but the disaster has made me feel I'm a useful human being again. Everything and everyone I once knew and loved is no more, but I'm happier and more fulfilled now than I've ever been. Does that shock you?"

"Not in the least. In some ways I share your feelings. For the first time in my life I'm doing something that really matters, something that's of benefit to those around me and the world in general. I guess it's called job satisfaction. In a way though it's not surprising I feel like that. I had nobody close to grieve over other than a few casual friends. I know it must be harder for those who've lost loved ones."

"It's a strange feeling," she said thoughtfully. "I've spoken to others and many agree with me. That past world is so remote now, almost like an old film that you've seen. I think that the scale of the loss and the fact that everyone suffered that loss at the same time somehow dulls the pain. If Roy, that's my husband, had dropped dead suddenly I would have been overcome with grief, but knowing that he died at the precise moment that five million other people in the country died in some way makes it acceptable. Or maybe I'm just a muddle-headed female," she concluded with a laugh.

I didn't sleep too well that night. Worry about Lindsay dominated my mind and in vain did I try to reassure myself that she was perfectly capable of looking after herself. I hoped that the baby wouldn't arrive before the following afternoon. More than anything I wanted to be there at the birth. It must have been nearly three o'clock before I fell into an uneasy doze. By contrast Danny must have slept like a log, for he was bright and breezy when we met up for breakfast. At half past nine we reassembled in the conference room for a final few words from Captain Phillips.

"Once again I feel this has been a useful exercise. We've had the chance to exchange information, discuss problems and bring all the communities closer together. There are hard times to come, but always remember that help is at hand wherever you are. If it's possible I'd like to have one more meeting this time next year, but that depends on the availability of fuel to fly the copters and run road transport. In the meantime we'll stay in constant touch by radio. I wish all of you a safe journey home."

I let Danny drive us back. I still wasn't fully functional after my lack of sleep. In fact I would have nodded off within five minutes but for his constant chatter.

"Thanks so much for bringing me with you, Dean," was his main theme. "You know, back when I was fourteen a party of us were taken to Holyrood by some of the teachers one day. We had a tour round the building and then sat in on one of the debates. Most of the other kids were bored stiff, but I loved it, seeing where all the decisions were taken. This has been similar. I feel as though I've been in the corridors of power.

"Hardly power, Danny," I laughed. "We can't pass laws and even if we could there'd be no way of enforcing them. All we can really do at these sessions is talk and compare problems and suggest solutions. It'll probably be a couple of hundred years before any meaningful government can take shape. My hope is that we can all stick together until that happens. It would be a tragedy if we copied history and descended into tribes fighting each other all the time."

"Surely that won't happen," he protested.

"Not in our lifetime, I wouldn't think, but who knows what will happen in the future? Disaster will always be just round the corner. Crop failures, an outbreak of disease among cattle and sheep and a hundred other problems could arise. A community falling on hard times could well decide that their only chance of survival is to attack their neighbours. You know the old saying about history repeating itself. Who knows? In the distant future we might well find ourselves at war with England again." I uttered the last sentence mainly in jest, then wondered if I was wide of the mark after all.

My first action after we reached home was to check on Lindsay. Thankfully the baby hadn't decided to make an appearance. In a morning examination Myra had predicted Thursday or Friday as the likely arrival time. In fact it was three o'clock on the Friday morning when Lindsay wakened me by the simple expedient of digging her elbow sharply into my ribs.

"I think it's starting," she murmured.

Quickly I dragged on shirt and trousers. "Can you walk to the medical suite or shall I get a wheelchair?" I asked solicitously.

"Of course I can walk," she snapped. "It's a baby I've got, not a broken leg. Pack a change of clothing for me and don't forget my cigarettes and lighter."

"You're surely not going to smoke," I said, horrified. I'd wanted her to stop while she was pregnant. It was a vain hope, though she had cut down considerably.

"Not in front of the baby. If I'm able I'll go outside; if not they can take the baby out for ten minutes."

Almost from day one Ling had insisted on the medical centre being staffed twenty-four hours a day. That morning it was Myra and Lily on duty. They put Lindsay to bed and Myra gave her a check-up. "You can relax," she told me. "Nothing's likely to happen for a few hours. Get a job indoors or near the house and I'll send for you when the time comes." I offered to stay but Lindsay told me firmly to go and get some sleep and leave her in peace. I did just that. In the morning I had a word with Danny and then swapped jobs with Esme. Instead of weeding on the other side of the main road I found myself cleaning bathrooms and toilets.

The call came five minutes before noon. Ling had joined Myra in the makeshift delivery room and Selma was also on hand. I found Lindsay in some pain and for once she was happy to hold my hand. The baby, a girl, arrived at ten to one. It was a natural and uncomplicated birth. Less than ten minutes later I was cradling my daughter in my arms. I felt close to tears and full of joy. She looked so perfect. I could have stayed there all day, but Ling more or less ordered me to leave after half an hour. "There's nothing you can usefully do now and Lindsay needs some rest," he told me. "Come back at five o'clock."

I was walking on air for the rest of the afternoon. At various times people came up to congratulate me, but afterwards I couldn't remember them individually. My mind was firmly centred on the medical suite. By five o'clock when I returned Lindsay was almost back to her normal self. She was sitting beside the bed with the baby in her arms, but as soon as she saw me she gave a big smile.

"Good. Now you can look after the wee one while I go out for a smoke," she beamed. "Ling wouldn't agree to taking the baby out and I haven't had a cigarette all day." So saying she thrust the tiny bundle into my arms and left. I stayed for an hour before going for a quick bite to eat. Then it was back to spend the rest of the evening with my newly enlarged family.

"I suppose we ought to decide on a name," I said at one point. If it had been a boy we'd already agreed on Robert, but Lindsay had been so sure it was going to be a boy that we'd never once discussed girls' names. "I think we should choose one that nobody else here has."

For once Lindsay was in agreement. "I'd like something a little bit out of the ordinary. Nothing stupid like Flower or Petal or Hyacinth but one that's not in common use." I suggested a dozen or more, each one getting a shake of the head. "What about Tamara?" Lindsay said eventually. "It's unusual and it has a nice ring to it."

"I like it," I said. "In fact I like it very much. So that's settled." I got up, went to the sink and ran a little water from the tap on to my finger. Very solemnly I dabbed some on the baby's forehead. "I hereby christen you Tamara Stevenson," I intoned.

"Are you not going to call her Barclay?" Lindsay queried.

"I've been thinking about that," I responded. "With so few people left we want to preserve as many surnames as possible. I'm going to suggest that all girls take their mother's surnames and the boys their father's."

Lindsay raised her eyebrows and grinned at me. "You know, sometimes you're so sensible you amaze me." Luckily for her she was holding Tamara at the time or she'd have been hit with a pillow.

With all the furore of the birth I saw little of Barton Phelps, the engineer who came as promised on Thursday morning. I met him as he arrived, said hello, introduced him to Tony and left them to it. We had another brief word at lunchtime.

"Yon lad of yours has done a reet good job," he informed me. "But there's nothing that perfect that can't be improved and we're going to work on a few ideas I've got." Over the next couple of days I saw him and Tony in the distance from time to time engaged in some sort of activity in the field where the greenhouses had been erected. Phelps left at some time late on Saturday, though I didn't see him leave. Tony, however, gave me a full report.

"The man's amazing," he told me, his eyes shining. "I won't go into the technical details, but briefly what he's done is set up a series of relays and switches that control our use of electricity. It means we can heat another dozen greenhouses at least for part of the time. The supply to the water pump is the first priority, and after that the heating in the hotel. When the temperature in the hotel drops below sixty-four degrees the supply to the greenhouses is cut off, the big one last. On top of all that we've fixed up a pump on the far bank of the river and installed a one hundred gallon water tank with a tap. That'll make it easier to draw water for the greenhouses. Barton also gave me a couple of manuals and taught me a lot more about maintenance."

It was Sunday afternoon before Myra judged Lindsay was fit to leave the medical suite and return to our room. By that time I was proficient in the age old art of changing nappies. Lindsay breast fed most of the time, but to me went the privilege of administering the occasional bottle. I suppose I wasn't any different from the vast majority of men in revelling in the joys of fatherhood. My only worry was whether Lindsay felt the same pride. She seemed to accept motherhood philosophically rather than embracing it. At least she showed no signs of post natal depression.

CHAPTER TWENTY-SEVEN

Meantime there were other things to worry about. We'd had nearly three weeks without rain and Alec was becoming increasingly concerned about our newly planted crops. Large scale irrigation was out of the question and we faced the prospect of losing much of that which we'd planted. It was a case of all hands to the pump except that we had no pump, other than the one Barton Phelps had installed. Every single person that could be spared spent the hours of daylight carrying water to the fields in every conceivable type of receptacle. Even so we could only cover a small area of each field. Our main handymen Ross, Gary, Robbie and Tony worked as a team and spent the hours discussing possible ways of laying on some kind of irrigation system but to no avail. The best that they could come up with was to dig a series of ditches connected to the river. Even that suggestion had to be abandoned when we calculated how much work would be involved. So we spent the long dry days praying for rain. There was nothing else to do. Alec's face grew longer with every day that passed. After more than a week had passed he and Jamie, Danny and I held a crisis meeting.

"We're going to have to prioritise," Alec insisted. "The most important crop we have is the sugar beet, even though it doesn't contribute to our food supply. This will likely be the last chance we have to get sugar, not only ourselves but for the rest of Scotland as well. Luckily it's only a small area so it won't take long to water it. Second come the greenhouses. These will need to be done every day and sometimes twice a day, drought or no drought. That's a full time job for at least two and more, probably three or four people. The cereal crops I'm not too worried about. With so few birds about we're not likely to lose much seed and it can lie there until the rain comes. It just means our harvest will be a little later this year. After the greenhouses I suggest next in importance are the potato fields, followed by the vegetable areas. We'll just have to do the best we can with those."

We spent more than two hours that evening checking on our stores of various items. Wheat and maize emerged as the main concerns. The latter was vital for feeding the ever increasing number of poultry, the former, of course, for bread making. At the end of the check it was obvious that if the harvest was delayed for more than a month we would have to consider rationing bread from early in July. Thankfully our stock of potatoes was more than sufficient, though an evening meal of potatoes rather than the usual soup and bread was not a prospect I relished. Our meals were boring enough without this additional blow.

In the end it was a full twenty-seven days before the drought broke. Even then we only had a few light showers over a forty-eight hour period. Another dry day followed and then the heavens really opened and a torrential downpour for over a full day solved all our problems. Alec calculated we'd lost around ten per cent of our grain and cereals, but the prized sugar beet plants emerged strong and healthy.

I'd hoped that the April meeting and the ensuing vote on the management of the group would go some way to relieving the tensions and the whispering campaign against me. Sadly that hadn't happened and if anything those who wanted change redoubled their efforts. Things came to a head in the middle of June. For some time many of us, instead of going to the restaurant for our evening meal, had taken to collecting sandwiches from the kitchens and eating in our own rooms. Though there was a little tea and coffee still available several of us, including Lindsay and I, had switched to drinking water instead. For our part we found it easier to dine in the room rather than carry Tamara down to the restaurant. It was a Wednesday evening as I recall and we were just starting on our meal when a knock came to the door. Danny came in looking ill at ease.

"Sorry to interrupt," he apologised, "but I thought I ought to have a word. There's been more rumblings about your leadership. Several more people seem to have gone over to the opposition in the last few days, including most of Alec's family and Claire and Brian. Claire's up in arms because she thinks Brian has enough to do in the conservatory and shouldn't be given other jobs and of course Brian thinks what she tells him to think. I've spoken to Jamie, who's still on side, and he says Sophie and Hester have been making noises about you and I interfering in the farming set-up. I feel I've kind of let you down with the duty rosters, but I wanted them to be as fair as possible."

I clapped him on the shoulder. "Of course you haven't let me down and don't think it for a minute. You've done a first class job. I appreciate your telling me all this. I know it can't be easy for you." I thought for a moment. "Ask everybody to come to the restaurant at half past seven will you? We'll need to get this sorted once and for all."

When he'd gone Lindsay looked at me with some concern. "What are you going to do?" she asked.

"What I've been wanting to do all along," I replied testily. "Tell them what they can do with the job. All the responsibility I want is right here in this room."

"Do you want me to come and support you?"

I shook my head. "I'll be less than five minutes. It's not worth disturbing the wee one."

Promptly at seen thirty I walked into a crowded room. As far as I could see everyone was there including the medical staff. I leaned against the bar and looked round. "I won't keep you long," I began. "If this community is to survive and grow we need to be united. It's become increasingly obvious over the past months that I have lost the confidence of the majority of you and that by staying in charge I risk causing a permanent rift. I'm therefore resigning my position as unofficial," I stressed that word, "leader as of now. I'll leave you to decide on the way forward." Without looking at anyone I marched out of the nearest door.

When I got back to the room Lindsay asked me how they'd taken my decision.

"Haven't a clue," I said cheerfully. "I said what I had to say and walked out and left them to it."

"How do you feel about it?" she asked next.

"I feel as though a weight has been lifted from my shoulders. As you well know I never wanted the job in the first place."

"But you've done so much," she wailed. "We wouldn't be half as well off if you hadn't taken charge of things."

I went over and sat beside her as she fed Tamara. "It's simply history repeating itself," I explained. "Anyone in authority is there to be shot at. No matter how good a job they do there's always someone who finds things to complain about, real or imaginary. Whoever takes over will find that out very soon." I sighed. "I suppose we'll be getting more visitors later on. I'd better tidy up the room. After that I'll radio Jack Phillips and let him know what's happened."

For a long time I'd known how to set up the radio for transmission, so I was able to get in touch with Turnberry very quickly. It took a few minutes for the duty officer there to contact the captain and when he did get to the microphone I told him briefly what had happened. He sounded shocked. I assured him that I'd try and ensure that whoever took over maintained the contact we'd made. When I'd finished talking to him I called up Archie in Thurso and had a chat to him as well.

"I suppose we'll all face opposition sooner or later," he remarked philosophically. "There's one or two people here that don't see eye to eye with me, so I might be the next one in the doghouse. What say we get together and start a new group of our own with a few handpicked friends."

I laughed. "Too much like hard work. Anyway, where else would we find somewhere with a built in electrical supply?"

"Aye, I suppose you're right," he acknowledged. "Keep in touch."

We managed a couple of hours of peace before the first caller came knocking. It was Robbie and he was vitriolic. "Talk about midsummer madness," he growled. "God only knows what they think they've achieved by hounding you out. I gave them a piece of my mind, I can tell you and when I'd finished Alec Geddes gave them another broadside, including some of his own family."

"Past history, Robbie," I said with a grin. "Tell us what happened after I left."

"They've elected a committee of three, Sophie, Ross and Jamie. Someone, I didn't see who, proposed me, but I told them in no uncertain terms that the only person I'd work with was you. Esme and Duncan proposed Danny, but he said the same thing. In the end the other candidates were Lewis and Gary, but they only got two votes each. I suspect those two votes were Hester and Sophie."

"Who stayed loyal?" Lindsay wanted to know.

"They didn't take a vote on whether to accept Dean's decision," he replied. "But I know that Esme and Duncan, James and Margaret, Danny and Selma, Alec, Jamie, Kirsty and Jan would have voted against it. Apart from Selma the medical staff stayed aloof as before."

"It's Danny I feel sorry for," I reflected. "He's been a rock from day one and I always expected that he'd take over from me eventually. Ah well, such is politics."

Esme, Alec and Kirsty all arrived in quick succession and spent a few minutes with us. It was well after midnight before we finally got to bed. Even then we lay for half an hour or more just talking. Lindsay was worried.

"I don't like the sound of that new committee," was her main theme. "You could find yourself getting all the dirty jobs from now on."

"I doubt it," I reassured her. "Sophie's the only one on it with a real grudge and Jamie and Tony won't let her away with too much. Anyway I'm used to the dirty jobs. I've never shirked my share of them. Let's not anticipate trouble. Don't forget, if things get too bad there's nothing that says we have to stay here. We can always move out. Turnberry or Arbroath would more than welcome us and so would Archie up at Thurso. I don't think it will come to that, though. As long as they don't take it out on you I can handle anything they throw at me."

"Don't you worry about me," said Lindsay emphatically. "I can more than take care of myself, as you should know by now."

When I came down to breakfast next morning I saw that all but one of the notices had been removed from the notice board in Reception. The day's duty roster had been moved to one side and a new missive occupied the centre of the board. It was headed 'Areas of Responsibility' in bold type. Below this came a list of names. I scanned through them quickly. Coordination—Sophie Laird; Farming—Jamie Geddes; Maintenance—Tony Kane; Catering—Margaret Tulloch; Fisheries—Donald Geddes; Duty Rotas—Gary Laird; Education—Christine Vaughan; Medical—Dr. Sen Chi Ling; Communications—Lewis Miller.

"Too many chiefs and not enough Indians," came an acid comment from behind me. I turned to find that Robbie had come up unheard.

"I don't know," I responded. "When you look into it that's pretty much what everyone's been doing unofficially anyway. The only changes are Gary for Danny on the duty lists and Jamie for Alec on the farms. And everybody knows that Jamie won't lift a finger without consulting Alec first.

Robbie snorted. "I still think it's a recipe for disaster."

I had a few words with Danny before heading off to the Gleneagles farm to join the team there. He didn't seem too upset at having been relieved of his duties, though Selma had had a few harsh words to say about the new regime. At the mid morning break Alec came over for a chat.

"I've been told to abandon the idea of getting the Gleneagles hotel fit for living in." He smiled and gave me a broad wink. "Unfortunately the order came in my left ear and I'm a bit deaf in that one when I need to be. In any case we've done everything needed except for the heating. Tony and I fixed up the water supply pumping system last week. I was thinking that if things get too unpleasant a group of us could move over to Gleneagles."

"That's the best idea I've heard today," I told him. "As far as the heating's concerned, if I can get into the radio room when Lewis isn't there, I'll contact Turnberry and see if they can let us have Barton Phelps again for a couple of days or so. If he can work with one of us so that Tony's not involved he should be able to fix us up with a heating system. Mind you, I don't think Tony would raise any objections to helping, but I don't want to test his loyalty to Sophie too far. We may find that things settle down and we don't need to move, but it would be nice to have the option."

In actual fact little changed in the weeks that followed my resignation, apart from the duty rostering. Gary decided to make it fortnightly instead of daily. This drew another caustic comment from Alec. "I don't require the same number of people every day. O.K., I can always find work for them weeding and hoeing but I'm sure there's more important things they could be doing. I'll be giving Jamie a piece of my mind. He should realise that more than anyone."

I didn't get the dirtiest job after all for the first fortnight. Instead I got the hardest one: greenhouse duty! This involved opening all forty-eight greenhouses early in the morning, watering them all at least once a day and closing them at night. The only source of water was the tank that Barton Phelps and Tony had set up on the north bank of the river. It was nearly a quarter of a mile to the farthest greenhouse so we had to walk a fair distance carrying full cans. In reality it was a job for at least four people but only two were allocated. I found myself paired with Louise. Nowadays she was a very different person from the one I'm met first at the A9 barrier. The arrogance and the superior look were long gone and though she still had plenty of self-confidence she didn't parade it as a virtue. There'd been a little initial resentment that she'd been allowed to stay at Muirton, but that melted completely once Robbie had taken her under his wing. Her recovery from her injuries had been little short of miraculous and she showed no signs of fatigue despite the work we were doing. Most of the time we had little opportunity for conversation, but on the second day a heavy shower of rain when we were at the far end of the field drove us to take shelter in one of the greenhouses. We found a space to sit down cross-legged on the floor.

"Pity there isn't a sliding roof," Louise remarked as she lit a cigarette. "It would save us a lot of watering."

I thought the time was ripe for making a confession. "There's something I've been meaning to tell you, Louise. I should have done it long ago but I was waiting for the right moment. I was the one that shot you. I'm sorry. My job was to take out the second lorry and its driver. I swear though that I never realised it was you in the passenger seat."

She took it better than I thought she would. "It's all water under the bridge now," she said airily. "I'm still alive, I've got my strength back and the only leftovers are the scars. I will never be able to flaunt my body again, but I don't suppose bikinis and low cut dresses will make a comeback during my lifetime. In a way you brought me luck. Life is better now than it has been for a long time."

"Not so long ago you told me that you wished we'd finished the job and let you die," I reminded her.

"That was before I got to know Robbie," she countered. "He's made such a difference to my outlook." I'd have liked to chat for longer, but the rain eased off and we had to get back to work.

Any hopes I'd had that by resigning the unity of the group would be restored were soon dashed. If anything the divide became greater. I had no problems with Sophie. By mutual consent we avoided each other. She and Alec, however, were constantly clashing. I overheard one such confrontation one day when I was in the stables for a reason I've since forgotten. I was out of sight when Alec drove up with a load of barley for the brewery. Just as I was about to make my presence known I heard footsteps approaching and Sophie calling Alec's name. I stayed hidden.

"I want you to stop shooting foxes," Sophie said without preamble. "There are few enough animals left in the world without going out of our way to kill them. They're such beautiful creatures."

Alec was scathing in his reply. "Those beautiful creatures as you call them ravage our crops, steal our chickens and attack our cats and dogs. Given the chance they'll attack our children too. Give what orders you like but I for one will continue to shoot every fox I see." He finished unloading and drove off with an angry clash of gears.

It was well into July before I got the chance to contact Captain Phillips. When I explained what I wanted he was very cooperative and promised to send Barton Phelps to Gleneagles at the first opportunity. Luckily I was working close to the hotel when the engineer arrived with an assistant four days later. They'd brought a low loader with them heaped with solar panels and four medium sized wind turbines. I explained what we needed. After consultation the two of them got to work and completed the job within three days without any of the committee being the wiser.

"It's not as refined a system as you've got over at Muirton," Phelps told me as he was leaving. "But it should provide you with enough power to get by. The only problem will come on windless winter nights and thankfully we don't get too many of them."

The second anniversary of the disaster was celebrated in similar fashion to the first with a barbecue of roast pork and roast chicken. Somehow the atmosphere wasn't the same, even though everyone tried to put their differences aside for the one day. Instead of one big party little groups formed here and there and kept strictly to themselves. On a visit to the toilet I was joined by Alec.

"I've got a feeling the new management isn't going to last much longer," he confided. "More than one of those that supported them at the beginning are having second thoughts. Don't be surprised if there's a move to put you back in charge."

"They'll be wasting their time," I said decisively. "There's no way I'd ever take up sole responsibility again. Depending who's on it I might be prepared to serve on a committee but that's as far as I'd go. Personally I think the best solution may in the end be to split into two groups with some of us moving into Gleneagles. Let's leave things for another couple of months and talk again at the end of the summer."

Tamara was fractious that evening. Her first two teeth were coming through and the poor wee mite was obviously in some pain. It was nearly eleven before she dropped off to sleep and Lindsay put her in her crib. She came and sat beside me with a sigh. "I wonder if we did the right thing bringing her into the world," she reflected. "She's not going to have much of a life, is she?"

"It'll be a hard life, certainly," I admitted. "But it will also be a healthy one. She'll spend her time in the open air instead of being hunched over a terminal in a stuffy office. She'll make friends and fall in love like any other girl in any past time."

"But look at all the things she'll never have," Lindsay countered. "She'll never taste chocolate, cola, pasta, rice and a hundred other things. She'll never go to the movies or on foreign holidays, never go to a proper school or a dance or a disco."

"But don't you see," I said patiently. "Because she'll never have these things she'll never miss them the way we do. In years to come she'll hear us mention things like chocolate or discos and wonder what on earth we're talking about. And look at the bad things she'll never have to encounter. No exams, no peer pressure to have the latest fashions, no politicians to confuse her, no drugs to tempt her, no fear of crime or assault, no struggle to find employment. I could go on and on. Life for her will be simple and straightforward compared to what it was for us."

"I suppose that means you want us to have more children."

"Let me put it this way," I said as mildly as I could. "I would like to have more children but the decision is yours and yours alone. You're the one that has to put up with the problems of pregnancy and the pain of childbirth. It would be nice to have a big family but I'm more than happy with what I have now." I grinned. "If Tamara turns out to be anything like you it'll be a full time job just coping with the two of you." I managed to dodge the pillow that she threw at me!

Long after Lindsay's regular breathing proved she was asleep I lay awake thinking about the future. Should we split the group and relocate to Gleneagles? Should we tough it out and try and build bridges that had been demolished? Should I take any sort of responsibility again? It took me a couple of hours to realise a simple truth. There was nothing I could do to change the future anyway. What was destined to happen would happen and would depend on circumstances way beyond my control. There was only one certainty in my mind. Whatever that future held my prime concern throughout would be the welfare of my partner and my daughter. Everything else paled into insignificance.

THE END